HELLFIRE

B.C. HOLLYWOOD

Edited by Danielle Yeager, Hack & Slash Editing.

ISBN-13: 978-1068675744

"The greatest trick the Devil ever pulled was
convincing the world he didn't exist."
Charles Baudelaire

"Hell is empty and all the devils are here."
William Shakespeare, "The Tempest"

"The Devil is not as black as he is painted."
English Proverb

CHAPTER 1
THE SPOT

Vincent Burke sat on his custom Yamaha XVS1300, his broad frame taking up most of the narrow country road. His helmet dangled forgotten from one hand as a persistent drizzle seeped into his leather jacket, trailing icy fingers down his spine. Vincent gave no hint that he noticed the cold, his intense blue eyes fixed on the old oak standing in the field across the hedge.

From this distance, he could make out the jagged scar on the tree's trunk – a reminder of that night almost a year ago. Beneath the blemish lay a colourful mound of dead flowers, each bloom a witness to a life cut short. His daughter's life. Rose.

A car approached from behind and halted, its engine idling. Vincent didn't move, lost in his thoughts.

BEEP! BEEP!

The sudden noise broke the silence, but Vincent remained indifferent, his attention never leaving the tree.

BEEP! BEEP! BEEP!

Vincent lifted his free hand, waving for the car to pass.

Plenty of room, you cunt, he thought, a flicker of annoyance disturbing his grief.

The vehicle inched forward, the whir of an electric window announcing a confrontation. *Oh, here we go.* He braced himself, turning to meet the driver's gaze. A man's face, flushed with rage, but something in Vincent's look – perhaps the pain inscribed in every line – made him reconsider.

"You're taking up the whole road," the driver said lamely, as if Vincent wasn't acutely aware of his position.

For a moment, Vincent considered dragging the man from his vehicle and beating him to a bloody pulp. He clenched his fist, then stopped himself. *There's been enough blood spilled here.* Before he could respond, the window had already closed, and the car sped away, horn blaring in impotent protest.

Vincent turned back to the tree, thinking about the stories he'd heard. The locals called this bend The Devil's Corner, a place where the unwary could find themselves in Auld Nick's embrace before they knew what hit them. The old oak tree had claimed more lives than anyone cared to count, earning the grim moniker.

He'd thought about burning it to ashes in those dark days after Rose's death. But he couldn't bring himself to follow through with the task. Despite the pain its presence caused, the tree stood as a living monument to his daughter. *It wasn't the fucking tree's fault.*

Vincent kicked out the side stand and dismounted, hanging his helmet on the handlebar. He moved to the right saddlebag, fingers deftly unbuckling the strap to retrieve a single, perfect red rose.

Pushing through the familiar gap in the hedge, Vincent crossed the muddy field. His heavy boots and leathers protected him from the brambles. At the base of the tree, Vincent reached out, his calloused fingers gently tracing the ragged scar on the trunk. He could almost hear the screech of tires, the sickening crunch of metal, the terrified screams cut short. His stomach lurched, and he squeezed his eyes shut, forcing the memories back down into that dark place where all his pain lived.

"Every day is harder without you," the words caught in his throat, a hoarse whisper. He placed the rose atop the others – nearly a year's worth now. "I miss you, Rose."

Vincent's voice broke on his daughter's name, and he turned away, hurrying back to his bike. *I'll mewl like a fucking baby again if I don't leave now.*

Back on the road, he mounted up, donned his helmet, and gunned the engine. The Yam's roar shattered the quiet, and Vincent sped away, desperate to outrun his grief.

In his haste, he failed to notice the dark shape observing from farther up the road, its eyes gleaming with an otherworldly interest.

CHAPTER 2

BAR FIGHT

Vincent stood at the entrance to Murph's, his muscular tattooed arms folded across a broad chest. He eyed the punters lining up. *Mostly kids*, he thought, resisting the urge to roll his eyes. At forty-two, he was a relic compared to this lot. They wore their best gear, queueing to pay over the odds for watered-down drinks and shite music that made his head pound.

What the fuck am I doing here? The thought hit him like a hammer, and he almost laughed. He'd been asking himself the same question for the past year, since . . . Vincent pushed the thought away, unwilling to deal with that particular pain again so soon after visiting the tree. His memory had other ideas.

The fairground materialised around him: Rose perched on his shoulders, her tiny hands gripping his hair. "Faster, Daddy!" she squealed, her five-year-old excitement piercing the carnival din. Cotton candy perfumed the air. Tinny calliope music clashed with the rhythmic clank of the approaching carousel. Vincent's fingers twitched, muscle memory reaching for a small hand that wasn't there. He blinked, and the fairground dissolved, leaving him empty and aching.

Why is it always the old memories that cut the worst? They'd filled him with joy right up to the moment when Rose was gone forever. After that moment, each recollection was a stab wound. He forced his head back to the present.

Murph's wasn't a bad gig, as far as these things went. Decent money for a few hours of standing around, glowering at youngsters, and stopping the odd fight. Only he was sick of it. Sick of the noise, the lights, the fights, the vomit. *Christ, I'm too old for this shite.*

A group of lads, just old enough to drink, approached. One of them, with a shock of ginger hair and a face like a slapped arse, looked up at him. "All right, big man?"

Vincent stared at him, one eyebrow cocked. The lad's bravado wavered under the large doorman's flat stare, and he looked away.

"IDs," Vincent said in a low rumble. The lads fumbled for their wallets, handing over their driving licences. "Didn't I see you over on Willow earlier?" Vincent thought so, but he couldn't be sure.

They shook their heads in unison and mumbled their denials. Willow Lane was a rough part of town and they weren't likely to admit it.

Vincent hardly glanced at the IDs before handing them back and letting the group in. "Behave yourselves." It wasn't a friendly reminder.

As he watched them disappear into the club, a hand settled on his shoulder. He turned to see Murph, a concerned look on his weathered face. "All right, Vinny?"

Vincent shrugged. "Aye, you know how it is."

Murph nodded. He did know. He'd been there for

Vincent this past year, through the worst of it. "Look, why don't you take the night off? I can handle things here."

He was tempted but shook his head. "Nah, I'm good. Need to keep busy, you know?"

Murph looked like he wanted to argue, but he only patted Vincent's shoulder and headed back inside.

Vincent turned back to the queue, his mind drifting again. What was he doing here, indeed? Standing in the pissing rain, listening to shite music, dealing with drunken kids. It was a far cry from the life he'd once imagined for himself.

IT NEARED CLOSING time when Vincent heard the unmistakable sound of a scuffle breaking out inside the club. He sighed, pushing himself off the wall he'd been leaning against, and headed inside.

The music blared on, but the dance floor stood empty as people gathered around the edge, watching the action unfold. Vincent shouldered his way through the crowd, his imposing frame making it easy to part the sea of bodies.

In the centre of the circle, he found Murph grappling with the ginger lad from earlier. The kid swung wildly, his face twisted with rage, as Murph tried to restrain him. Another lad, sporting a rapidly swelling eye, struggled against the grip of his mates.

"Oi!" Vincent's voice cut through the noise like a knife. "What's all this, then?"

Murph looked up, relief evident on his face. "Vinny! Give us a hand, will you?"

Vincent waded in, grabbing the ginger lad by the scruff

of his neck and hauling him bodily toward the exit. The lad struggled, spitting curses, but Vincent's grip was iron.

"Get the fuck off me, you prick!" the lad snarled as Vincent shoved him out into the street.

"Watch your mouth, son. Or I'll do more than throw you out."

The lad scrambled to his feet, his face flushed with anger and humiliation. He pointed a shaking finger at Vincent. "You'll fucking regret this, you wanker! You don't know who you're messing with!"

Vincent stared at him, unimpressed. "I think I'll take my chances. Now fuck off before I lose my patience."

For a moment, it looked like the lad might take a swing at him. But then he thought better of it, spitting on the ground at Vincent's feet before turning and stalking off into the night.

Vincent watched him go, shaking his head. *Little prick.* He turned to head back inside, but Murph was already there, a worried look on his face.

"You good, Vinny?"

"Aye, I'm grand. What was that all about?"

Murph shrugged. "Fuck knows. Probably an argument over a lass or something. You know what these young lads are like."

Vincent nodded, but he had an inkling it wouldn't be the last he'd be hearing of the ginger prick. He pushed the thought aside. It wasn't his problem. He was there to do a job, not get involved in whatever shite the kids were into.

"Come on," he said to Murph, clapping him on the shoulder. "Let's get this place closed up. I'm fuckin' wrecked."

As they walked back inside, Murph hesitated. "Listen,

Vinny . . . I've been meaning to talk to you about something."

Vincent tensed, sensing the shift in Murph's tone. "What's that, then?"

Murph sighed, running a hand through his thinning hair. "I'm worried about you, mate. You've been different since Rose, and with the anniversary coming . . . I know you're hurting, but—"

"Don't," Vincent cut him off, sharper than he'd intended. "Just . . . don't, Murph. Not tonight."

Murph held up his hands in surrender. "All right, all right. But we need to talk about it sometime, Vinny. You can't keep going on like this."

Vincent didn't respond. He pushed past Murph and went back into the club. While he helped clear out the stragglers, worry settled in his chest, as if his carefully constructed world crumbled around him. And he didn't know how to stop it.

CHAPTER 3
CONSEQUENCES

Vincent walked along the empty street, his heavy footsteps echoing off the surrounding buildings. The cool night air was a relief after the stifling heat of the club. He was exhausted, his body aching from standing all night, dealing with pissed-up kids and breaking up fights. The confrontation with the ginger lad left a sour taste in his mouth.

The low rumble of an engine came from behind him and he looked back. A sleek black car turned onto the street, its headlights cutting through the darkness. Vincent kept walking, but the car slowed, pulling up alongside him.

Tinted windows made it impossible to see who was inside. Vincent's gut tightened. In his experience, nothing good ever came from a mysterious car rolling up on you in the middle of the night.

Vincent teetered on the edge of lashing out, fist cocked to smash the window when it rolled down. He blinked in surprise. The ginger lad from the club, the one he'd thrown out earlier, sat in the passenger seat. A smug look plastered his face, as if he'd won the fucking lottery.

But it was the man in the driver's seat that really caught Vincent's attention. He was older, maybe in his fifties, with slicked-back ginger hair and a well-tailored suit. He had the look of money about him, the kind of bloke used to getting what he wanted.

"Well, well, well," the older man said, smooth as silk. "If it isn't the big, bad bouncer himself."

Vincent tensed. "The fuck do you want?"

The ginger lad leaned forward, a sneer on his face. "Told ya you'd regret messing with me, you wanker. This is my da. He's going to sort you out good and proper."

Vincent looked between the two of them. He didn't like the look of this. Not one fucking bit. But he wasn't about to let some rich cunt and his little shite of a son intimidate him.

He took a step toward the car, his eyes locked on the older man. "Listen, mate," he said in a threatening tone. "I don't know who the fuck you think you are, but you'd best be on your way. I'm not in the mood for games."

The older man smiled, unfazed by Vincent's menacing manner. "Oh, I think you'll want to hear what I have to say, Mr Burke. It concerns your daughter."

Vincent froze, his blood turning to ice. "What the fuck did you say?"

The older man's smile widened, revealing teeth too perfect to be natural. "Rose, wasn't it? Such a tragedy, what happened to her. It would be a shame if something similar were to befall someone else you care about."

Vincent's vision blurred with rage. He was ready to lunge for the car door and rip that smug prick out. But before he could move, the older man cut in, "I see your rage, Mr Burke. But whatever you're thinking of doing, you'd be wise to reconsider." His eyes flicked to the ginger lad, then back to Vincent. "I'm not someone you want to mess with. One wrong move, and your life could become very complicated."

Vincent shook with pent-up fury. "Who the fuck are you?"

The older man sneered. "Let's just say I'm someone who doesn't appreciate my son being manhandled by lowlife thugs. Consider this a friendly warning, Mr Burke. Cross the line with my boy again, and you'll wish you'd died in that accident with your daughter."

With that, the car sped away, leaving Vincent alone in the street.

CHAPTER 4

SLEEPLESS NIGHT

Vincent fumbled with his keys, his hands still shaking from the encounter. The lock clicked, and he stumbled into his dark house, slamming the door behind him. He leaned against it, his heart thumping in his ears.

"Fuck."

He flicked on the lights, wincing at the sudden brightness. The house was a mess, clothes strewn about, empty takeaway containers littering the coffee table in the lounge. He hadn't bothered to clean in weeks. What was the point?

Vincent shrugged off his leather jacket, tossing it onto the back of a chair. He made his way to the kitchen, his movements automatic, driven by habit rather than conscious thought. The fridge door opened with a soft *whoosh*, and he grabbed a beer, deftly popping the cap off.

He took a long swig, the cold liquid doing little to calm his nerves. The ginger lad's face kept flashing in his mind, that smug grin mocking him. And the older man, the lad's dad . . . His grip tightened on the bottle. How did he know about Rose?

Vincent's gaze fell on a framed photo on the kitchen counter. Rose, smiling at the camera, her eyes bright with life. He remembered taking the picture on the night she died. She looked so beautiful – a girl of sixteen with her whole life ahead of her. He turned it face down, unable to bear her gaze.

He shuffled to the bathroom, flicking on the harsh fluorescent light. The man in the mirror looked like a stranger – unkempt beard, bloodshot eyes with dark circles scored under them. Vincent splashed cold water on his face, a poor attempt to wash away the night's events.

Back in the living room, he collapsed onto the sofa, kicking off his boots. He thumbed the remote, and the TV flickered to life, filling the room with a dull glow and mindless chatter. Vincent stared at it blankly, not really seeing or hearing anything.

His nightly routine continued on autopilot – finishing his beer, brushing his teeth, stripping down to his boxers, and going to bed. He lay there staring at the ceiling, but sleep eluded him. The faint glow of streetlights seeped through the curtains, casting eerie shadows across the room. He shifted, trying to find a comfortable position, but his body refused to settle. The concrete-like mattress unyielding and cold beneath him.

He replayed the night's events in an endless loop. The ginger lad's face twisted with anger. The sleek black car pulling up beside him. The older man's words echoed in his head, a sinister lullaby that kept him wide awake. *You'd do well to remember your place, Mr Burke.*

Vincent's fists clenched involuntarily, bunching up the sheets. How dare they threaten him? He'd faced down worse in his time. But then—

Your daughter. Rose, wasn't it? Such a tragedy, what happened to her. It would be a shame if something similar were to befall someone else you care about.

A chill ran down Vincent's spine. The casual mention of Rose's death tossed out like a throwaway comment. It made his blood boil. What did they know? Who were these people?

He rolled onto his side, trying to get more comfortable.

Vincent wracked his brain, trying to think of anyone else who might be in danger because of him. Truth be told, he didn't give much of a fuck about anyone now. He should've decked that smug bastard right there in the street. Grabbed him by his fancy collar and showed him what an actual threat looked like.

"Fucking cowards," he said in a rough growl.

The older man's face swam before his eyes. That condescending smirk burned into his memory. Vincent's blood boiled. He should've demanded answers, pinned the bastard against his expensive car, and made him explain what he was getting at. Explain what he knew about Rose.

Vincent jolted up and swung his legs out of bed. He reached for his mobile on the nightstand, fingers hovering over Murph's number. Murph would know what to do. He always had a level head in a crisis.

But the glowing numbers on the bedside clock gave him pause: 3:47 a.m. Too late, or early, to be waking anyone. Murph had his own problems; he didn't need Vincent's shite on top of everything else.

He flopped back onto the bed and squeezed his eyes shut, willing sleep to come. But every time he drifted off, he saw that black car sliding up beside him, heard that silky voice dripping with menace.

He twisted again, punching his pillow into submission. Sleep. All he wanted was some goddamn sleep. Everything would look different in the morning. It had to.

~

Vincent's eyelids grew heavy, his body succumbing to exhaustion, and he drifted toward slumber. A voice shattered the surrounding stillness.

"Are you going to let them get away with it, Vincent?"

The words, deep and smooth, almost seductive, jolted him awake. Vincent's eyes snapped open, his heart hammering against his ribs. He bolted upright in bed, chest heaving as he gulped in air.

"Who's there?" he growled, the words scraping from his throat.

Silence answered him.

Vincent's eyes darted around the darkened room, squinting to make out shapes in the gloom. Shadows reached from every corner, seeming to shift and dance in his peripheral vision. He strained his ears, listening for any sound: a creaking floorboard, a rustling curtain, anything to betray an intruder's presence.

Nothing.

The hair on the back of his neck bristled. Vincent fumbled for the bedside lamp, knocking over an empty beer can in his haste. It clattered to the floor, impossibly loud in the night's stillness.

Light flooded the room, momentarily blinding him. Vincent blinked rapidly, his eyes adjusting as he scanned every inch of his bedroom. The wardrobe door stood ajar, and for a heart-stopping moment, he imagined someone hiding inside. But as his vision cleared, he saw only rumpled clothes and old boxes.

Vincent scanned from corner to corner, his pulse gradually slowing as familiar bedroom items formed out of the darkness. The battered dresser piled high with discarded clothes. His cracked mirror reflecting his haggard face. The faded poster of a motorcycle he'd meant to replace years ago. Everything appeared normal, yet the voice clung to his thoughts, refusing to fade.

He swung his legs over the side of the bed, wincing as his bare feet touched the cold floorboards. Vincent stood, his knees creaking in protest. He padded across the room, each step cautious.

The curtains. Vincent yanked them aside, half-expecting to find someone crouched on the window ledge. Nothing but the dim glow of a streetlight and the patter of rain against glass.

He turned to the partially open wardrobe, hesitated, then wrenched it open in one swift motion. Clothes hung limply from their hangers and shoes lay scattered across the bottom. No intruder, only the musty smell of neglected clothing.

Vincent dropped to his knees, ignoring the twinge in his back. He peered beneath the bed, where dust bunnies and a lone sock greeted him. Nothing more.

Exhausted and slightly embarrassed, Vincent sank back onto the mattress. He let out a long, shaky breath. "You're losing it, old man," he muttered. "It's stress. You need some bloody sleep."

But even with his self-reassurance, doubt gnawed at him. The voice had been so clear, so . . . present. Vincent shook his head to dispel the lingering unease.

He flicked off the light and sank back into bed, still on

edge. The darkness enveloped him, but sleep remained elusive. That voice, so coherent and yet impossible, echoed in his mind.

"Are you going to let them get away with it?"

He squeezed his eyes shut, willing the words away, but they persisted. Vincent's thoughts drifted to the ginger lad, his sneering face imprinted on memory. The boy's father – all expensive suit and cold eyes – loomed larger still. Their threat hung in the air, as tangible as the musty smell of his bedroom.

It concerns your daughter. Rose, wasn't it? Such a tragedy, what happened to her. It would be a shame if something similar were to befall someone else you care about.

Vincent ground his teeth at the memory. How dare they speak her name? His sweet Rose, taken too soon. The image of her laughing face morphed into the twisted metal of the crash, the ancient oak stained with blood.

The ginger lad's smug expression swam before Vincent's eyes. His father's cold threat.

It concerns your daughter. Rose, wasn't it? Such a tragedy, what happened to her. It would be a shame if something similar were to befall someone else you care about.

What were they implying? It had been an accident, plain and simple. Hadn't it? But now, doubt crept in like a poisonous fog.

Vincent pieced together fragments of memory. Rose's excitement about her new job. The mysterious phone conversations she'd stopped when he entered the room. Her nervous glances in the weeks before the crash.

"Are you going to let them get away with it?"

The question pounded in his head, relentless as a migraine. Vincent pressed his palms against his temples, trying to silence the voice, but it only grew louder.

"Are you going to let them get away with it?"

As Vincent lay in the darkness, his fear melted away, replaced by a seething anger that caused his muscles to tighten. The ginger lad's smug face followed by the cold, calculating eyes of his father. Their threat hung in the air, a challenge left unanswered.

He got out of bed again and paced. With each step he took, the old floorboards emitted a distinct creaking sound, filling the small room. The thought of action, of doing something, anything, to push back against their intimidation grew more appealing with each passing moment.

Vincent paused, a memory surfacing: The rundown house on Willow Lane, its peeling paint and overgrown garden a blight on the neighbourhood. He'd asked them about it at the club earlier and they kept quiet, but he'd seen the ginger lad and his mates lounging there, smoking and drinking, causing trouble. It was their hangout.

He looked at the bedside clock. The red digits glowed in the darkness: 4:07 a.m. Vincent's lips curled into a grim smile. Now that the streets were deserted, it was the perfect time for Vincent to attend to some unfinished business.

A dangerous resolve formed in his eyes and a surge of dark energy coursed through him, as if the voice in the darkness approved of his decision. He moved to his wardrobe, pulling out dark clothes suitable for moving unnoticed in the night. Black jeans, a navy jumper, and his old leather jacket. Vincent dressed rapidly.

As he laced up his boots, a flicker of doubt crossed his mind. Was this really a good idea? He paused, hand on the doorknob, considering his options.

Before he had time to talk himself down, another whisper filled the room.

"They sullied your daughter's memory. Are you going to stand for that?"

Vincent thought of Rose, and then the sneering ginger lad, and his hesitation evaporated. No, he wouldn't stand for it. *I'll teach that cunt a lesson he won't forget.*

CHAPTER 5
DARK DEEDS

Vincent stepped into the pre-dawn darkness. The chill air nipped at his exposed skin. The street lay silent, houses dark and still in the early morning hours. His mood matched the gloom but with a simmering anger beneath the surface.

He strode toward the Yam parked in the driveway. The bike's chrome gleamed dully in the faint light from the streetlamps. Vincent swung his leg over the seat, settling onto the familiar leather. He slid the key into the ignition and turned it to the ON position.

Vincent paused for a heartbeat. The gravity of what he was about to do pressed down on him, but the memory of the ginger lad's smirk and his father's threat steeled his resolve.

He pushed the starter.

The engine thundered to life, piercing the silence of the neighbourhood. Vincent revved it once, twice. The powerful vibrations coursed through his body. The low rumble spoke to something primal within him, echoing his caged fury.

Vincent eased out of the driveway, the bike's headlight

cutting a swath through the darkness. As he accelerated down the empty street, the wind on his face carried away the last trace of doubt.

The familiar streets of the village passed by in a blur as Vincent replayed the confrontation with the ginger lad and his father. Their comments about Rose twisted in his gut, stoking the fire of his anger.

He leaned into a turn, the bike responding smoothly to his touch. The thrum of the engine and the rush of the wind filled his ears, drowning out the voice of reason whispering that this might be a mistake.

VINCENT STOPPED the Yam a few doors down from the ramshackle house on Willow Lane. He cut the engine and lights, plunging himself into darkness. The dilapidated hovel stood across the street, its peeling paint and boarded windows showing years of neglect.

He dismounted, his boots crunching on loose gravel. A damp chill clung to the darkness, tinged with the subtle rot of fallen leaves. Vincent settled in to wait.

Time crawled by, each minute stretching into an eternity. The eastern sky was still inky black; he'd have the cover of darkness for hours yet. Vincent shifted his weight, muscles stiff from standing motionless for so long.

A flicker of movement caught his eye. The front door of the house creaked open, and a figure stumbled out onto the porch. Vincent's breath caught in his throat; he recognised the shock of ginger hair, now mussed and sticking up at odd angles.

The lad looked worse for wear, his clothes rumpled and stained. He swayed, fumbling in his pocket, likely searching for a smoke. Even from this distance, Vincent could see the bloodshot eyes and pallid complexion of someone nursing a vicious hangover.

Vincent's pulse quickened as the lad stumbled down the street. He waited until there was a bit of distance between them before starting his bike, following at a cautious pace. The streets were empty, amplifying the rumble of his Yamaha, but the lad was too out of it to notice. He weaved his way through the village, occasionally stopping to steady himself against a wall or lamp post.

Vincent kept back, his eyes never leaving the shock of red hair bobbing ahead. His grip tightened on the handlebars.

As they approached the outskirts, the lad turned down a secluded side street. Vincent's heart leapt. This was his chance. He parked his bike in a nearby alley, cutting the engine and dismounting in one fluid motion.

On foot, Vincent moved swiftly and silently. Years of working as a bouncer had taught him how to move without drawing attention. The lad was only a few metres ahead, oblivious to his presence. What would he do when he caught up? The anger that had driven him there now mixed with uncertainty. But second thoughts were no longer an option.

"Oi!" Vincent's rough bark cut through the silence.

The ginger lad spun around, nearly losing his balance. His bleary eyes widened in surprise, then narrowed as recognition dawned. A sneer spread across his face, transforming his youthful features into something ugly and spiteful.

"Oh, it's Big Balls," the lad drawled, his words slurred. "What are you doing here, Big Balls? Bit far from your usual patch, ain't ya?"

Vincent clenched his fists, fighting the urge to wipe that smirk off the prick's face. He took a step forward, towering over the youth.

Vincent's blood boiled as the lad swayed on his feet. His cocky grin widened, but his eyes gleamed with malice.

"Me da warned you, didn't he?" The lad chuckled, his words slurring. "Told you to back off. But here you are, Big Balls Burke, thinking you're hard."

Vincent's fists clenched tighter, his knuckles white beneath his gloves. He took another step forward, looming over the ginger youth.

"You made a huge mistake bringing your auld fella into this." The words rumbled from deep in his chest, a sound more animal than human, each syllable laced with threat.

But the lad didn't flinch. If anything, his smirk grew wider, fuelled by liquid courage and youthful bravado.

"Mistake?" He barked out a laugh. "Nah, mate. The mistake's all yours. Wait till me da hears about this. You'll be six feet under before the day's out."

Vincent's jaw tightened, a muscle twitching in his cheek. The lad was playing with fire, and he didn't even know it.

"You think you're untouchable because of your daddy?" Vincent spat. "You're nothing but a snot-nosed brat who—"

"Speaking of brats," the lad interrupted, his eyes glinting with cruel amusement. "How's that girl of yours? Oh wait, that's right. Poor little Rosie can't play anymore, can she?"

Something snapped inside Vincent. The world around him faded to a dull roar, his vision tunnelling until all he could see was the lad's mocking face. Rose's name on those sneering lips ignited a fury unlike anything he'd ever known.

Vincent lunged forward, his hands closing around the lad's throat. The cocky grin vanished, replaced by wide-eyed terror as the youth realised his mistake. Vincent's grip tightened, his fingers digging into the soft flesh.

The lad's hands clawed at Vincent's arms, nails raking across leather. He kicked out, catching Vincent in the shin, but the older man brushed it off. Rage coursed through Vincent, drowning out everything else.

They stumbled backwards, the youth's back slamming against a brick wall. His eyes bulged, face turning an alarming shade of red. Beneath Vincent's fingers, a rapid pulse throbbed, accompanied by the desperate struggle for air.

Something primeval took over. Rage clouded Vincent's mind, his muscles tensing as a hot flush spread across his skin. His vision constricted, zeroing in on the terror-stricken face. The lad's mouth gaped and shut like a beached fish, his strangled throat unable to produce a sound.

Vincent lifted the youth off his feet, legs kicking wildly, feet scrabbling against the wall. His hands beat weakly against Vincent's chest, strength fading fast.

In a burst of desperate energy, the ginger lad broke Vincent's grip. He gulped in air, coughing violently. But before he could cry out, Vincent's hand shot out, grabbing a fistful of that bright red hair.

With a roar, Vincent slammed his head against the brick wall. A sickening, wet *CRACK* resounded through the quiet street. The lad's body slumped and slid down the wall like a broken doll.

Vincent stared at the crumpled form below him. The

red haze of rage dissipated, replaced by a cold, creeping dread. Kneeling beside the motionless body, his hands trembled as they desperately searched for a pulse at the lad's throat.

Nothing.

For a moment, panic clawed at Vincent's insides. He was unable to process what he'd done. But then, as if someone had flipped a switch, an eerie calm washed over him. His racing thoughts slowed, his breathing steadied.

Vincent's eyes darted around the alley, taking in every detail with unnerving clarity. A nearby streetlight cast long shadows, but the street remained mercifully empty. No windows overlooked this spot. No CCTV cameras in sight.

With mechanical efficiency, Vincent grasped the lad's ankles and dragged him deeper into the alleyway. The youth's head flopped, leaving a faint smear on the rough concrete. Vincent's mind registered this dispassionately as if observing someone else's actions.

He spotted a large wheelie bin tucked against the wall. Perfect. Vincent heaved the body behind it, arranging the limbs to make it less visible from the street. He stood back, surveying his work.

Vincent's icy gaze swept over the scene one last time. Without a flicker of emotion, he returned to his bike. The engine roared to life, filling the night. In seconds, he was gone.

As Vincent navigated the empty streets, he planned. He needed a car. Something inconspicuous. Something that wouldn't be missed for a while. And he knew exactly where to get one.

The familiar outline of Murph's Bar stood ahead. Vincent pulled into the back alley, killed the engine. He'd helped Murph close up countless times. He knew where the spare key was hidden.

VINCENT'S HANDS gripped the steering wheel of Murph's old Ford in a vise grip as he travelled the country road, winding through dense woodland. He'd driven this route countless times but seldom with such cargo.

Ahead, Vincent spotted the side road he was looking for. He turned off the main road, an old memory guiding him along the overgrown path. With each bump and obstacle, the suspension creaked and groaned, adding to the roughness of the journey.

After a few minutes, he reached a small clearing. Vincent switched off the engine, plunging the world into silence. He sat for a moment, listening to the soft tick of the cooling engine and the rustle of leaves in the breeze.

Vincent stepped out of the car. The boot opened with a soft groan, revealing the ginger lad's lifeless form. Vincent hefted the body over his shoulder, grunting at the dead weight. He bent his knees and reached in to grab a shovel with his free hand.

He trudged deeper into the woods, fallen leaves crunching beneath his boots. The ground sloped gently downward, leading to a secluded hollow. Vincent's eyes scanned the area, settling on a spot beneath an aged oak tree.

He dropped the body to one side without ceremony and got to work, the shovel biting into soft earth with ease. Vincent fell into a steady rhythm, the physical labour a welcome distraction. While he dug, his thoughts drifted to the echoes of previous nights, of other bodies. The hollow held its share of secrets.

When the hole was deep enough, Vincent rolled the lad's body into it. He paused, looking down at the pale face framed by that shock of ginger hair. For a moment, remorse threatened to overwhelm him. But Vincent pushed it aside, burying it along with the body.

With the grave filled and the ground smoothed over, Vincent returned to the car. He wiped down every surface, erasing any trace of his presence. The cleaning supplies went into a plastic bag; he'd dispose of them later.

Back at Murph's Bar, Vincent parked the Ford back where he'd found it. He gave it a last once-over before retrieving his motorcycle. Riding home, the first rays of sunlight peeked over the horizon. Another long night, another secret buried in the woods.

VINCENT TRUDGED INTO HIS BATHROOM, peeling off his sweat-soaked clothes. He cranked the shower to its hottest setting and stepped under the scalding spray. Desperate to wash away the night's events, he scrubbed his skin raw as billows of steam rose around him.

Stepping out of the shower, Vincent wiped the condensation from the mirror. His reflection stared back at him, haggard and haunted. Dark circles ringed his eyes, and his beard seemed greyer than ever. He didn't recognise the man looking back at him.

"What have you become?" The question hung in the air, unanswered.

As Vincent stumbled to his bedroom, exhaustion settled on him like a concrete slab. He collapsed onto the unmade bed, not bothering with nightclothes. As his eyes closed, sleep claimed him.

As unconsciousness threatened to engulf him, a whisper slithered through the silence. Smooth and seductive, it caressed his ear.

"Well done, Vincent. You're one step closer."

Vincent's eyes snapped open, but the room was empty. He shook his head, trying to clear the cobwebs of fatigue. As he fell into a troubled sleep, the voice reverberated in his mind, casting an eerie spell like a haunting lullaby.

CHAPTER 6
UNEASY PEACE

Wide awake, Vincent's chest heaved as his heart pounded against his ribcage. For a moment, he couldn't remember where he was. Then it all came crashing back – the ginger lad, the voice, the woods. He groaned, rubbing his face with calloused hands.

Sunlight streamed through the gaps in the curtains, painting stripes across his rumpled bedsheets. Vincent fumbled for his mobile on the nightstand, squinting at the bright screen. Several missed calls from Murph glared back at him.

His thumb hovered over the call back button, but Vincent hesitated. He didn't want to deal with anybody before he got his head on straight about the previous night.

He tossed the phone aside, ignoring the calls for now. He swung his legs over the side of the bed, wincing as his feet hit the floor. Every muscle was sore, a reminder of the night's exertions.

He shuffled to the kitchen, desperate for a cup of coffee to clear his head. As the kettle boiled, Vincent leaned against the counter. He thought about the risks he'd taken.

What if someone saw me on Willow Lane or when I took Murph's car? What if the lad's father comes asking questions?

The kettle clicked off, startling Vincent from his thoughts. He poured the steaming water over instant coffee granules, watching them dissolve. The familiar aroma went a little way in calming his thoughts.

As he sipped the bitter brew, Vincent's gaze fell on the calendar hanging on the wall. Today's date was circled in red – the anniversary of Rose's death. His stomach churned. How had he forgotten? The guilt of this lapse in memory far outweighed his guilt for sorting out that ginger cunt.

Vincent reached for the remote, flicking on the telly. The sudden burst of noise in his quiet kitchen made him flinch. He'd meant it as a distraction, but fate had other plans.

" . . . local youth, Declan Kenny, has been reported missing . . ." The newsreader's crisp voice cut through Vincent's thoughts like a knife.

His eyes snapped to the screen, coffee mug frozen halfway to his lips. The world tilted on its axis as a familiar face filled the television – ginger hair, freckled cheeks, cocky grin. It was him.

Declan Kenny. The name echoed in Vincent's mind, giving shape to the nameless spectre he'd dumped in a shallow grave.

Vincent's hand shook, hot coffee sloshing over the rim of his mug and splashing onto the counter. He scarcely noticed the scalding liquid seeping into his shirt, his eyes fixed on the screen as he listened.

" . . . Declan was last seen leaving a friend's house in the early hours of this morning. His family are appealing for any information . . ."

The mug slipped from Vincent's numb fingers, clattering into the sink. He stumbled back, his legs carrying him to the sofa where he sat.

The telly droned on, but Vincent couldn't make out the words anymore. His gaze remained fixed on the screen, unseeing, as images from the previous night flashed through his mind. The confrontation, the struggle, the sickening *THUD* as the lad – Declan – hit the ground.

His phone buzzed, vibrating against the coffee table. Murph's name flashed on the screen, persistent and demanding. Vincent stared at it. He couldn't avoid Murph forever. He reached for the phone, hesitating for a moment before answering it.

"All right, Murph?" Vincent's voice sounded strange to his own ears, but he forced himself to keep it steady.

"Vinny, where the hell are you? Your shift started an hour ago." Murph's gruff voice crackled through the speaker.

He couldn't go in. Not today. He'd be too paranoid. He cleared his throat, buying himself a moment to think.

"Sorry, mate. I'm not well. Must've caught something." The lie slipped out easily, surprising Vincent with how natural it sounded.

"You're sick? You never get sick."

"Yeah, well, there's a first time for everything, eh? Stomach's been giving me grief since last night."

A pause on the other end of the line. Vincent held his breath, waiting.

"All right, then," Murph said. "Get some rest. I'll find someone to cover your shift."

"Cheers, Murph. I owe you one."

After hanging up, Vincent paced his living room, his heavy footsteps echoing in the empty house. He replayed the events of the previous night over and over, looking for weak points. The confrontation, the struggle, the sickening *THUD* as Declan's head hit the wall.

He caught sight of himself in the mirror above the fireplace and froze. The man staring back at him was a stranger – hollow-eyed, unkempt, haunted. Vincent hardly recognised himself.

His gaze drifted to the liquor cabinet. Without thinking, he strode over and yanked it open, pulling out a bottle of whiskey. He poured a generous measure into a tumbler. The amber liquid sloshed, creating small ripples.

Vincent lifted the glass to his lips and tossed it back in one swift motion. The whiskey burned its way down his throat, settling like liquid fire in his stomach. He grimaced, welcoming the sensation. It was something tangible, something real to focus on.

As the alcohol took effect, dulling the sharp edges of his thoughts, Vincent rationalised his actions. Declan had been a threat. The lad and his father had cornered him, had sullied Rose's memory. What was Vincent supposed to do? Let them get away with it?

He poured another drink, sipping it slowly. The more he thought about it, the more convinced he became. It had been self-defence. Declan came at him first. Vincent had been protecting himself. And if things had got out of hand, well . . . that wasn't his fault, was it?

Vincent nodded to himself, the alcohol lending false confidence to his reasoning. He'd done what he had to do. It was regrettable, sure, but necessary. He couldn't have known things would end up the way they did.

Vincent's phone buzzed again, vibrating against the coffee table. He eyed it warily, the whiskey glass hovering halfway to his lips. He set the tumbler down and reached for the device.

An unknown number flashed on the screen. Vincent's brow furrowed, and he swiped to open the message. With each word he read, his blood grew colder and colder.

Well done. You've taken the first step.

He blinked hard, hoping the message would somehow change when he looked again. But the words remained, plain and unsettling, on the bright screen.

Who would have sent this? How did they know? He'd been careful, hadn't he? No one was in the woods, and it was too late for witnesses on the street. Yet someone knew what he'd done.

His thumb hovered over the message. With a sudden, decisive movement, he hit delete. The text vanished, leaving his inbox empty once more. Vincent tossed the phone aside as if it had burned him.

"Wrong fuckin' number," he muttered to himself, reaching for his whiskey glass again. "Has to be."

But even as the words left his lips, Vincent knew he didn't believe them. The message had been too specific, too timely to be a mere coincidence. Someone out there knew his secret, and the thought sent panic coursing through him.

He drained his glass, grimacing at the burn. The alcohol did little to calm his nerves. Vincent's gaze darted around the room, suddenly exposed. Were they watching him even now? He stood abruptly, stumbling to the windows to yank the curtains closed.

～

Vincent spent the rest of the day in a fog, his mind oscillating between frantic worry and an eerie, unnatural calm. One moment, he'd pace the living room, imagining police sirens wailing in the distance. The next, he slumped on the sofa, staring blankly at the wall, his thoughts oddly quiet.

As the light outside faded, Vincent's stomach growled, reminding him he hadn't eaten all day. He dragged himself to the kitchen, opening cupboards and the fridge without seeing their contents. Eventually, he pulled out a tin of beans and some bread, going through the motions of preparing a meal.

The beans bubbled in the saucepan, filling the kitchen with their rich, tomato-y scent. Vincent stirred them mechanically. He popped two slices of bread into the toaster, the familiar routine bizarrely out of place given the circumstances.

When the toast popped up, Vincent jumped. He let out a shaky breath, annoyed at his own nervousness. Placing the beans on the toast, he carried the plate to the dining table and sat down heavily.

Vincent stared at the food, his appetite vanishing as quickly as it had appeared. He forced himself to take a bite, chewing slowly. The toast was sawdust in his mouth, the beans tasteless and unappealing. But he made himself continue, knowing he needed to keep up some semblance of normalcy.

As he ate, Vincent's look kept drifting to his phone lying face down on the table. The mysterious text message nagged at him. Who sent it? And more importantly, what did they want?

Vincent pushed his half-eaten supper away, his stomach churning. He couldn't shake the sensation of being watched, even in the privacy of his own home. With a heavy sigh, he reached for the remote.

The screen flickered to life, and Vincent's blood ran cold. A familiar face stared back at him – Declan Kenny again. The news anchor's voice droned on.

". . . still missing. Police are urging anyone with information about Declan Kenny's whereabouts to come forward. The eighteen-year-old was last seen . . ."

Vincent gripped the remote tighter. Images of Declan's smiling face flashed across the screen, interspersed with footage of worried family members and grim-faced police officers.

He watched, transfixed, as Declan's father – the man who had threatened him –appeared on the screen. The once intimidating figure now looked haggard and desperate, pleading for his son's safe return. Vincent wondered who the Kennys were; it hadn't been twenty-four hours since Declan had gone missing and it was all over the news. That would take leverage.

Sick of looking at them, Vincent jabbed at the power button. The screen went black, leaving him in silence. He stared at his reflection in the darkened TV, a blank face that looked back at him.

Vincent got to his feet, swaying more than a little. Without bothering to clean up, he made his way to the bedroom, hoping that sleep might offer some respite.

He lay in the darkness, his body heavy with exhaustion, but his mind playing the events of the past twenty-four hours on repeat, a twisted film he couldn't shut off. He squeezed his eyes shut, willing sleep to come, but it remained elusive.

"It was necessary," he whispered into the void. "I had no choice."

The words hung in the air, seeming to mock him with their hollow ring. Vincent repeated them, again and again, like a mantra. Each repetition was less convincing than the last.

He rolled onto his side, pulling the duvet tighter around himself as if it could shield him from his own thoughts. In the midst of finding solace in the familiar warmth, a small voice of doubt crept into his mind.

Was it really necessary? Did you truly have no choice?

Vincent pushed the questions away, burying them deep. He couldn't afford to second-guess himself now. What was done, was done. There was no possibility of going back.

As he drifted off, that nagging voice persisted. It whispered that perhaps he was trying to convince himself of a lie, that maybe there had been another way. But exhaustion won out, and Vincent slipped into an uneasy sleep.

CHAPTER 7

SIXTEEN AND GONE

Vincent jolted awake, his daughter's name tearing from his throat. "Rose!"

Heart hammering, he sat bolt upright in bed, sheets tangled around his sweat-soaked body. The darkness of his bedroom pressed in on him, thick and oppressive. Vincent struggled to catch his breath, the remnants of the nightmare clinging to him like cobwebs.

As his pulse slowed, the fog of sleep lifted, only to be replaced by a different haze. Memories, intentionally suppressed, bubbled to the surface of his consciousness.

That night. One year ago.

Vincent squeezed his eyes shut, but it did nothing to stem the tide of images flooding his mind.

VINCENT STOOD BEFORE THE MIRROR, adjusting his collar. The din of Rose's excited chatter filled the small bathroom, her words tumbling over each other in a rush.

"Dad, you won't believe it! Saoirse's having this massive party tonight. Everyone's going to be there!"

He glanced at his daughter's reflection. Rose's eyes sparkled with anticipation, her hands gesticulating wildly as she leant against the doorframe.

"Everyone, eh?" Vincent raised an eyebrow, a knot of worry tightening in his gut. "And who's everyone?"

Rose rolled her eyes, a gesture that reminded him so much of her mother it made his chest ache. "You know. People from school. It's not a big deal."

Vincent turned, fixing her with a look. "Sounds like a bit of a big deal."

"Dad," Rose grumbled. "I'm sixteen. It's just a party."

He sighed. The thought of Rose out there, surrounded by hormone-addled teenagers, made his skin crawl. "I don't know, love. It's a school night, and I've got to work."

"But Saoirse's parents will be there," Rose countered quickly. "And I promise I'll be back by eleven. Please, Dad?"

Vincent hesitated, torn between his instinct to protect and the knowledge that he couldn't keep her locked away forever. The pleading look in Rose's eyes was almost enough to crumble his resolve. She was growing up, and it scared the hell out of him.

"You're sure Saoirse's parents will be there?" he asked, searching her face for any hint of deception.

Rose nodded. "Absolutely. Mrs O'Brien is even making her famous apple tart for us."

Vincent gave her another long look before sighing. "All right. But you're back by eleven, no exceptions. And you call me if you need anything, yeah?"

Rose's face lit up, her smile as bright as a summer's day. She threw her arms around him, almost knocking him off balance. "Thank you, thank you, thank you! You're the best dad ever!"

He chuckled, wrapping his arms around her slight frame. "Don't you forget it," he mumbled into her hair.

Vincent finished getting ready for his shift at the club as Rose got ready in her bedroom. He grabbed his leather jacket from the hook by the door and stepped into the hallway.

He paused. Rose stood in there, dressed for the party in a flowery dress that made her look older than her sixteen years.

"You look beautiful, love." He drank in the sight of his little girl somehow transformed into a beautiful young woman. He thought his heart might burst with pride.

Rose beamed at him. "Thanks, Dad. Have a good night at work."

Vincent stepped forward, pulling her into a tight embrace. He breathed in the scent of her shampoo, committing it to memory. The nagging sense of disquiet returned, making him reluctant to let go.

"Dad." Rose laughed, the sound muffled against his chest. "I can't breathe."

He released her, forcing a smile onto his face. "Sorry, love. B-be careful, yeah?"

Rose rolled her eyes, but her expression was fond. "Always am. Don't worry so much."

As Vincent opened the front door, he turned back for one last look at his daughter. She stood in the hallway waving goodbye, her smile bright and carefree. The image burned itself into his mind as he stepped out into the cool evening air, unaware that it would be the last time he'd see her alive.

LATER THAT NIGHT, Vincent leant against the wall near the club's entrance, his eyes unfocused. The thump of bass from inside reverberated through his body, but his mind was elsewhere. He checked his watch for the umpteenth time, the hands crawling toward eleven o'clock.

A gentle nudge to his shoulder snapped him back to reality. Murph stood beside him, concern plain on his weathered face.

"You all right there, Vinny? You've been miles away the entire night."

Vincent shook his head, trying to clear the fog of worry. "Yeah, it's just . . . Rose is out at a party. Can't stop thinking about it."

Murph's expression softened. "Ah, I see. First time letting her out on a school night?"

"First time letting her out to a big party like this," Vincent admitted. "I know I'm being stupid, but I can't shake this feeling . . ."

"Listen, mate," Murph said, clapping a hand on Vincent's shoulder. "Rose is a good kid. Smart as a whip, that one. She won't do anything stupid."

Vincent nodded, wanting to believe his friend's words. "I know, I know. But the world out there, Murph. It's not always kind to young girls, is it?"

Murph's face grew serious. "No, it's not. But Rose has got a sound head on her shoulders. And she's got you looking out for her. That counts for a lot."

Vincent checked his watch again: 10:45. "She promised she'd be home by eleven."

"And she will be," Murph reassured him. "You've raised her right, Vinny. Trust in that."

Vincent took a deep breath, trying to let Murph's words sink in. But the knot of worry in his gut refused to loosen.

VINCENT'S EYES darted to his phone for the hundredth time that night. It was 11:05. No texts, no calls. With each refresh of his messages, his heart thumped against his ribs.

Nothing.

He dialled Rose's number, his fingers trembling. The phone rang, each unanswered tone increasing his dread.

Voicemail. Again.

"Rose, it's Dad. You're late. Call me back. Now."

Vincent hung up and pocketed his phone, scanning the thinning crowd outside the club. No sign of her.

It was 11:15.

Still nothing.

He pulled out his phone again, dialled her number. Straight to voicemail this time.

"Rose, where are you? I'm worried sick. Please, call me."

Vincent's breath came in short bursts. He shouldered his way through the club's entrance, searching for Murph. The pulsing lights and thunderous music only heightened his anxiety.

He found Murph behind the bar.

"Murph!" Vincent yelled over the din. "I need to go. Rose isn't back. She's not answering her phone."

Murph's face creased with concern. "Go, mate. I'll cover for you. Let me know when you find her."

Vincent nodded, already turning away. He burst out of the club, the cool night air doing nothing to calm his frayed nerves. His motorcycle stood waiting, a gleaming promise of speed.

As he swung his leg over the seat, Vincent's hand shook so badly he could barely get the key in the ignition. The engine roared to life, matching the panic surging through him.

He tore through the village streets, heading for Saoirse's house. Each second ticked by like an eternity. Each darkened street a potential hiding place for his worst fears.

~

GRIPPING THE HANDLEBARS, the vibrations of Vincent's roaring motorcycle reverberated through his body, his knuckles turning pale with intensity. One thing consumed his entire being: finding Rose.

Saoirse's house was ahead, dark and silent. As Vincent pulled up, a heavy feeling settled in his chest. No lights, no music, no teenagers stumbling about. He leapt off his bike, pounding on the front door.

No answer.

"Rose!" he shouted. Her name echoed in the night.

Nothing.

Back on his motorcycle, Vincent tore through the town. He checked the park, the late-night café Rose and her friends frequented, even the old abandoned mill where kids sometimes hung out. Each location crushed his hope further.

As he circled back toward the village centre, his phone buzzed in his pocket. Fumbling to answer it, Vincent almost crashed before he pulled in on the verge.

"Rose?" he gasped.

"Dad?"

Relief flooded through him, followed by anger. "Where are you?"

She spoke with a slurred and confused voice, saying, "I-I don't know. Everything's spinning."

Vincent took a deep breath, forcing himself to stay calm. "Okay, sweetheart. Look around. What do you see?"

"Trees. Lots of trees. And there's a big rock. It looks like a face."

Vincent knew that place – the old quarry on the outskirts of town. "Stay where you are, Rose. I'm coming for you."

He ended the call and gunned the engine, accelerating back onto the road. Relief warred with anger inside him. She was alive but drunk in a dangerous place.

Who the fuck is with you?

Vincent sped toward the quarry, determined to bring his daughter home.

VINCENT'S HANDS tightened on the handlebars as he approached The Devil's Corner. The notorious bend loomed ahead, its reputation as black as the night sky above. Rain pattered against his visor, distorting his view of the road.

Memories flooded back, unbidden. That night, so many years ago, when Deirdre vanished without a trace. Vincent had come home late from a shift at the club, exhausted and looking forward to crawling into bed beside his wife. Instead, he'd found an empty house and a crying toddler.

"Dee?" he'd called out, an echo through the silent rooms. But there was no answer, only Rose's frightened wails from her crib.

Vincent shook his head, trying to focus on the road. The rain lashed down, drumming against his leather jacket. He eased off the throttle, all too aware of how treacherous this stretch could be.

The night of Deirdre's disappearance had changed everything. He'd become both mother and father to Rose overnight, fumbling through nappies and bottles, desperate phone calls to his own mum for advice.

Vincent's phone buzzed in his pocket, vibrating against his thigh. He cursed under his breath, knowing he shouldn't check it while riding, but the thought that it might be Rose overrode his caution. Slowing the bike further, he fumbled with one hand to pull the mobile from his jacket.

The screen lit up, revealing a text from Rose. Vincent's heart leapt as he read:

> Dad, I'm ok. Figured out where I am. Getting a ride. Don't worry.

Relief washed over him, chased by a surge of anger. He'd been out of his mind with worry, and she'd been fine all along? Vincent imagined the lecture he'd give her when she got home.

So focused was he on the text that Vincent failed to notice the approaching headlights until they were upon him. The car rounded the bend at breakneck speed, its tyres screeching on the wet tarmac.

Vincent's head snapped up, his eyes widening in horror as the vehicle bore down on him. Time slowed as Vincent wrenched the handlebars, trying to avoid the oncoming headlights. The Yam's tyres lost their grip on the slick tarmac, and the bike slid out from under him.

His world tilted sideways, the road rushing up to meet him. The screech of tyres filled his ears, mingling with the thunderous pounding of his own heart.

Through the chaos, Vincent caught sight of the car as it swerved wildly. It ploughed through the hedge bordering the field, branches and leaves exploding in its wake. The ancient oak tree stood in its path, a silent sentinel in the darkness.

Vincent's breath caught in his throat as he watched, helpless. The car hurtled toward the tree, its headlights illuminating the gnarled trunk for a split second before impact.

The crash was deafening. Metal crumpled like paper, glass shattered, and the night air filled with the acrid smell of burning rubber and petrol.

Vincent's eyes widened in horror, his mouth open in a silent scream. Then darkness engulfed him as his head struck the ground, and consciousness flowed away like water through his fingers.

Vincent's eyes fluttered open, his vision blurry and unfocused. Pain radiated through his body, each throb matching the pounding in his head. He blinked, trying to make sense of his surroundings. The cold, wet grass beneath him came into focus.

A wave of relief washed over him as his muddled mind pieced together what had happened. Rose wasn't with him. She was safe somewhere else. Thank God for small mercies.

But as Vincent's gaze swept across the field, his blood ran cold. The car. It was there, wrapped around the ancient oak tree like some grotesque metal sculpture. Smoke rose from the crumpled bonnet, wisps curling into the night air.

"No," Vincent croaked.

Ignoring the protests of his battered body, Vincent pushed himself to his feet. The world tilted dangerously, and he staggered, nearly falling. But the sight of the wrecked car spurred him on.

Vincent stumbled through the field, his legs leaden. Each step sent shockwaves of pain through his body, but he pressed on. The wet grass squelched beneath his boots, threatening to trip him with every step.

As he drew closer to the wreckage, Vincent's heart hammered in his chest. The car's frame was twisted beyond recognition, its once sleek lines now a jagged mess of metal and shattered glass.

"Hello?" Vincent rasped. "Is everyone all right?"

Silence answered him, broken only by the soft hiss of steam escaping from the ruined engine. Vincent reached the driver's side, his hands shaking as he peered through the shattered window.

What the hell? The driver's seat was empty.

Vincent's heart stopped as his eyes fell on the passenger seat. There, slumped against the cracked window, was Rose. Blood matted her long brown hair, and her face appeared pale and lifeless.

"Rose!" Vincent's voice cracked as he called out to her, "No, no, no."

He grabbed the door handle, yanking it with all his might. The metal groaned in protest but refused to budge. Vincent's panic increased, threatening to choke him.

"Rose, sweetheart, can you hear me?" He pressed his face against the shattered window, ignoring the sharp edges that cut into his skin. "Please, Rose. Open your eyes."

Vincent's fingers scrabbled at the twisted frame, searching for any way to reach his daughter. Blood trickled down his hands, but he didn't notice. All he could see was Rose, so still, so silent.

"I'm here, Rose. Daddy's here. Just hold on, please." His

voice broke, tears mixing with the rain on his face. "I'm sorry. I'm so sorry."

In the distance, sirens wailed, growing louder with each passing second. But to Vincent, they seemed a lifetime away. His vision swam, the edges of the world growing dark.

"No," he said, fighting against the encroaching darkness. "I have to— Rose—"

But his body betrayed him. Vincent's knees buckled, and he slumped against the wrecked car. As consciousness slipped away, his last sight was of Rose, unmoving in the passenger seat.

OPENING his leaden eyelids was a battle for Vincent. The harsh fluorescent lights above seared his retinas, forcing him to squint. A dull ache throbbed through his body, and the sharp scent of disinfectant filled his nostrils. Hospital. He was in the hospital.

As his vision cleared, Vincent noticed a figure slumped in a chair beside his bed. Murph. His face looked drawn and haggard, with dark circles under his eyes.

"Murph?" Vincent's voice came out as a hoarse whisper.

His friend's head snapped up, relief flooding his features. "Vinny, thank Christ. You're awake."

Vincent tried to sit up, but a sharp pain in his ribs forced him back down. "What happened? Where's—"

And then the memory hit him like a truck: A rain-slicked road. The sudden glare of headlights. The sickening crunch of metal. And Rose. Oh God, Rose.

"No," Vincent choked out, his eyes wide with horror. "No, no, no."

Murph reached out, his hand hovering uncertainly over Vincent's arm. "Vinny, I—"

But Vincent didn't hear him. His mind was trapped in that moment, seeing Rose's lifeless form slumped in the passenger seat, the cold metal and sharp glass beneath him as he'd struggled to reach her.

"Rose," he gasped, his breath coming in ragged bursts. "Where's Rose? I need to see her. I need—"

The look on Murph's face said it all. Vincent didn't need to hear the words. He knew. Rose was gone.

A cry tore from Vincent's throat. He thrashed in the bed, ignoring the pain that lanced through his body. Monitors beeped alarms as Vincent's heart rate spiked.

"She can't be gone," Vincent sobbed, his fingers clawing at the sheets. "Not my little girl. Not Rose."

Murph stood, trying to calm his friend. "Vinny, please. You need to—"

But Vincent was beyond reason. Grief and guilt consumed him, leaving no room for anything else. He'd failed her. He was supposed to protect her, and he'd failed.

Vincent blinked, the hospital room fading away. He found himself back in his dimly lit bedroom, the sheets twisted around his legs. His cheeks were wet, and he realised he'd been crying.

The memories crushed him. He struggled to catch his breath, his heart hammering. He sat up, running trembling hands through his sweat-damp hair.

"I'm sorry, my little flower," he whispered into the darkness. "It should have been me who died in that field."

The words hung in the air, heavy with regret and

sorrow. Vincent's gaze fell on the framed photo on his bedside table. Rose's bright smile beamed back at him, frozen in time. He reached out, his fingers tracing the outline of her face.

A sob caught in his throat. The grief remained a constant ache that refused to fade away, just as it had been in the hospital. Vincent tried to make sense of it all. How had he gone from that broken man in the hospital bed to this?

He squeezed his eyes shut, but Rose's face remained imprinted in his mind. What would she think of him now? She'd think he was a monster, and the thought made his stomach churn.

"I've lost my way, Rosie. I don't know who I am anymore."

The silence that followed was deafening. Vincent half-expected to hear that mysterious voice again, whispering dark promises. But there was nothing. Only the hollow echo of his own guilt.

CHAPTER 8
SORRY

Vincent's eyes cracked open, the dim light of dawn filtering through the curtains. His head throbbed, a dull ache that matched the heaviness in his chest. He blinked, his eyes swollen and sore. The nightmare enveloped him, with Rose's face haunting his every thought.

He groaned and hauled himself out of bed. His joints protested, reminding him of the years that had settled into his bones. Vincent shuffled to the bathroom, avoiding his reflection in the mirror. He knew what he'd see – a broken man, a far cry from the father Rose had known.

The shower did little to wash away the taint of the dream. Vincent went through the motions, scrubbing his skin robotically. As he dressed afterward, his movements were mechanical, his mind elsewhere.

In the kitchen, he fumbled with the kettle and made a cup of instant coffee. The aroma filled the air, but it stirred no appetite in him. He added a splash of whiskey. It couldn't do any harm. The first sip barely registered on his tongue.

Vincent stood at the kitchen window, staring out at the grey morning. The mug warmed his hands, but the chill inside him remained. He took another sip, not tasting the bitter liquid. His thoughts drifted back to Rose, to happier mornings filled with her laughter and chatter.

The silence in the house pressed in on him, a reminder of what he'd lost. Vincent's gaze fell on the calendar hanging on the wall. The date mocked him, another day without his daughter. Another day living with the result of his actions.

Vincent downed the rest of the coffee and returned to his bedroom. At the closet, he reached inside, his fingers seeking a box tucked away in the corner. Finding it, he pulled it out, hesitating for a moment with his hand hovering over the lid. With a deep breath, he opened it, revealing a treasure trove of memories he'd locked away.

Nestled among Rose's old drawings and school awards sat Huggs, her favourite teddy bear. Vincent lifted it out with care, as if it might crumble in his hands. Running his fingers over the soft, worn fur, a wave of familiarity washed over him. He brought it close to his face, inhaling deeply. A faint trace of Rose's scent still lingered.

Vincent cradled the bear against his chest, his eyes closed tight against the onslaught of emotions. Rose's laughter reached his ears, and her hugs enveloped him. The teddy bear in his arms was a comfort and a torture.

He stood there for a long moment, lost in memories. When he opened his eyes, his gaze fell on the window again. The grey sky outside mirrored his mood. Without realising his decision, Vincent moved toward the door, Huggs still clutched tightly in his arms.

～

VINCENT SWUNG his leg over the Yam and started the engine, the familiar rumble doing little to calm his nerves. He tucked Huggs securely into his jacket, ensuring the bear wouldn't fall during the journey. As he pulled away from the kerb, a knot formed in his stomach, tightening with each mile that brought him closer to his destination.

The route was imprinted upon his memory, every turn a reminder of that fateful night. At this stage, he could ride it blindfolded. Vincent's grip on the handlebars tightened as he approached The Devil's Corner. The ancient oak tree materialised ahead, its gnarled branches reaching out like accusing fingers.

He brought the bike to a stop, the sudden silence deafening. Vincent dismounted, his movements slow and hesitant. He retrieved Huggs from his jacket, clutching the bear to his chest like a shield against the onslaught of memories.

Each step toward the tree was slow and laborious, as if wading through thick, sticky treacle. The closer he got, the harder it became to breathe. Vincent's vision blurred, tears threatening to spill over. He blinked hard, forcing himself to focus on the base of the tree.

His breath caught in his throat. Amidst the withered remains of his accumulated offerings, fresh flowers bloomed. Vibrant colours stood out against the tree's dark bark; a bouquet of daisies tied with a pink ribbon. He hadn't brought them. Someone else had been here, someone else still remembered Rose.

Realisation struck him. He wasn't alone in his grief. Others carried Rose in their hearts, keeping her memory alive. Vincent sank to his knees before the tree, Huggs still pressed against his chest. His tears flowed freely, soaking the bear's worn fur.

Vincent's lips trembled as he spoke in a whisper over

the rustling leaves, "Rose. My sweet girl," his throat constricting around the words. "I'm so sorry. I should've protected you. I should've been there."

He paused, drawing a shaky breath. The guilt rushed at him, threatening to knock him down.

"It's my fault you were on that road. If I hadn't let you go to that party, if I'd picked you up myself . . ."

Vincent's fingers dug into Huggs' soft fur, seeking comfort from the familiar texture. He closed his eyes, picturing Rose's smiling face, her eyes alight with excitement as she'd talked about the party.

"I was so caught up in work, in my life. I should've put you first, always. You were everything to me, Rose. Everything."

An involuntary sob escaped him. Vincent hunched forward, pressing his forehead against the rough bark of the tree.

"I'd give anything to trade places with you. Anything to bring you back."

The words poured out of him now, a torrent of regret and sorrow he'd kept bottled up for too long.

"I miss you so much, sweetheart. Every day without you is . . . It's like living in darkness. I don't know how to go on without you. I don't know who I am anymore."

Vincent's voice cracked.

"I've done terrible things, Rose. Things that would make you ashamed of me. I'm not the father you deserved. I never was."

He pulled back, gazing up at the branches swaying above him. The dappled sunlight filtering through the leaves reminded him of the way light used to dance in Rose's hair.

"I wish I could speak to you one more time. To tell you how much I love you. To beg for your forgiveness."

Vincent carefully nestled Huggs among the vibrant flowers, his hands shaking with delicate precision. The worn toy looked small and vulnerable against the vibrant blooms, much like Rose had in her final moments. He smoothed the bear's fur one last time, his fingertips lingering on the soft material.

A sudden gust of wind disturbed the branches above, sending leaves rustling in a frenzied dance. Vincent's breath caught in his throat as the sound morphed into something eerily familiar. Whispers floated on the breeze. He strained his ears, searching for the sound again.

Then he heard it. Clear as day, Rose's laughter rang out, carried on the wind. It was unmistakable: that bright, tinkling sound that had once filled their home with joy. Vincent's head snapped up, eyes wide and searching. He spun around, gaze darting from tree to tree, half-expecting to see Rose's smiling face peeking out from behind a trunk.

"Rose?" he called out, voice hoarse and desperate. "Sweetheart, is that you?"

But the area remained empty. No sign of his daughter, no trace of her presence beyond the fading echo of her laughter in his ears. Vincent's shoulders sagged, the brief flicker of hope extinguished as quickly as it had ignited.

He turned back to the tree, eyes falling on Huggs nestled among the flowers. Had he imagined it? Was his grief playing cruel tricks on him? Vincent's hand grazed his weathered face, a reminder of the years he'd lived and the burdens he carried.

He clung to that moment, to the sound of Rose's laughter carried on the wind. Real or imagined, it had brought her close for a heartbeat. In this place of sorrow and regret, he'd sensed her presence more strongly than he had in months.

Vincent closed his eyes, his lips moving in silent supplication. He begged for Rose's forgiveness, not only for his failures as a father, but for the darkness that had consumed him since her death. His latest transgression was just another stain on his soul.

Soul, my fucking arse, he thought as he opened his eyes. Something flickered in the corner of his vision. A dark shape, indistinct but undeniably there. Vincent's head snapped around, eyes searching for the source of the movement. But as quickly as it had appeared, the shape vanished, leaving nothing but empty air and swaying branches.

Vincent's heart rate quickened, a chill creeping up his spine despite the warmth of the day. He scanned the area, gaze darting from tree to tree, searching for any sign of the mysterious shape. The forest held its breath, an unnatural stillness settling over the clearing.

He stood, muscles tensed and ready for . . . for what? Vincent wasn't sure. But every instinct screamed that something was off. The hairs on the back of his neck stood on end, his skin prickling with the sensation of being watched.

Vincent turned in a slow circle, eyes narrowed as he scrutinised every shadow, every patch of undergrowth. The impression intensified, as if unseen eyes bore into him from all directions. He swallowed hard, his mouth dry.

"Who's there?" he called out, too loud in the eerie silence. No response came, save for the faint rustle of leaves in the breeze.

Vincent cast one last glance at Huggs nestled among the flowers. The peaceful moment he'd shared with Rose's memory had shattered, replaced by an unsettling sense of being watched. He swallowed hard, forcing his legs to move.

Each step away from the tree was heavier than the last, as if invisible tendrils sought to hold him in place. Vincent shook his head, trying to clear the fog of unease. He focused on the familiar shape of the Yam on the roadside, using it as an anchor to reality.

The ground beneath his boots seemed unnaturally loud in the field's stillness. Vincent's shoulders tensed, half-expecting something to leap out at him from the shadows beneath the tree. He quickened his pace, eager to put distance between himself and the ancient oak.

Reaching for the bike's handlebars, a whisper drifted past his ear, so faint he almost missed it.

It's not your fault, Dad.

Vincent whirled around, his eyes scanning the hedge and field, searching for any sign of movement. But the area was empty, save for the gently swaying branches and the distant chirping of birds.

He tried to steady his breathing. It couldn't have been real. Rose was gone, buried in the cold earth. His mind played tricks on him, his guilt manifesting in the worst possible way.

"It's the wind, you daft cunt," Vincent muttered, the words sounding hollow even to his own ears. "Just the bloody wind."

Vincent swung his leg over the Yam, his movements mechanical as he settled onto the familiar seat. He turned the key, and the engine roared to life.

He cast one final glance toward the old oak, his eyes seeking the slight form of Huggs nestled among the flowers. The sight of the teddy bear, so small and vulnerable against the massive trunk, sent a fresh wave of pain through his chest. For a moment, Vincent considered turning back, snatching up the bear, and clutching it to him like a lifeline.

But he couldn't. He'd made his choice, leaving a piece of Rose behind in this haunted place. Vincent swallowed hard, forcing his gaze away from the tree and onto the road ahead.

As he pulled away, the wind caressed his face, carrying with it the faintest echo of Rose's laughter. Or was it his imagination? Vincent couldn't distinguish between reality and the tricks of his grief-stricken psyche.

As the rumble of Vincent's bike faded into the distance, a figure materialised from the lengthening shadows beneath the ancient oak. Tall and lithe, clad in the deepest black, the stranger exuded an aura of otherworldly power. His eyes, glinting with an unnatural fire, followed the path Vincent had taken.

A smile played across full lips, revealing teeth that were a touch too sharp. He strode toward the base of the tree, his movements fluid and predatory. Stooping, he plucked Huggs from its resting place among the wilting flowers and held the stuffed bear up to eye level.

"*Oh, Vincent,*" he said, his silken voice caressing the air. "*You've no idea what you've set in motion, have you?*"

The figure's fingers traced the worn fabric of the bear, lingering over a small, dark stain near its left paw. His smile widened, a mixture of satisfaction and anticipation clear in the curve of his mouth.

"*Your grief, your guilt, your rage,*" he mused, speaking to the absent Vincent as if he could hear. *"Such delicious emotions. And now . . . now you've added another murder to the mix."*

An icy wind blew through the clearing, causing the branches of the oak to creak and groan. The figure remained unmoved, his attention fixed on the stuffed bear in his hands.

"Did you think I'd forgotten our little arrangement all those years ago, Vincent?" he asked, his tone conversational. *"A soul freely given. And now, it's finally ripe for the picking."*

THE ROAD UNFURLED BEFORE VINCENT, each bend and stretch a reminder of that fateful night a year ago. His thoughts churned, a maelstrom of conflicting emotions. Guilt gnawed at him, not only for Rose's death, but for the darkness that had consumed him since. Yet, amidst the turmoil, a spark of something else flickered. The whispered words he'd heard replayed in his mind.

It's not your fault, Dad.

Had it been Rose's voice? Or his own desperate need for absolution manifesting itself?

Vincent wrestled with the possibility. If it had been Rose, if she didn't blame him . . . The thought was almost too much to bear. It offered a glimmer of hope, a chance at redemption he wasn't sure he deserved.

CHAPTER 9
MURPH'S BAR

Vincent pushed open the heavy wooden door of Murph's Bar, the familiar creak a welcome sound after days of self-imposed isolation. The smell hit him first: stale beer, whiskey, and the lingering scent of last night's punters. The aroma comforted, evoking nights filled with companionship and memories.

He shuffled toward the bar, aware of Murph's eyes on him. The barkeep's concern showed in the deep lines of his weathered face. Vincent knew he looked a sight – unshaven, eyes bloodshot, clothes rumpled from nights of fitful sleep.

"All right, Vinny?" Murph asked, his tone a careful blend of caution and curiosity.

Vincent grunted in response, sliding onto his usual stool. The worn leather creaked beneath him, moulded into his form after years of patronage. He raised two fingers.

Murph hesitated for a moment before reaching for the bottle of Jameson. "Double Jemmy?"

Vincent nodded, his gaze fixed on the scratched surface

of the bar. Murph was worried. Questions brewed behind those kind eyes, but Vincent couldn't face them. Not yet.

Murph poured the amber liquid into a glass, the familiar clink of the bottle against the rim echoing in the near empty bar. As Murph slid the drink across the polished wood, he leaned in close, concerned.

"How are you feelin'?"

Vincent's fingers closed around the glass, and he suppressed the urge to fidget. He lifted it to his lips instead, taking a long swig before answering.

"I'm grand, Murph. Been under the weather."

The lie tasted bitter on his tongue, and Vincent couldn't bring himself to meet his friend's eyes. If he looked up, he'd see the doubt there, the questions he wasn't ready to answer.

Vincent's gaze drifted around the bar instead. The early hour found only a few regulars occupying their usual spots. Old Tom nursed a pint in the corner, his rheumy eyes fixed on the racing results. At a nearby table, Mary and her husband bickered in hushed tones over a shared pot of tea.

The normalcy was surreal. The world just carried on when he, a man responsible for the death of his own daughter, a man capable of snuffing out a life in a fit of rage, could walk into a bar and order a drink unworried about any consequences.

Vincent took another gulp of whiskey, willing the burn to wash away the thought. But it clung to him, a shadow he couldn't shake. The guilt ate at his insides.

He glanced at the door, half-expecting the Guards to burst in. But there was only the gentle creak of the hinges as another patron entered, seeking solace in a midday drink.

Vincent's fingers tightened around his glass. He'd killed

a man – a boy, really, for Declan had been only a child – for all his bravado and threats. And now he lay cold in the earth, while Vincent sat here, drowning his conscience in whiskey.

The irony wasn't lost on him. He'd taken a life to avenge his daughter's memory, but what would Rose think of him? That was the root of his shame. He signalled Murph for another drink.

Before Vincent saw the cause, he noticed a shift in the surrounding atmosphere. The usual hum of conversation died away, replaced by a tense silence that prickled the back of his neck. He lifted his gaze from his glass, catching Murph's sudden, worried glance.

The heavy tread of boots on worn floorboards drew Vincent's attention to the door. His stomach clenched as he recognised the tall, imposing figure of Detective Moriarty. The detective's steely look swept the room before locking onto Vincent, his expression unreadable.

Vincent's hand death-gripped his glass. He forced himself to remain still, to breathe steadily, even as his heart drummed against his ribs. Had they found something? Did they know?

As the detective stalked toward the bar, Vincent's chest tightened. He ignored the darting glances from the other patrons that ricocheted between him and the advancing detective. Willing his hands still, he locked eyes on Moriarty's stone-faced approach.

Murph busied himself with polishing a glass, his movements jerky and unnatural. Vincent knew his friend was trying to appear nonchalant, but the tension in his shoulders betrayed his unease.

As Moriarty drew closer, Vincent caught a whiff of cigarette smoke and cheap aftershave. He steeled himself, willing his face to remain impassive. The detective stopped short of Vincent's stool, close enough that Vincent could see the faint stubble on his chin, the lines of fatigue around his eyes.

"Mr Burke." Moriarty's voice was low, but in the bar's silence, it carried clearly. "I was hoping I might have a word."

Vincent nodded, careful to keep his expression neutral. "Of course, Detective. What can I do for you?"

Moriarty turned to Murph, offering a casual nod. "Evening, Murph. Quiet enough?"

"Aye, Detective. Sure, it's early yet," Murph said, steady despite the tension Vincent saw in his shoulders.

Moriarty's attention swung back to Vincent, his gaze sharp and probing. "Mr Burke, I'd like to ask you a few questions about the night Declan Kenny disappeared."

Vincent nodded, forcing himself to remain calm.

"You were working at the club that evening, correct?"

"What evening was that, Detective?"

Moriarty looked at him, poker-faced, for a handful of seconds before answering, "Three nights ago."

"Aye, I worked that night."

"There was an altercation, I understand. Between you and young Declan."

A cascade of thoughts tumbled through Vincent's mind, invisible behind his neutral mask. "There was a minor incident, yes. The lad was causing trouble, so I escorted him out of the premises. Standard procedure."

Moriarty's eyes narrowed. "And after that?"

"I advised him to go home. Told him to sleep it off."

The detective's gaze bore into him, searching for any crack in his story. Vincent met his eyes, willing himself not to flinch. This was a battle of wills and Vincent was fucked if he'd let Moriarty win it.

"That's the last you saw of him?" asked Moriarty, conceding that match.

Vincent nodded, his throat dry. "Last I saw of him."

Murph piped up, cutting through the tension. "Vinny was here most of that night, Detective. After his shift, I mean. We had a few pints, didn't we, Vinny?"

Vincent glanced at Murph, a mix of gratitude and surprise washing over him. He hadn't expected his friend to provide an alibi, partial though it was.

"Aye," Vincent agreed, seizing the lifeline. "Came straight in here after work. Needed to unwind after dealing with that crowd."

Moriarty's gaze flicked between them, his expression unreadable. Vincent held his breath, wondering if the detective would accept Murph's account or press further.

Vincent's stomach clenched as Moriarty's eyes narrowed, the detective's disbelief plain in the tense air of the bar. He fought to keep his expression neutral.

"Mr Burke," Moriarty began, his tone deceptively casual, "I've been looking into your background. You've a colourful past."

Vincent's jaw tightened. He'd known this was coming, had dreaded it from the moment he'd seen Moriarty walk through the door. The ghosts of his youth, the mistakes he'd thought long buried, rising up to haunt him once more.

"That was a long time ago, Detective," Vincent said. "I was a different person then."

Moriarty nodded, a mirthless smile playing at the corners of his mouth. "Oh, I'm sure. But old habits, as they say . . ." He paused, letting the implication hang in the air.

"Tell me, Mr Burke, do you remember that incident back in ninety-five? The one with the stolen car?"

Vincent's fingers tightened around his glass. Murph's gaze spoke of concern. The other patrons strained to hear his response. "Like I said, Detective, that was a lifetime ago."

Moriarty leaned in closer, dropping to a near whisper. "Your wife, Deirdre. She vanished without a trace, didn't she? Never found a body for that one either."

The mention of Deirdre's name sent a jolt through Vincent. He hadn't heard it spoken aloud in years, had done his best to bury those memories along with everything else. The pain, the confusion, the guilt . . .

"I don't see what that has to do with anything," Vincent growled, struggling to keep his anger in check. "Deirdre left. She chose to go. I had no say in it."

Moriarty's eyes glinted, a predator sensing weakness. "Did she now? And you've no idea where she might have gone? No clue at all?"

"I told the police everything I knew about Deirdre. She left. End of story."

Moriarty leaned in closer, his eyes boring into Vincent's. "Is it, though? Because I'm seeing a pattern here, Mr Burke. People disappearing around you. No bodies, no evidence. Just . . . gone."

Vincent held the detective's gaze. Sweat beaded on his forehead, his heart racing beneath his calm exterior. The urge to lash out, to defend himself, was almost overwhelming. But he figured that's what Moriarty wanted.

"I don't know what you're implying, Detective. I had nothing to do with Declan Kenny's disappearance. Or Deirdre's, for that matter."

Moriarty opened his mouth to respond, but Murph cut

in, louder than necessary in the tense atmosphere of the bar, "Vinny's been through enough, Detective. Losing his wife, then his daughter. He's a good man. He doesn't deserve this."

Vincent shot Murph a grateful look, touched by his friend's defence. However, Moriarty remained undeterred.

"A good man, is he?" the detective asked. "Then perhaps Mr Burke won't mind coming down to the station to answer a few more questions. A chance to clear things up properly."

Vincent sensed the other patrons' stares, sensed their curiosity and suspicion. The walls of the bar closed in around him, the air thick with tension.

He took a deep breath, bracing himself against the force of Moriarty's accusation. He'd faced this before, enduring the crushing burden of perceived guilt. But this time, he couldn't afford to crack.

"Am I being charged with something, Detective?" Vincent asked. He met Moriarty's look, refusing to flinch under the intensity of it.

Moriarty's eyes narrowed, searching Vincent's face for any sign of weakness. Finding none, the detective's shoulders sagged almost imperceptibly. Vincent suppressed a flicker of relief. He couldn't let his guard down. Not yet.

"Not at this time, Mr Burke," Moriarty said, his tone clipped. "But I strongly advise you not to leave town. This investigation is far from over."

Vincent nodded, careful to keep his expression neutral. "Understood, Detective. I've no plans to go anywhere."

Moriarty leaned close. In a low growl, he said, "You won't get away with it again, Burke. Mark my words."

As the detective turned and strode toward the door, all eyes were upon him. The bar had gone eerily quiet, the usual hum of conversation replaced by tense silence. Whispers arose around him, and suspicious glances pierced him from all sides.

Anger flared in Vincent's chest, hot and sudden. He turned, fixing the other patrons with a hard stare. One by one, they dropped their gazes, finding their drinks far more interesting than the drama unfolding before them.

Vincent turned back to the bar, his jaw clenched tight. Tension sparked the air. He knew the whispers would resume the moment he left.

He stared into his glass, the amber liquid within reflecting the dim light of the bar. Murph fixed his eyes on him and concern radiated from his friend, followed by the creak of the barstool beside him before the man's weathered hand came to rest on Vincent's shoulder.

"Vinny." Murph's voice was low, meant only for Vincent's ears. "What's really going on here?"

Vincent tensed. He wanted to unburden himself, to share his guilt with someone who might understand. But the words stuck in his throat. How could he drag Murph into this mess? How could he ask his friend to carry the burden of his crime?

"It's nothing, Murph," Vincent muttered, not meeting his friend's gaze. "Moriarty's being a prick."

Murph sighed, the sound heavy with disbelief. "Come on, Vinny. I've known you too long for that shite. Something's eating at you, has been for days now. This isn't just about Rose anymore, is it?"

Vincent tensed at the mention of his daughter's name. He took a long swallow of whiskey, letting the burn distract him from the memories threatening to surface.

"I appreciate the concern, Murph," Vincent said. "But there's nothing to tell. Moriarty's fishing, same as always."

Murph was silent for a long moment. When he spoke again, it was with a sadness that made Vincent's chest ache, "You know I'm here for you, right? Whatever's going on, whatever you've done . . . you can trust me, Vinny."

The words hit Vincent like a punch in the guts. He wanted to confess, to pour out the whole sordid tale. But the image of Declan's lifeless body flashed through his mind, and he knew he couldn't. He couldn't ask Murph to share in that knowledge, to become complicit in his crime.

"I know, Murph," Vincent said, finally meeting his friend's eyes. "And I appreciate it. More than you know. But there's nothing to tell. Really."

Murph searched for something in Vincent's eyes. Whatever he saw there made him nod, a mix of resignation and concern on his face.

"All right, Vinny," Murph said, squeezing Vincent's shoulder. "I won't push. But be careful, yeah? Moriarty's like a dog with a bone. He won't let this go easily."

Vincent drained the last of his whiskey and set the glass down, aware of Murph's concerned look still fixed upon him.

Vincent was miles away, Declan's lifeless eyes staring back at him from a dark pit. He wondered why it bothered him so much. Was it the lad's age, so close to Rose's? It wasn't the first time he'd crossed that line, but perhaps each new crossing was its own journey.

And now, Moriarty was sniffing around. The same detective who investigated Deirdre's disappearance all those years ago.

Just. Fucking. Great.

He glanced around the bar, noting the furtive looks and hushed whispers of the other patrons. Word would spread. By morning, everyone would know about Moriarty's visit, about the suspicions surrounding him. Perhaps that was part of the detective's strategy.

The investigation hung over him like a dark cloud, ready to unleash a storm at any moment. Vincent was aware that it was only a matter of time before Moriarty would come back armed with more questions and accusations. The detective was relentless. Vincent had to give him that. No matter how deeply it was buried, he would uncover the truth.

And who knew what Declan Kenny's father would do?

Vincent stood, his legs unsteady. The whiskey had done little to calm his nerves or ease the burden of his guilt. If anything, it had only sharpened his awareness of the precarious position he found himself in.

"Heading off?" Murph asked.

Vincent nodded, not trusting himself to speak. He could sense his friend's concern, knew that Murph wanted to help, but this was a burden he had to bear alone. He couldn't drag anyone else into the darkness he'd created.

As he made his way to the door, the eyes of the other patrons followed him. Their silence spoke volumes, filled with unasked questions and unvoiced suspicions. He squared his shoulders, forcing himself to walk tall.

Fuck the lot of them.

CHAPTER 10
THE MRS

Vincent stumbled into his faintly lit living room, the half-empty whiskey bottle sloshing in his unsteady grip. The world tilted and swayed around him as he lurched toward the battered armchair in the corner. His legs gave out, and he collapsed into its worn embrace.

The room spun, shadows dancing at the edges of his vision. Vincent blinked hard, trying to focus his bleary eyes. The whiskey dulled the sharp edges of his guilt, but it couldn't erase the resurfaced memory of Rose in the crashed car.

He took another swig, grimacing as the liquor burned its way down his throat. The warmth spread through his chest, a poor substitute for the comfort he craved. Vincent looked around the room, taking in the faded photographs on the walls, the dust-covered trinkets on the mantle. Each item held a memory, a fragment of a life that could belong to someone else.

Vincent's bleary eyes settled on the drawer across the

room. A sudden urgency gripped him, cutting through the drunken haze.

He heaved himself out of the armchair, swaying as he found his feet. The room tilted alarmingly, but Vincent pressed on, stumbling to the drawer like a man possessed. He fumbled with the handle, yanking it open with more force than necessary.

There, nestled among old papers and forgotten knick-knacks, lay a worn photograph. Vincent's breath caught in his throat as he pulled it out, his hands trembling. Deirdre stared back at him, frozen in time, her smile as radiant as the day he'd fallen in love with her.

The sight of her hit Vincent like a physical blow. Anger surged through him, hot and vicious. It twisted in his gut, intertwining with an unexpected grief so profound it threatened to bring him to his knees.

But beneath it all, guilt troubled him. Vincent's eyes followed the contours of Deirdre's face, remembering the warmth of her touch, the sound of her laughter. He'd failed her, the same as he'd failed Rose. Like he was failing now, with Declan's blood on his hands.

His grip on the photograph tightened. Conflicting emotions warred within him, each fighting for dominance. He slumped to the floor, his back pressed against the hard wall. The photograph of Deirdre shook in his unsteady hands as the room whirled around him. He squeezed his eyes shut, trying to still the nauseating spin, but it only made things worse.

～

TEN YEARS AGO.

A younger Vincent walked up the path to his front door,

his shoulders sagging with exhaustion. The night had been long, filled with rowdy punters and too many fights. All he wanted was a hot meal and the comfort of Deirdre's arms.

He fumbled with his keys, the porch light flickering above him. He made a mental note to get it fixed, forgotten as soon as he pushed open the door. Something was not right.

"Deirdre?" he called out, echoing in the empty room.

Vincent's eyes adjusted to the dim interior, and his heart sank. The living room was a mess, empty bottles strewn across the coffee table and floor. A half-eaten meal lay forgotten on the arm of the sofa.

"Dee? You here, love?"

No response. He moved through the house, his footsteps heavy on the creaking floorboards. His concern grew with each passing moment. The kitchen was in a similar state of disarray, unwashed dishes piled in the sink.

A knot formed in Vincent's stomach as he climbed the stairs, taking them two at a time. "Deirdre?" he called again, urgently.

The bedroom door stood ajar. Vincent pushed it open, his breath catching in his throat. The floor was littered with clothes and the bed was unmade. Deirdre's favourite perfume bottle lay shattered on the dresser, its scent hanging heavy in the air.

Vincent's heart pounded as he rushed to Rose's room, fear clawing at his insides. He flung open the door, his eyes scanning for his little girl.

"Daddy?" A small voice came from the corner.

There she was, huddled in her bed, clutching her stuffed bear, Huggs. Vincent crossed the room in two long strides.

"Rose, sweetheart, are you okay?"

The five-year-old's bottom lip trembled as she looked up at him with wide, frightened eyes. "I'm hungry, Daddy. Mommy didn't make dinner."

A knot of anger toward Deirdre formed in his chest. He pushed it down, focusing on his daughter's needs.

"It's okay, love. Daddy's here now." He scooped her into his arms, her small body trembling against his chest. "Let's get you something to eat, yeah?"

Troubled, Vincent carried her downstairs. How long had Rose been alone? Where the hell was Deirdre?

In the kitchen, he sat Rose on the counter, rummaging through the cupboards for something quick and easy. He found a tin of beans and some bread.

"How about beans on toast, Rosie? Your favourite."

Rose nodded, her little face brightening, the first peep of the sun from behind the clouds. As Vincent prepared the simple meal, he kept glancing at his daughter. He should've been here earlier. He should've known something was wrong.

"Mommy said she'd be back soon," Rose said matter-of-factly, swinging her legs. "But she didn't come."

Vincent's hand tightened on the spoon he was using to stir the beans. His anger toward Deirdre flared again, hotter this time. How could she leave their child alone like that?

"It's all right now, sweetheart," he said, forcing himself to remain calm. "Daddy's home, and I'm not going anywhere."

He placed the plate of beans on toast in front of Rose, watching as she tucked in eagerly. As she ate, Vincent's mind churned with worry and rage. Where was Deirdre? Had something happened to her?

Vincent's fingers trembled as he dialled Deirdre's number for the umpteenth time. The monotonous ring echoed in his ear, each unanswered tone twisting the knot in his stomach tighter.

"Come on, Dee," he muttered, pacing the kitchen floor. "Where are you?"

The call went to voicemail once again. Vincent fought the urge to hurl the phone across the room. He glanced at Rose, still perched on the counter, her small legs swinging as she finished her food.

"Daddy?" Rose's voice was small, uncertain. "Where is Mommy?"

Vincent's heart sank. He forced a smile, hoping it didn't look as strained as it felt. "I don't know, sweetheart. But I'm sure she'll be back soon."

He hated lying to her, but he didn't know where Deirdre was or when, or if, she'd return. He wouldn't let Rose see his fear, his anger.

"Did she go to the shops?" Rose asked, her forehead creased in childish concern.

Vincent swallowed hard as he grasped for a plausible explanation. "Maybe, love. Or perhaps she's visiting a friend. You know how Mommy likes to chat."

He ruffled Rose's hair, hoping the gesture would reassure her. But as he looked into her wide, trusting eyes, guilt stabbed his insides. He should've been here, should've known something was wrong. He turned away, pretending to wash up the few dishes in the sink while concealing the worry on his face.

～

VINCENT TUCKED ROSE INTO BED, his heart heavy as he kissed her forehead. "Sweet dreams, love," he said, but she was fast asleep and didn't hear him. The bath and mug of hot milk he'd given her had worked. Ten millilitres of Dozol helped too.

Back downstairs, he paced the living room, his emotions swinging between worry and rage. Where was Deirdre? How could she leave Rose alone like that? His fists clenched and unclenched as he wore a path in the carpet.

The clock ticked incessantly, each passing hour intensifying Vincent's anxiety. He called everyone he could think of, but no one had seen Deirdre. His imagination conjured increasingly dire scenarios.

The front door creaked open in the early hours of the morning. Vincent spun around, his heart in his throat.

Deirdre stumbled in, her hair a tangled mess, makeup smeared across her face. The stench of alcohol hit Vincent's nostrils as she swayed in the doorway.

"Where the hell have you been?" Vincent hissed, mindful of Rose sleeping upstairs.

Deirdre blinked at him, her eyes unfocused. "Out," she slurred, attempting to push past him.

Vincent grabbed her arm, his grip tight. "Out? You left our five-year-old daughter alone for hours! She was hungry, scared—"

"Oh, for God's sake," Deirdre interrupted, rolling her eyes. "She's fine, isn't she?"

"Fine?" In his tone, a war raged between disbelief and anger as Vincent's voice grew louder. "She's five, Deirdre! Anything could have happened!"

Deirdre yanked her arm free, stumbling slightly. "Don't be so dramatic, Vinny," she sneered. "It's not like I abandoned her in the woods."

Vincent stared at her, aghast. "How can you be so fucking heartless? She's our daughter!"

To his shock, Deirdre let out a bitter laugh. "Our daughter? Please. She's your obsession, Vincent. Your precious little Rose." She spat the words like they tasted foul.

"What are you talking about?" Vincent demanded, his anger rising at her dismissive tone.

Deirdre's laughter grew louder, more manic. "You don't get it, do you? Poor, clueless Vincent." She stumbled toward him, her breath reeking of whiskey. "I needed a break. From her. From you. From all of this."

Vincent stared at Deirdre, unable to comprehend the venom in her words. She was like an alien to him.

"What are you saying?" he asked in a whisper.

Deirdre's laugh was harsh, grating. "I'm saying I'm sick of it, Vincent. Sick of playing happy family. Sick of pretending I wanted any of this."

Her words hit him like physical blows. Vincent stumbled back, gripping the edge of the sofa for support. "But . . . Rose . . . she's our daughter. We wanted her. We—"

"You wanted her," Deirdre spat. "You and your ridiculous dreams of fatherhood. I never wanted kids, Vincent. I told you that from the start."

Vincent shook his head, desperately trying to reconcile this bitter, angry woman with the Deirdre he'd fallen in love with. "That's not true. You were happy when Rose was born. You—"

"I was drugged up to my eyeballs!" Deirdre shouted, then glanced guiltily at the stairs. She lowered her voice, but the intensity remained. "I was in pain and pumped full of drugs. Of course, I smiled and cooed. What choice did I have?"

The ground was crumbling beneath him. He reached out, grasping for Deirdre's hand. "Please, love. Think about Rose. She needs her mum. We can work this out, we can—"

Deirdre yanked her hand away, her face twisting in

disgust. "Fuck off, Vincent," she snarled. "I'm done. Done with you, done with Rose, done with this whole fucking life."

Vincent watched in frozen horror as Deirdre left the room and came back moments later, shoving clothes into a bag. He was unable to process the sudden shift in his world.

"Deirdre, please," he said, his voice cracking. "You can't leave. What about Rose?"

She ignored him, continuing to stuff items into her bag with frantic energy. Vincent's heart pounded in his chest, panic rising like bile in his throat.

He reached out, grabbing her arm. "Dee, stop. We need to talk about this."

Deirdre whirled around, her eyes flashing with anger. "Let go of me, Vincent," she hissed, trying to wrench her arm free.

Vincent tightened his grip, desperation lending him strength. "No, not until you listen. You can't walk out on us, on Rose. She needs you!"

"I said, let go!" Deirdre snarled, swinging her free arm at him.

Vincent ducked, narrowly avoiding her wild swing. They grappled, Deirdre's nails raking across his neck as she fought to break free. Vincent winced at the sharp pain but held on, terrified that if he let go, she'd disappear forever.

"Please, Dee," he begged. "We can work this out. Whatever's wrong, we can fix it. Please don't go."

BEEP! BEEP! from outside.

Vincent glanced out the window, his grip on Deirdre's arm loosening. A sleek black car idled at the kerb, its headlights cutting through the darkness. He could see the faint silhouette of a man behind the wheel.

"Who's that?" Vincent demanded, eyes wide in disbelief.

Deirdre's lips curled into a cruel smirk. "My ride," she spat. "Now let me go."

The realisation hit him like a slap. All those late nights at work, the hushed phone calls, the growing distance between them . . . it all made sickening sense now. His stomach churned as the full extent of her betrayal crashed over him.

"You're leaving us for him?" Vincent's voice cracked, a mixture of hurt and rage bubbling up inside him.

Deirdre's eyes flashed, cold and furious. "I told you, I'm done with this life. Now get your hands off me!"

She lashed out again, her nails raking across Vincent's cheek. He hissed in pain, tightening his grip on her arm. Deirdre snarled, twisting in his grasp like a wild animal.

"Let go of me, you bastard!" she shrieked, her free hand striking at him.

Vincent ducked, avoiding her fist. He grappled with her, trying to restrain her flailing arms without hurting her. But Deirdre fought like a woman possessed, kicking and scratching at every inch of him she could reach.

"Deirdre, stop!" Vincent pleaded, struggling to hold on to her. "Think about Rose!"

At the mention of their daughter's name, Deirdre's fury intensified. She brought her knee up, catching Vincent in the stomach. He doubled over, gasping for breath, but refused to release his grip on her.

Vincent's head snapped up as the front door creaked open. A tall, well-dressed man stepped inside, his eyes darting between Vincent and Deirdre.

"Everything all right in here, love?" the stranger asked, smooth and confident.

Vincent's vision blurred, rage consuming him as he stared at the intruder. This man – this stranger – had waltzed into his home, ready to tear his family apart.

"Who the fuck are you?" Vincent snarled, releasing Deirdre and advancing on the newcomer.

The man raised his hands, taking a step back. "Now, let's all calm down here—"

"Calm down?" Vincent's laugh was harsh, unhinged. "You're in my house, trying to take my wife, and you want me to calm down?"

Deirdre darted between them, her face flushed. "Vincent, don't—"

But Vincent was beyond reason. He lunged forward, grabbing the man's expensive shirt and slamming him against the wall. The stranger grunted, his calm facade cracking.

"You think you can walk in here and destroy my family?" Vincent roared, his fist clenching.

"Vincent, stop it!" Deirdre shrieked, clawing at his arm.

The man struggled against Vincent's grip, his composure evaporating. "Get off me, you fucking psycho!"

Vincent's world narrowed to a pinpoint of rage. He drew back his hand, ready to unleash years of pent-up frustration and betrayal. His fist trembled in the air, his rage pulsing through every fibre of his being. The stranger's eyes widened, a flicker of fear breaking through his bravado. Deirdre's shrieks faded into white noise as Vincent prepared to unleash his fury.

Suddenly, a thought cut through the red mist of his anger, startling in its clarity: *They'll destroy everything you love. Stop them.*

Vincent hesitated, his fist frozen mid-swing. Where had

that come from? It wasn't him, wasn't his thought, and yet . . .

The moment of confusion passed as quickly as it had come. Vincent's fury surged anew, drowning out all reason. His muscles tensed, ready to deliver the blow that would shatter more than the stranger's face.

VINCENT'S HANDS moved methodically across the living room floor, scrubbing with an intensity that bordered on manic. The acrid smell of bleach stung his nostrils, but he ignored it. His mind was blank, focused solely on the task at hand. Scrub, rinse, repeat. The monotonous rhythm helped keep the memories of the night at bay.

The house was unnervingly quiet, save for the occasional squeak of the sponge. Vincent paused, listening. Had he heard . . .? No, only his imagination. He shook his head and resumed his cleaning.

A small voice pierced the silence. "Daddy?"

Vincent's head snapped up. Rose stood in the doorway, her teddy bear clutched to her chest. Her eyes were wide with confusion, darting around the room as if searching for something, or someone.

"Where's Mommy?" she asked, her lower lip trembling slightly.

He set down the sponge and crossed the room, kneeling before his daughter. How could he explain? How could he make her understand?

"Sweetheart," he began, full of emotion. "Mommy . . . Mommy had to go away for a while."

Rose's brow furrowed. "But why? When will she be back?"

Vincent swallowed hard, fighting back the lump in his throat. "I don't know, love. But it's just you and me now, okay? We'll be all right."

He pulled Rose into a tight hug, stroking her hair as she buried her face in his shoulder. As he held her, Vincent's gaze drifted back to the living room floor. His eyes locked onto a dark spot on the carpet, barely visible beneath the foam of cleaning solution. He'd been scrubbing at it for hours, but it refused to disappear.

Vincent's stomach churned as he stared at that stubborn stain. He tightened his embrace around Rose, as if he could shield her from the truth with his own body.

VINCENT BLINKED, the vivid memories fading as he found himself back on the cold floor of his living room. The photograph of Deirdre lay crumpled in his fist, edges digging into his palm. His chest heaved as he struggled to catch his breath, the past rushing down on him.

The room spun, whiskey and guilt churning in his stomach. Vincent pressed his forehead against the cool floorboards, trying to anchor himself in the present. But the ghosts of his past refused to be silenced.

"I did what I had to do," he said. The words echoed in his mind, a haunting refrain from that fateful night a decade ago. It was the same phrase he'd repeated to himself countless times since, a mantra to keep the guilt at bay.

But now, with Declan's blood on his hands and Detective Moriarty's suspicions hanging over him, the old justifications rang hollow. Vincent uncurled his fist, staring at Deirdre's crumpled photograph. Her frozen smile mocked him, a reminder of all he'd lost and all he'd done.

"I did what I had to do," he said more forcefully. But even as the words left his lips, doubt bit at him. Did he truly have no choice? Or had he simply been too weak, too angry, too afraid to find another way?

Vincent's gaze drifted to the spot on the carpet where that stubborn stain had once been. He'd scrubbed it clean years ago, but in his mind's eye, it still gleamed dark and accusing. Just like the fresh blood he'd spilled, a new stain on his conscience that no amount of cleaning could erase.

Vincent struggled to his feet, the room spinning around him like a demented carousel. His legs wobbled, threatening to give way at any moment. He blinked hard, trying to focus his bleary vision on something, anything, that might steady him.

His gaze fell upon the coffee table, where his keys glinted in the dim light. The sight of them sparked a reckless idea in his alcohol-addled mind. A ride, that's what he needed. The wind in his hair, the roar of the engine drowning out the voices in his head.

Vincent lurched forward, his hand outstretched toward the keys. The world tilted dangerously, forcing him to grab the edge of the table to keep from toppling over.

The rational part of his brain, buried deep beneath layers of whiskey, screamed at him to stop. To lie down, sleep it off, anything but what he was considering. But Vincent was beyond reason now, driven by a desperate need to escape, if only for a little while.

Vincent's fingers brushed against the cold metal of his keys, the contact sending a shiver through his alcohol-numbed body. As he grasped them, a whisper slithered through the room.

"End it all, Vincent. You know where to go."

He froze. The voice came from everywhere and nowhere

at once, filling his head with its seductive promise of release.

Vincent's grip tightened on the keys, their jagged edges digging into his palm. The pain was grounding, a reminder of his corporeality in an unreal world.

His legs moved of their own accord, carrying him to the front door. Images flashed before his eyes: Rose's smile, Deirdre's accusing stare, Declan's glazed, dead eyes. Each step was a battle of wills against his shame, yet something pushed him forward, an inexorable force guiding him toward his fate.

The cool night air hit Vincent's face as he stumbled out onto the driveway, the sudden change making his head spin even more. His bike stood waiting, its chrome gleaming in the moonlight. It beckoned to him, promising escape, oblivion, an end to the torment that had become his life.

Vincent lurched toward the motorcycle, his destination crystallising in his mind with terrifying clarity. He knew where he needed to go, where it all had to end. The Devil's Corner waited for him, that cursed stretch of road where he'd lost Rose, where his world had shattered beyond repair.

As he swung his leg over the seat, a small part of Vincent screamed in protest, begging him to reconsider. But the whisper in his head grew louder, drowning out all reason, all hope. With shaking hands, he inserted the key into the ignition.

CHAPTER II
HITTIN' A TREE

Vincent bolted out of his driveway, the Yam's engine growling beneath him. The bike wobbled, and he struggled to keep it upright, his alcohol-addled brain unable to process the simple act of steering. He gripped the handlebars, arms straining with the effort of maintaining control.

The cool night air rushed at his face as he picked up speed, cutting through the fog of whiskey that clouded his mind. In a moment of clarity, a warning bell rang in the back of his head. But the whisper that had driven him from his house grew louder, smothering all reason.

Empty streets stretched out before him, the village slumbering in blissful ignorance of the turmoil raging within its most troubled resident. Vincent twisted the throttle, urging the bike faster. The engine's noise echoed off silent buildings, a beast roaring at the night.

Vincent leaned into a turn, the bike's tyres screeching in protest. The rear wheel slipped and his heart lurched as he fought to regain control. The world spun, a dizzying kaleidoscope of shadows and streetlights. Somehow, he righted himself.

As he sped down the main street, memories assaulted him with each familiar landmark he passed. At the pub, he shared pints with Murph, laughing about Rose's latest antics. In the school where, proud and terrified in equal measure, he'd watched his daughter grow. The church where he'd sought absolution before his sins became too much to bear.

Rose's laughter echoed in his ears, a phantom sound that pierced his heart. He could almost see her running alongside his bike, pigtails bouncing, eyes bright with joy.

The image shattered, replaced by Deirdre's sneering face. Her cold eyes bored into him, filled with contempt. "You're pathetic, Vincent," a hiss in his mind. "You couldn't even keep your own wife happy."

Vincent twisted the throttle more, the engine's roar drowning her out. But the mysterious voice cut through it all, a silken whisper.

"You know what you have to do, Vincent. It's the only way to make it right."

He shook his head, trying to dislodge the intrusive thoughts. The bike wobbled again, but Vincent took no notice. He was beyond caring about his own safety.

The last streetlight faded behind him as he left the town limits. The road ahead stretched into darkness, winding through the countryside like a black ribbon. Vincent leaned into the curves, pushing the bike to its limits. With each turn, he played a dangerous game, a lively tango with fate that set his pulse racing and his senses alive.

Trees loomed on either side of the road, their branches reaching out like gnarled fingers. Vincent's eyes darted from shadow to shadow, half-expecting to see Rose's ghost or Deirdre's accusing stare. But there was nothing but the night and the relentless jabbing of his own guilty conscience.

Vincent leaned into another curve, the Yamaha's engine growling beneath him. The full moon hung low in the sky, casting an ethereal glow across the countryside. Shadows danced and shifted along the roadside, transforming familiar landmarks into grotesque, alien shapes.

As he rode, Vincent's thoughts drifted inexorably to Rose. He could almost see her standing by the roadside, her face a mask of disappointment. Her eyes, once so full of love and admiration, now loaded with accusation.

"How could you, Dad?" Her ghostly voice sighed on the wind. "What have you become?"

Shame washed over him. What would Rose think if she could see him now? Drunk, reckless, fleeing from the consequences of his actions. He'd always taught her about responsibility, about facing up to your mistakes. Now here he was, the worst kind of hypocrite.

Vincent approached The Devil's Corner. The bend ahead, a dark serpentine twist in the moonlit road.

Through a gap in the hedge, he caught sight of the ancient oak tree standing sentinel in the field beyond. Bathed in ethereal moonlight, its gnarled branches reached for the sky like skeletal arms.

Vincent swore he saw Rose standing beneath the tree, beckoning to him, but he blinked away the vision. Grief and longing threatening to overwhelm him.

"I can't do this anymore, love," he said, his words lost in the wind. Tears blurred his vision. "You were the best part of me."

He gunned the engine; the bike surging forward as he approached the bend. The Yam's powerful motor roared beneath him, vibrating through his entire body. A heady mix of fear and exhilaration coursed through him.

Instead of following the curve, Vincent aimed straight for the hedge.

The roar of the engine faded to a dull hum in his ears. He could see every leaf, every twig of the hedge rushing at him. The rational part of his mind screamed at him to turn, to brake, to save himself. But Vincent was beyond reasoning.

The Yam ploughed through the hedge with a deafening crash. Branches whipped at Vincent's face and body, leaving stinging welts in their wake. Then a fleeting sense of weightlessness as the bike was airborne.

He sailed over the field, his eyes locking onto the oak tree. It grew larger in his vision, its gnarled branches stretching out like welcoming arms. The old tree that had witnessed so much of his pain now waited to receive him.

The ground rushed up to meet him, the bike's suspension rattling under the impact. Vincent fought to keep it steady, his muscles straining against the violent bucking of the machine. Clods of earth flew up around him as the tyres tore into the soft grass.

Time slowed down as Vincent hurtled toward the oak. The world around him blurred into a smear of moonlit shadows, but the tree stood in sharp focus, growing larger with each passing heartbeat. Vincent's grip on the handlebars loosened, a strange calm washing over him as he accepted his fate.

In this elongated moment, Vincent's life flashed before his eyes. He saw himself as a boy, running through fields with wild abandon, his father's laughter echoing behind him. The image shifted, and he was a young man, nervous and excited, walking into Murph's Bar for his first shift as a bouncer.

Deirdre's face swam into view, beautiful and carefree as she had been when they first met. Her smile was so full of promise and love.

His vision blurred as memories flooded his mind, transporting him back to the hospital room where he'd first held Rose. Her tiny body cradled in his arms had been overwhelming, a mixture of pure love and abject terror.

"She's so small." He was overcome with emotion. Rose's eyes, unfocused and new to the world, had locked onto his face. In that moment, Vincent had felt a fierce protectiveness unlike anything he'd ever known.

The memory shattered as the bike hit a rut in the field. Vincent's teeth rattled with the impact, his arms struggling to maintain control. The Yam lurched violently, its trajectory becoming erratic as it bounced across the uneven ground.

Part of him wanted to let go, to surrender to the inevitable crash. But his hands clenched tighter, muscle memory taking over as he fought to keep the bike upright.

Another memory flashed before his eyes: Rose, almost a year old, taking her first tentative steps across their living room floor. Her chubby legs had wobbled, much like the bike beneath him now. But her face had been alight with determination, a toothless grin spreading across her features as she'd reached out for him.

"That's it, baba." Vincent held out his arms. "Come to Daddy."

Rose had giggled, her tiny fingers grasping at the air as she'd tottered toward him. When she'd finally collapsed into his arms, Vincent's heart might have burst with pride and love.

The rush of the wind against his face brought Vincent back to the present. The oak tree came ever closer, its gnarled branches reaching out for him. He set his jaw, a grimness settling over him. He maintained his course, pushing aside the instinct for self-preservation.

Another memory intruded: Vincent's hands trembled as he scrubbed furiously at the carpet, the acrid smell of bleach burning his nostrils. Sweat beaded on his forehead, mingling with tears he hadn't realised he'd shed. The stain refused to budge, a dark reminder of the night's events that mocked his efforts.

"Come on, come on," he muttered.

He paused, listening for any sound from Rose's room. The house remained silent, save for the rhythmic scrubbing of bristles against the fabric. He looked at the clock on the mantel. Its ticking grew louder with each passing second.

Another memory surfaced: Rose on her sixteenth birthday, her face alight with joy as she blew out the candles on her cake. Vincent had watched her, his heart swelling with pride and love. She'd turned to him, her smile radiant, eyes sparkling with excitement for the future.

"Thanks, Dad," she'd said, wrapping her arms around him in a tight hug. "This is the best birthday ever."

Vincent had held her close, savouring the moment, unaware that it would be one of their last happy memories together.

The roar of the motorcycle's engine brought Vincent back to the present. The oak tree was impossibly large now, filling his entire field of view. He could make out every crevice in its aged bark, every leaf rustling in the night breeze.

Vincent closed his eyes, bracing for the impact. A strange sense of peace settled upon him, replacing the turmoil that had driven him there. In this last moment, he was closer to Rose than he'd been since her death.

"I'm coming, love," he said, his words whipped away by the wind.

Vincent's world narrowed to a single point as the ancient oak rushed at him. In that suspended moment, his mind catapulted him back to that fateful night a year ago: The screech of tyres on wet tarmac pierced the air. Vincent's hands gripped the handlebars of his bike, desperately trying to regain control. He saw the car appear as if from nowhere, headlights blinding in the rain. The accident unfolded in slow motion as he watched on, helpless to prevent it. The sickening crunch of metal filled his ears as the car slammed into the tree. Glass shattered, raining down like deadly confetti.

Vincent's eyes snapped open. The oak tree, impossibly close. The moment of impact, eternally suspended. His heart thundered, each beat echoing in his ears like a countdown. The roar of the motorcycle's engine faded as if the world held its breath.

In this warped moment, Vincent experienced a startling moment of clarity. The finality of what he was about to do hit him with the force of a physical blow. This was it. There would be no coming back from this, no second chances.

A flash of regret hit him. Images appeared before his eyes: Murph's concerned face, the unfinished bottle of whiskey on his kitchen table, Rose's teddy bear left at the base of this very tree.

For a fleeting instant, Vincent's hands twitched on the handlebars. The tidal wave of grief and guilt that had driven him to this point overwhelmed an instinctive urge to turn, to live. But his actions – both past and recent, viewed as he perceived Rose viewing them – bore down on him, extinguishing any glimmer of self-preservation.

Vincent braced for impact; his body tensed as he stared at the gnarled bark of the old oak. The world around him faded away, leaving only the tree.

The front wheel of the Yam inched closer, the distance shrinking with each passing millisecond. Vincent's heart pounded in his chest, a frantic drumbeat counting down his last moments. A bead of sweat trickled down his temple, cool against his flushed skin.

In this last, unending fragment of a second, Vincent's mind cleared. The chaos of guilt, grief, and anger that had brought him there fell away, leaving a pure and painful clarity. He saw Rose, not as she had been at the end, but as she had been in life – vibrant, full of love and laughter.

His lips parted, and in a whisper against the howling wind, he said, "I'm sorry, Rose."

The words hung in the air, his last plea for forgiveness. Vincent's eyes remained fixed on the tree. The bike's front wheel hovered inches from the trunk, poised on the knife's edge between life and oblivion. He waited for his own end.

CHAPTER 12
"NOT SO FAST, VINNY."

Vincent's eyes remained wide open, unflinching, as he stared down his chosen fate.

A maelstrom of emotions churned within him. The determination that had driven him to this point warred with a sudden, sharp pang of regret. His body was tense, as if bracing for the impact that hovered just out of reach. The bike vibrated beneath him. He smelled the petrol and leather mingling with the earthy scent of the surrounding field.

In this stretched moment, Vincent experienced clarity. The fog of grief and guilt that had clouded his mind parted, leaving behind a painful awareness. He saw with sudden, brutal honesty the path that had led there – every choice, every mistake, every moment of weakness.

His lips parted, a whisper lost to the wind, "Rose . . ."

The name hung in the air.

Without warning, a mysterious and commanding figure materialised from behind the tree. Vincent's eyes widened, his focus shifting from the impending collision to this unexpected apparition.

The figure's eyes glowed with an otherworldly light, cutting through the darkness. A chill ran down Vincent's spine, his grip on the handlebars loosening. The world around him faded, leaving only himself, his bike, and this mysterious presence.

Vincent's perception shifted, his focus moving from the tree to the figure. The glowing eyes held him captive, stabbing into his soul. The penetrating gaze exposed him, as if every dark secret he had ever harbored was laid bare.

Maddeningly, time continued to stretch as Vincent hurtled toward the figure. As his eyes adjusted, he could see more details – a tall, broad-shouldered silhouette that absorbed the surrounding darkness. The figure radiated power and primeval malevolence, sending waves of dread washing over Vincent.

The figure's deep voice reverberated through him. "*Not so fast, Vinny.*"

His mind struggled to comprehend what was happening. One moment, he'd been hurtling toward oblivion, the next . . . this. The ancient oak tree was so close, yet still untouched. Time slowed to a crawl, the front wheel of his Yamaha suspended mere inches from the gnarled bark.

Vincent wanted to look away from those glowing eyes, to focus on the impact he sought, but it was impossible to tear his gaze from the strange new arrival.

"*This isn't part of our deal,*" the figure intoned in a disconcerting mix of amusement and warning.

The figure expanded, filling Vincent's vision until it was all he could see. The glowing eyes bore into him, peering into the darkest corners of his soul. All of his sins laid bare before this enigmatic being.

Vincent struggled to comprehend the figure's words.

Deal? What fucking deal? He had no recollection of any

agreement, let alone one with this otherworldly being. His confusion deepened, a frown etching itself across his weathered features.

Vivid scenes came to him: A dimly lit room, thick with incense smoke. Candles flickering in a draft. His own voice, younger and desperate, chanting words in a language he didn't understand. The memories were alien, as if they belonged to someone else.

Another flash: Standing at a crossroads at midnight, the taste of copper on his tongue. A shadowy figure leaning over him, its eyes glowing just like this one's. Words exchanged, promises made. But about what? The details slipped away like smoke in the wind.

Was it a dream, perhaps? He saw himself kneeling before an altar, blood dripping from his palm onto a strange symbol carved into the wood. The air thrummed with power, making his skin prickle.

These visions were both familiar and completely foreign. Vincent's breath came in short, sharp gasps. He couldn't reconcile these flashes with his own history. Had he done these things? Made some sort of pact? The very idea seemed absurd, yet the memories were undeniably real.

A wave of nausea washed over him as another memory surfaced, this one more recent: Standing in his living room, whiskey bottle in hand, rage and grief consuming him. He'd shouted into the empty room, demanding . . . something. Help? Vengeance? The details blurred, but he remembered a voice answering, smooth and seductive, offering . . .

Vincent shook his head, trying to clear it. These couldn't be actual memories. He hadn't done these things, had he? Doubt gnawed at him, eroding his certainty about his own past.

Vincent watched in stunned disbelief as the figure – the Devil, his mind supplied with horrifying certainty – reached out to the aged oak. The movement was fluid, almost graceful, yet entirely wrong. It defied natural laws, bending reality around it.

As the Devil's hand contacted the gnarled bark, Vincent's breath caught. The air thickened, pressing in on him with an oppressive weight. A swirling vortex of darkness formed, centred on the point where the Devil's fingers touched the tree.

Vincent's eyes widened, unable to look away from the impossible sight. A portal grew, pulsing with an eerie, otherworldly energy. It drew in the surrounding light, creating a void darker than the blackest night. The edges of the vortex shimmered and writhed, defying description.

The portal pulled him. It wasn't just light being drawn in, but something more fundamental. The essence of reality bent *into* the swirling darkness. Vincent's grip on his motorcycle tightened instinctively, as if it could anchor him against the portal's inexorable draw.

The pulsing energy emanating from the vortex set Vincent's teeth on edge. It resonated at a frequency just beyond human perception, a discordant hum that vibrated through his bones. The rhythmic throbbing within his chest matched the portal's pulsations.

The world Vincent thought he knew crumbled around him, replaced by this nightmarish reality where the Devil stood before him and portals to God-knows-where opened at a touch.

The Yam's front wheel touched the edge of the swirling vortex, and Vincent's world tilted on its axis. The muted roar of his motorcycle faded further, replaced by an otherworldly hum that vibrated through him. His stomach lurched as reality warped around him, the edges of his vision blurring and stretching.

Vincent fell and flew simultaneously, his body weightless yet heavy with dread. In front of him, the ancient oak tree, the field, and the starry night sky above all melted away, replaced by a kaleidoscope of impossible colours and shifting patterns. He could no longer tell up from down, past from present.

Time lost all meaning as the front half of his bike disappeared into the pulsing darkness. His skin tingled. He tasted copper on his tongue, sharp and metallic.

In that moment of vertigo, suspended between two worlds, Vincent faced a choice. He could fight against the portal's pull, try to wrench his bike back from the brink of the unknown. Or he could surrender to it, plunge headlong into whatever lay beyond.

Every instinct screamed at him to resist, to cling to the familiar world, no matter how broken it had become. Yet a small part of him, buried deep beneath layers of guilt and grief, whispered of possibility. Of answers. Of redemption.

As Vincent teetered on the edge of decision, the figure cut through the chaos. Its voice reverberated not just in his ears but through his very being, each word engraved upon his soul.

"Your journey is far from over, Vincent Burke. Go back and save the girl. She's one of us."

Vincent looked over his shoulder. His gaze swept across the moonlit field behind him, drinking in the familiar world he was about to leave. The hedge he'd just driven through and the road beyond, the distant lights from scattered houses, pinpricks of warmth in the darkness, and the stars above, cold and indifferent to his plight.

More memories: Rose's laughter, Murph's concerned

face, the despair of the past year. All of it, the good and the bad, the joy and the pain, crystallised in this single moment of decision.

Vincent clenched his jaw. He'd come too far to turn back now. Whatever lay beyond that portal, be it answers or oblivion, he would face it head-on.

"Fuck it!" The words tore from his throat, rough and defiant.

Vincent twisted the throttle. The Yamaha's engine roared to life – a final, thunderous battle cry against the encroaching darkness. The bike surged forward, plunging into the swirling vortex.

Reality warped around him as the portal engulfed both him and the bike. The familiar world vanished. Vincent's body stretched and compressed, and his atoms screamed in protest as they were pulled apart and reassembled.

The roar of the engine stopped completely, swallowed by the deafening silence of the void. Vincent's last coherent thought was a mixture of terror and exhilaration as he hurtled into the abyss, leaving behind everything he'd ever known.

THE VORTEX SWALLOWED Vincent and his motorcycle, leaving behind a sudden, eerie silence. The air crackled with residual energy, and the oak leaves rustled in an otherworldly breeze. As quickly as it had appeared, the portal collapsed, vanishing with a thunderous clap that echoed across the field.

Where Vincent had been moments before, only flattened grass remained. The field lay empty, save for the dark figure standing in the shadow of the gnarled oak.

The Devil's eyes glowed with an unearthly light, his lips curling into a satisfied smile. He examined the spot where Vincent had disappeared, savouring the moment.

"*Godspeed, Vinny,*" he said, amused.

With those words uttered, the Prince of Darkness melted back into the shadows. His form shimmered and twisted, becoming one with the darkness beneath the ancient oak's sprawling branches. In mere seconds, he had vanished, leaving no trace of his presence.

The field fell still once more. Moonlight bathed the scene in a soft, silvery glow, casting long shadows across the grass. The aged oak stood as it had for centuries, its gnarled branches reaching toward the star-studded sky. No evidence remained of the supernatural event that had occurred. The fabric of reality had mended itself in the wake of the Devil's departure, leaving only the timeless serenity of the moonlit field.

CHAPTER 13
THE PAST

Vincent's stomach lurched as he and the Yam plunged through the swirling vortex. The world around him warped and twisted, reality bending in ways his mind rejected. Colours bled into one another, forming impossible hues that hurt his eyes.

The roar of his bike's engine distorted, stretching and compressing like a warped vinyl record. He fought to control the bike as the laws of physics refused to behave.

Shapes blurred and melted, reforming into grotesque parodies of familiar objects. Trees twisted like toffee, and the ground beneath him rippled like water, threatening to swallow him.

Vincent's head spun, overpowered by the sights and sounds. He squeezed his eyes shut, but the dizzying display continued behind his eyelids. His body experienced an intense pulling sensation, as if atoms were on the verge of tearing apart in a thousand different directions.

Time had no meaning. Vincent couldn't tell if he'd been in this nightmare for seconds or centuries. The only constant was the thrumming of his bike beneath him, a tenuous anchor to reality in this sea of chaos.

Vincent's breath came in ragged gasps as he fought against rising panic. He'd wanted an end, but this . . . this was beyond his wildest imaginings.

And then it did end.

Vincent's bike slammed onto solid ground, the sudden impact jarring his bones. He fought to keep control as the Yam skidded across damp leaves and loam. The world snapped back into focus, the unusual colours replaced by a sea of green and brown.

He blinked, his mind struggling to process the abrupt change. Gone was the familiar field, the ancient oak that had been his intended destination. Instead, dense woodland surrounded him on all sides. Towering trees reached for a night sky barely visible through the thick canopy above.

Vincent fought to control the Yam on the uneven forest floor. The bike's tyres slipped and slid over fallen leaves and exposed roots. Each bump and jolt threatened to throw him off balance. His muscles tensed, arms straining as he gripped the handlebars.

The machine slid sideways, its centre of gravity shifting. Panic flared; he was losing control.

The world tilted and spun as the Yam careened off course. Vincent's eyes widened as he saw a massive tree trunk rushing toward him. Panicked, he pushed himself off the bike, but it wasn't enough.

He hurtled toward a certain impact, the gnarled trunk filling his vision. His body slammed into the unyielding wood. The collision was brutal and pain exploded through him, a white-hot agony that overwhelmed his senses.

As consciousness slipped away, Vincent clung to an image of Rose. But even that comfort faded, her bright face dissolving into the encroaching darkness that swallowed him whole.

CHAPTER 14

THE HELLFIRE CLUB

Lord Edmund Blackwood looked into the dancing flames in the open fireplace, the warmth caressing his face as he contemplated the evening ahead. The crystal glass was cool against his palm, while within the growing heat of anticipation grew. He sipped the brandy, savouring its rich flavour as he listened to the soft rustle of fabric and the murmur of voices behind him.

Lady Scarlett's perfume reached him, a heady blend of jasmine and something darker. He turned, his eyes meeting hers as she glided into the room. Her emerald gown hugged her curves, the candlelight catching the rubies at her throat. With a playful smirk at the corner of her painted lips, she issued a challenge and a promise.

Inclining her head slightly, she addressed him as "My Lord."

"Lady Scarlett," he acknowledged. "I trust you are prepared for tonight?"

Mischievousness danced in her eyes. "I'm always excited at the prospect of excitement. One tires of the usual diversions."

Before Blackwood could respond, Sir Reginald shuffled in, his nose buried in an obscure tome. The man's dishevelled appearance stood out against the opulence surrounding him, but Blackwood knew better than to judge by appearances alone. Reginald's brilliance was invaluable, even if his social graces left much to be desired.

"Ah, Hawthorne," Blackwood called, drawing the scholar's attention. "Have you deciphered the text?"

Reginald's head snapped up, his eyes wide behind his spectacles. "Oh! Yes. Yes indeed. Quite fascinating, really. The ritual requires—"

Blackwood held up a silencing hand. "Later, old friend. We have guests arriving."

As if on cue, a group of lesser nobles entered, their chatter filling the room. Blackwood observed them coolly, noting the hunger in their eyes. They were here for thrills, for a taste of the forbidden. Little did they know how deep these waters reached.

Lord Blackwood raised his glass, and the crystal caught in the firelight, causing all eyes to be drawn to him like moths to a flame. Noise died away and he savoured the moment, aware of their expectations.

Let the show begin. "My friends," he began, his intonation rich with promise, "we stand on the precipice of greatness. Our recent acquisitions have yielded more power than we dared hope."

A ripple of excitement coursed through the room. Blackwood's gaze swept over his assembled followers, drinking in their eagerness, their hunger. Fools, the lot of them, but useful fools.

"The artefacts from the monastery have proven most efficacious," he continued, allowing a smile to play across his lips. "I daresay we've made more progress in the past month than in the previous year."

He paused, savouring the anticipation that hung thick in the air. These sycophants would lap up every word, never realising they were mere pawns in a game far beyond their comprehension.

"My Lord," Lady Scarlett cut in, smooth as silk and sharp as a blade. "While our recent gains are indeed impressive, perhaps we should discuss the young witch. Siobhan O'Connor, I believe her name is."

Blackwood turned to her, masking his irritation at the interruption. Scarlett met his gaze unflinchingly, a challenge glimmering in her emerald eyes. She was becoming bolder, this one. He made a mental note to watch her more closely.

"Ah yes, our Irish flower. Enlighten us. What news of our potential recruit?"

Lord Edmund Blackwood directed his question to Sir Reginald, ignoring the venomous look this elicited from Lady Scarlett. Sir Reginald cleared his throat, fumbling with a sheaf of papers.

"Yes, well, regarding the girl's father," Reginald began, reedy with excitement, "our agents report that Padraig O'Connor's drinking has spiralled out of control. He's amassed considerable debts to our local representatives."

A thrill of anticipation coursed through Blackwood. This was the opening they needed. He leaned in, dropping to an intense whisper, "How deep is he in?"

Reginald adjusted his spectacles, squinting at his notes. "By our estimates, he owes over two years' worth of his annual income. The man is drowned in debt with no reasonable recourse, my Lord."

Blackwood smirked. Victory was his. "Excellent. This

presents us with a unique opportunity. Wouldn't you agree, Lady Scarlett?"

Her emerald eyes glittered with understanding. "Indeed, my Lord. The girl's father is" – she paused – "most desperate."

Blackwood nodded, pleased by her quick grasp of the situation. He turned to address the room, loud enough to carry to their eager ears, "Friends. It seems fortune favours us once again. We shall offer to buy the witch from her father."

A ripple of excitement passed through them. Blackwood savoured their reaction as an intoxicating rush of power.

"The man's desperation and debt will be our leverage. We will present it as an act of charity, of course. A means for him to clear his debts while securing a better life for his daughter."

Blackwood considered the possibilities. Siobhan's untrained power was the key to unlocking even greater mysteries. And they had extensive knowledge of the means of extraction.

Lord Blackwood studied them as his words sank in. The reactions of his followers revealed their true natures, laid bare by the prospect of acquiring such power.

Lady Elizabeth, ever the hypocrite, feigned concern. "But surely, my Lord, to separate a child from her father is immoral."

Blackwood suppressed a sneer. As if the woman cared about the girl's welfare. She'd sacrificed her own niece in a ritual not two months past. Did she forget in whose company she stood?

Lord Ashworth did not hide his glee. "Oh, come now, Elizabeth. The girl will be far better off with us. Think of the . . . education we can provide." The lascivious glint in

Ashworth's eye made his true intentions clear. Blackwood filed that away for future reference. Useful leverage, should the need arise.

Lady Scarlett cleared her throat, drawing attention back to the matter at hand. "If I may, my Lord. I believe I have a figure in mind that would prove persuasive."

Blackwood nodded, gesturing for her to continue. He admired Scarlett's cunning, even as he remained wary of it.

"We offer twice the amount of Padraig's debts," she said, smooth as silk. "Enough to clear what he owes and leave him with a tidy sum. He'll see it as his salvation, not realising his damnation."

Blackwood allowed himself a small smile. Scarlett's proposal was perfect – generous enough to appear benevolent, yet not so extravagant as to arouse suspicion.

Sir Reginald, ever the voice of caution, spoke up, "What of potential resistance? The girl herself may prove difficult. And the villagers—"

Blackwood cut him off, "Your concerns are noted, Reginald, but ultimately unfounded. The local authorities are in our control, and as for the girl" – he paused for dramatic effect – "there are ways to ensure compliance, are there not?"

A dark chuckle rippled through the assembly. Blackwood experienced a surge of pride. These were his people, united in their pursuit of power, unbound by the petty moralities of the common folk.

Lord Blackwood raised a hand, silencing them. He turned to Sir Reginald, who was fidgeting with restrained enthusiasm.

"Now, Reginald," Blackwood said, "Perhaps you would enlighten us on the specifics of the ritual you've uncovered."

Reginald's eyes lit up behind his spectacles. He fumbled with his notes, clearing his throat. "Yes, well, it's quite fascinating, really. The ritual requires a conduit of immense power: a witch of considerable talent. Our research suggests young Siobhan would be ideal."

Blackwood listened intently as Reginald delved into the intricacies of the ritual. The scholar's scientific mind struggled to reconcile the occult elements, his explanation peppered with terms like 'energy transference' and 'metaphysical resonance.'

Lady Scarlett interjected, her voice sharp, "That is all fine, Reginald, but what are the risks? We can't afford another incident."

Blackwood noted the flash of irritation Reginald directed at Scarlett. The tension between the two was obvious, and he filed it away for future consideration.

"The risks are considerable," Reginald admitted. "But the potential rewards—"

Lord Ashworth cut in, his face flushed with excitement, "Damn the risks! Think of the power we will wield!"

A heated debate erupted among the members. Blackwood observed them, gauging the shifting alliances and power dynamics within the group. Lady Elizabeth argued for caution, while younger members clamoured for immediate action.

Throughout it all, Blackwood remained still, a pillar of calm amid the storm of raised voices. Their eyes darted to him, seeking his approval, his decision. He gave none.

When the argument reached its peak, Blackwood's words cut through the noise like a knife.

"We will proceed with the ritual."

The room fell silent. Blackwood allowed his gaze to sweep over the assembled members, daring anyone to challenge him. Only silence followed his declaration. He gloried in their expectations, their hunger for power, but most of all, their obedience. It intoxicated him, and he allowed himself a moment to bask in it before continuing.

"Lady Scarlett," he said. "Draft the offer letter for Padraig O'Connor. Make it irresistible. Appeal to his desperation, his desire to escape his debts. But be subtle. We don't want to arouse suspicion."

Scarlett nodded, a glint of anticipation in her eyes. "Of course, my Lord. I will ensure he views it as an act of charity rather than an ensnarement."

Blackwood turned to Sir Reginald, who vibrated with excitement. "Reginald. You will prepare for Siobhan's arrival. Set up a suitable space for her. And ensure you have made all preparations for the ritual.

"Yes. Of course." Reginald was already lost in thought. "I'll calibrate the focusing crystals and perhaps adjust the containment circle."

Blackwood looked at the rest of them. "As for you, I want increased pressure on Padraig O'Connor. Drive home the burden of his debts. Let him know that time is running out. But be discreet. We can't afford any . . . unfortunate incidents."

The lesser nobles nodded, relishing the opportunity to prove their worth. Blackwood saw the dark excitement in their eyes, the excitement of what lay ahead.

As the meeting concluded, the members filed out, their hushed conversations full of speculation. Blackwood watched them go, pleased with the unfolding events.

THE LAST OF the lesser members filed out and Lord Blackwood turned to Lady Scarlett and Sir Reginald. They were his trusted lieutenants and he gave them a genuine smile. "That went rather smoothly, wouldn't you agree?" He moved to the drinks cabinet and selected a bottle of his finest cognac, a vintage he reserved for only the most auspicious occasions.

Lady Scarlett settled into a plush armchair, her emerald gown shimmering in the firelight. "Indeed, my Lord. Though I must say, some of our colleagues seem a tad overeager."

Blackwood chuckled as he poured three glasses. "Fools and sycophants, the lot of them. But useful, in their own way."

Sir Reginald accepted his glass with trembling hands, his eyes still alight with intellectual fervour. "The ritual, my Lord . . . With the girl's power, we could unlock secrets beyond our dreams."

Blackwood raised his glass, the amber liquid catching the firelight. "To power, my friends. And to the future we shall shape with it."

Lady Scarlett and Sir Reginald echoed the toast, their glasses clinking in the quiet room. As Blackwood savoured the rich, smoky flavour of the cognac, he found his gaze drawn to the dancing flames in the hearth.

"It's remarkable, isn't it?" he mused. "How easily men's souls are bought and sold."

CHAPTER 15

PICKIN' MUSHROOMS

Siobhan crouched low, her skirts brushing the damp forest floor as she plucked a cluster of pale mushrooms from the base of a tree. The earthy scent of decaying leaves filled her nostrils, a comforting aroma that spoke of life and death intertwined. She placed the fungi in her woven basket, already half-full with an assortment of herbs and roots.

The forest whispered to her, the gentle rustling of leaves creating a symphony of nature's secrets. Siobhan listened. The forest's voice held more than just the wind for those who knew how to listen.

A flash of movement caught her eye, and she turned to see a robin hopping along a nearby branch. Its beady eye fixed on her, and for a moment, Siobhan felt a connection — a spark of understanding between them.

"What secrets do you hold, little one?" she murmured, reaching out a hand. The bird cocked its head and let out a trill causing Siobhan to shiver like somebody had walked on her grave. Warning or welcome, she couldn't tell.

She shook off the eerie feeling and focused back on her

task. She separated the delicate leaves of a yarrow plant from its stem, adding them to her growing collection. Each herb, each mushroom, each root held potential – for healing, for harm, for glimpsing beyond the veil that separated this world from the next.

Siobhan thought of the rituals she had planned. They'd have a full moon that night, perfect for enhancing her powers. Perhaps she'd succeed with the curse she'd been trying, the one that would make her father's drink turn to ashes in his mouth.

Her fingers stilled on the yarrow stem, a chill creeping up her spine. The forest's whispers changed, no longer a soothing murmur. Something was off, a discordant note in the usual harmony of nature.

She closed her eyes, reaching out with senses beyond the physical. The energy of the woods swirled around her, familiar yet altered. A ripple of . . . something . . . pulsed through the trees, setting her nerves on edge.

Siobhan rose, her basket forgotten at the base of the tree. She turned in a slow circle to pinpoint the source of the disturbance. It was otherworldly, yet achingly familiar, like a half-remembered dream.

Her feet moved of their own accord, drawn by an invisible thread. Siobhan pushed through a tangle of brambles, not noticing the thorns that snagged at her skirts. With each step, the feeling intensified, a blend of unease and excitement forming in her stomach.

The trees thinned, giving way to a small clearing bathed in dappled sunlight. Siobhan's breath caught in her throat as her eyes fell upon a crumpled form lying amid crushed ferns and wildflowers.

A man lay there, motionless. His strange clothes were unlike anything she'd seen before – dark leather and odd, heavy boots. A trickle of blood marred his temple, sharp against his pale skin, and a dark beard flecked with grey obscured much of his face.

Siobhan approached warily, her heart thumping. The disturbance in the forest's energy emanated from this stranger. Who was he? How had he come to be here?

She knelt beside him and held a hand over his chest. His life force was strong, yet something else enveloped him – a darkness clung like a shroud, whispering of pain, regret, and incomprehensible power.

Siobhan's eyes shifted between the unconscious man and the peculiar metal contraption resting close by. Her eyes widened as she took in its bizarre shape. It gleamed in the filtered sunlight, a tangle of metal and rubber.

The thing radiated an aura of menace that made Siobhan's skin crawl. Its shape reminded her of a horse, but twisted and unnatural. Two enormous wheels stood in place of hooves, and a long, sleek body stretched between them. A seat perched atop it, and odd protrusions jutted out at various angles.

Siobhan swallowed hard, her throat dry. This . . . this thing could be a demonic steed. What else explained its unnatural form, its otherworldly presence? She half-expected it to rear up, snorting fire and brimstone.

Forcing herself to look away from the metal monstrosity, Siobhan turned her attention back to the unconscious man. She would check him for injuries, regardless of the dark energy that clung to him. She leaned in and caught sight of his wrist, revealed by the jacket's accidental shift.

Siobhan's breath caught. There, marked on his skin in strong black lines, was a small pentagram. It sent a jolt through her, a shock of recognition, for she knew that symbol. Had she not seen it in the forbidden books she'd pored over in secret?

It symbolised power and alliances with dark forces. Who was this man to bear such a mark? And what did his presence, along with his demonic steed, mean for her quiet forest?

Siobhan stared at him, her mind a whirlwind. Fear coiled in her gut, urging her to flee. Yet an undeniable curiosity tugged at her, drawing her closer despite her misgivings.

She stepped back and forth, her hands grasping her skirts. The surrounding forest held its breath, waiting to see what she would do. Siobhan closed her eyes, reaching out with her other senses, gauging the true nature of this mysterious stranger.

The darkness that clung to him whispered of pain and power, of choices made and regretted. But beneath that, she sensed a flicker of warmth, of humanity. It called to her, resonating with her soul.

Siobhan opened her eyes, decision made. She couldn't leave him there, not without knowing his story. Carefully, she lowered herself to the ground a few paces away, her skirts pooling around her. She'd observe from there without getting too close.

A string of questions occurred to her. Who was he? Where had he come from? And most pressingly, what did his arrival mean for her? Siobhan's fingers absently traced the birthmark on her wrist, a mirror image of the pentagram printed on the stranger's skin.

The alleged coincidence sent a chilling sensation through her. Was there a link between this man and her past? To the powers that frightened her with their intensity?

Unwilling to leave herself vulnerable, Siobhan wove a protective charm. Her fingers moved deftly, braiding strands of grass and weaving in the few herbs she had tucked into her pockets. As she worked, she murmured words of power under her breath, imbuing the simple bracelet with layers of magical protection.

CHAPTER 16

THE DEVIL YOU DON'T KNOW

Vincent groaned as consciousness crept back. Pain throbbed in his head, intensifying as he regained his senses. His eyes fluttered open, and he squinted against the harsh daylight. "Fucking Hell."

The world spun as he tried to focus, trees blurring into green blobs above him. He blinked hard, willing his vision to clear. A wave of nausea hit, and he turned his head, retching onto the leaf-strewn ground.

Wiping his mouth with the back of his hand, he attempted to sit up. Pain shot through his ribs, forcing him back down with a grunt. He lay there, chest heaving, trying to piece together what happened.

Eventually, he looked around again and jumped in surprise at the young woman sitting a short distance away. Her wide eyes, filled with fear and awe, remained fixed on him. She didn't move. He blinked to clear his vision. Was he seeing things? The girl wore a dress that looked like it belonged in a museum.

"Who the hell are you?" he asked.

The girl flinched but didn't respond.

Vincent's head pounded, each throb sending waves of nausea through him. Perhaps he hallucinated her. He closed his eyes for the count of five and opened them again. She was still there, just as out of place as before.

Gritting his teeth, Vincent pushed himself onto his elbows. The world tilted, but he forced himself to focus on his surroundings. Fresh air, heavy with the scent of damp earth and lush growth. Unfamiliar bird calls sounded through the forest, a cacophony that set his teeth on edge. Trees towered over him, their gnarled branches stretching into a sky he couldn't quite see.

He looked around for anything familiar and spotted the Yam lying on its side a few metres away. The sleek lines of the motorcycle looked alien against the backdrop of the forest. Vincent stared at it, struggling to reconcile the modern machine with the archaic setting.

"What the fuck is going on?" he muttered, more to himself than to the girl.

Vincent's head throbbed as memories crashed over him like a tidal wave: The suicide attempt, the swirling portal that had swallowed him and his bike whole, the mysterious figure with glowing eyes – the fucking Devil? It all came rushing back, leaving him gasping for air.

Fighting against pain and nausea, he struggled to sit up. The world spun, trees becoming a nauseating whirl of green and brown. Vincent shut his eyes, willing the dizziness to pass.

"What fuckin' deal did I make?" he muttered.

The words slipped out unbidden, fragments of a conversation he couldn't quite remember. A forgotten arrangement, a price owed. Vincent shook his head so as to clear the brain fog.

A sharp intake of breath from close by and his eyes

popped open. The girl he'd almost forgotten stepped back, her eyes wide as saucers but curious too. She prepared to bolt.

She spoke, but Vincent struggled to understand. Her voice was soft, lilting, with a strange accent, but he suspected she spoke Irish. He was out of luck if that was the case. Years of school had ensured he knew nothing of his native language.

"Who are ye, sir? Are ye lost?" she asked.

That's English! Thank fuck! He opened his mouth to respond but then realised he couldn't find the words. How could he explain when he didn't understand what was going on himself?

Vincent cleared his throat, wincing at the post-session dryness. "Lost?" Was he lost? "Look, I don't know what's going on here," he said in a gravelled voice. "My name's Vincent. I'm from—" He paused, realising how ridiculous it would sound if he told her what had just happened to him. "Never mind where I'm from. Where the hell am I?"

The girl's eyes widened at the word 'hell'. She shook her head. "Yer accent is strange. Are ye an Englishman?"

Vincent groaned, frustration mounting. "My name is Vincent. I'm Irish, like you."

"And I'm Siobhan." She made a curtsy. "Did The Master send ye?"

Vincent shook his head, confused. "What?"

Siobhan reached over and grabbed his arm, twisting it so his palm was up. She pointed at the inverted pentagram tattoo on his wrist – a scar from his misspent youth.

"The Divil. Were ye sent by him?"

Vincent gave her a hard stare. "What do you know of the Devil?"

In answer, she showed him her own wrist. She had a

birthmark in the same location which bore an uncanny resemblance to his tattoo. She waited for him to answer.

"I don't know what you're on about," he said.

The girl's expression shifted, a spark of suspicion entering it. She stood up straight, squaring her shoulders. Vincent watched warily as she raised her hand, palm facing upward. Her lips formed words he couldn't hear, and a small stone near her feet rose.

Vincent blinked hard, certain his addled brain played tricks on him. But no, the stone rose to eye level and hovered in the air, defying gravity. He stared, mouth agape, as the girl guided it through the air with subtle movements of her fingers.

"Bloody hell," he said. He rubbed his eyes, but the floating stone remained. Vincent's head throbbed, the pain intensifying as he tried to make sense of the magic show.

Siobhan continued her impossible display, watching him as she did so.

Vincent couldn't process it. He'd seen plenty of street magicians in his time, but this was something else. What kind of place had he landed in? And who, or what, was this girl?

Trepidation clouded her face at his reaction. The stone dropped to the ground. She'd expected a different response, perhaps thinking him accustomed to such displays. For his part, Vincent didn't know what was going on. Attempted suicide and riding through a portal opened by the Devil instead wasn't his usual night out.

He recalled the Devil's words. *Your journey is far from over, Vincent Burke. Go back and save the girl. She's one of us.*

He guessed Siobhan was 'the girl' but she didn't look like she needed saving. And back to where? Vincent noticed the silence surrounding them. No distant hum of traffic, no blaring sirens, nor the faint whir of electrical lines. Just the rustle of leaves in the breeze and the occasional bird call. It was unsettling, akin to stepping into an alternate reality.

Instinctively, Vincent reached for his pockets, patting himself down. Relief washed over him as his fingers brushed against the familiar shapes of his wallet and phone. At least he had something familiar in this bizarre situation.

He pulled out his phone, his thumb moving to the power button. The screen lit up with a soft glow, illuminating Vincent's face in the dim forest. The phone emitted a series of beeps and notification sounds as it struggled to find a signal.

Vincent glanced up, catching Siobhan's reaction. Her eyes were wide with wonder and a hint of fear, fixed on the glowing device he held. Stepping back, she moved her lips and waved her hand in a warding gesture.

It dawned on Vincent that to her, his phone must appear as magical – or as demonic – as her floating stone had looked to him. He shoved it back into his pocket, not wanting to frighten her further.

"It's all right," he said, holding up his hands in what he hoped was a peaceful gesture. "It's just a pho— Well, I suppose you wouldn't know what a phone is, would you?"

The crease in Siobhan's forehead broadcast her lack of understanding. Vincent sighed. He was way out of his depth.

He considered her old-fashioned dress, her archaic manner of speaking, and remembered the Devil saying *Go back and save the girl.* He cursed himself for an idiot. This wasn't some unfamiliar forest in rural Ireland. He'd been flung into another time.

For a moment, a hysterical laugh bubbled up in

Vincent's throat, but he shook his head to banish it, wincing at the pain the movement caused. He looked at Siobhan, who was watching him warily.

"What year is it?" Vincent asked.

She cocked her head to one side as if to view him from a better angle, one that made him make more sense. "The year of Our Lord eighteen hundred, sir."

Vincent's jaw dropped. "Fuck me," he said after a moment. *Over two-fucking-hundred years in the past,* he thought.

He patted his jacket pockets, searching for something, anything. His fingers brushed against a familiar shape – his cigarette packet. He pulled it out, finding it crumpled but intact. Next to it, his trusty lighter. He'd been off the smokes, but the situation warranted an exception. His hands shook as he extracted one from the pack. He craved the familiar comfort.

Vincent raised the lighter to the cigarette, flicking it on. A small flame burst to life, and he heard a sharp intake of breath. He glanced up to see Siobhan staring at the lighter, her eyes fearful. It must have looked like he'd conjured fire from thin air.

He watched, bewildered, as the girl's demeanour transformed. Awe joined the fear that was in her eyes. She took a hesitant step forward, her gaze fixed on the lighter. He flicked the flame off, pocketing it. The girl's eyes followed his movement, as if expecting the fire to reappear at any moment. Vincent took a long drag of his cigarette, the familiar act grounding him in this surreal situation.

The girl sank to her knees. Her lips moved in what looked like a prayer, her eyes never leaving Vincent's face. He shifted, unsure how to react to the sudden reverence.

"Look, I'm not . . ." he trailed off. How could he explain he wasn't whatever she thought he was?

Below him, Siobhan reached into a pouch at her waist. Vincent tensed, half-expecting her to pull out a weapon. Instead, she withdrew a flat, smooth stone. It was unremarkable save for a series of intricate symbols inscribed on its surface.

She held it out to Vincent, eyes downcast. "For you, master."

What the fuck is this now? Vincent looked at the offering as he smoked. Siobhan saw it as significant, so he accepted it. As soon as his fingers touched the stone, she gasped and bowed her head lower, murmuring words Vincent couldn't understand.

Vincent turned the stone over in his hand, studying the strange symbols. They looked vaguely familiar, reminiscent of occult markings, but he had no clue where he'd seen them. Maybe a death metal album? The hair on the back of his neck rose as he realised what this might mean.

The girl thought he was a demon or the Devil. If he wasn't careful, she'd be worshiping him next.

Not knowing what else to say, he mumbled, "Thank you."

He took another long drag of his smoke and slipped the stone into his pocket.

Just fucking great, he thought.

CHAPTER 17
THE WITCH'S SECRET

Vincent dropped the cigarette butt and crushed it on the forest floor with his boot. It made him lightheaded, and he swayed. His stomach growled, a reminder that he hadn't eaten since yesterday.

Siobhan heard the sound and prepared to leave. "I will take ye to my home," she said, and motioned for him to follow. Her eyes darted to his motorcycle. "Well ye be needing that?"

He nodded. "I can't leave it here." Grabbing the Yam's handlebars, he heaved it upright, wincing at the pain the movement caused. He suspected he'd busted a rib, but there was nothing to do about it.

They set off through the dense forest. Vincent pushed his bike along the uneven ground. He was soon sweating and cursing profusely at the backbreaking work.

Siobhan walked ahead, glancing back to ensure he kept pace. "The farm isn't far," she said, by way of encouragement.

When they emerged from the dense forest, he shielded

his eyes from the sudden brightness. He struggled to adjust to it after the low light beneath the trees.

Siobhan's arm shot out, pointing at a ramshackle structure in the distance. "Tá sé sin mo theach," she said, then caught herself. "That be my home," she added.

The cottage had seen better days, its thatched roof sagging in places, the stone walls weathered and covered in creeping vines. It looked like something out of a historical drama, not a real dwelling.

The girl tugged at his sleeve, leading him away from the cottage to a dilapidated barn.

"We must hide yer . . . yer steed," she said, gesturing at the Yam. "The barn will keep it from prying eyes. Hurry now."

Vincent pushed the bike faster across the more even ground to keep up with Siobhan. She reached the barn and pushed open the creaking door, ushering him in. "We must hide ye afore the sun climbs and brings unwanted eyes."

Vincent wheeled his bike into the musty interior. His head swam from the exertion as he, helped by the girl, pushed the Yam into the darkened recesses of the barn. The rough-hewn wooden beams and piles of musty hay created an atmosphere of rustic charm, but the chrome and leather seemed out of place.

"Cheers for the help," Vincent said. "She's a beast to move."

The girl's eyes narrowed, and her forehead crinkled. "Cheers? Beast? Yer words make little sense."

Vincent rubbed his aching temples. "I just meant thank you. The bike is heavy."

Siobhan nodded, then pressed a finger to her lips. "Bí ciúin," she whispered, then, "Be silent, you must."

Vincent gave her a slight nod.

She crept to the barn door, her movements graceful and silent. She peered out, scanning the area before motioning for him to stay put. Then she left.

Through gaps in the weathered planks, Vincent observed her hurrying toward the cottage. Her long skirts swished around her ankles, so different from the jeans and trainers he was used to seeing. The reality of his situation sank in. This wasn't just some remote village stuck in the past. He'd travelled through time and found himself lost and alone in a world he didn't understand.

Vincent's ears perked up at the sound of a man's voice bellowing from the cottage. The words, a jumbled mix of Irish and English, carried through the still evening air. He pressed closer to the barn wall, straining to make sense of the angry tirade.

"Cá bhfuil tú, you useless girl?" the man yelled. "Out gallivanting while there's work to be done?"

Vincent's mood darkened as he caught snippets of the verbal assault. Though he couldn't understand every word, the tone was unmistakable. His fists balled at his sides as he listened to the girl's soft, placating responses drowned out by the man's continued abuse.

As dusk fell, casting long shadows across the barn's interior, Vincent paced. The musty smell of old hay filled his nostrils with each agitated breath.

"Bloody hell, what've I got myself into?" His modern English sounded out of place after Siobhan's speech. "Time travel? It's mental. Fucking mental."

He kicked at a pile of straw, sending it scattering across the dirt floor. "Right, Burke. Think. You've driven through what? A portal? A wormhole? And now you're stuck in bleeding nineteenth-century Ireland with a witch and some arsehole? Oh, and don't forget the Devil told you to save the girl from God-knows-what. Maybe her auld fella?" He rubbed the bridge of his nose. "Christ, I need a drink."

As night settled in, Vincent's pacing grew more frantic. He alternated between cursing his situation and trying to piece together a plan. But every scenario he conjured seemed more far-fetched than the last.

SIOBHAN CREPT THROUGH THE DARKNESS, a bundle clutched to her chest. The night air nipped at her skin, and she shivered, glancing over her shoulder every few steps. The moon hung low, casting long shadows across the farmyard. "Blessed Mother, protect us," she said. "Guide our path and shield us from harm."

She reached the barn door and paused, listening for any sign that her father stirred in the cottage. Satisfied all was quiet, she slipped inside and stopped to allow her eyes to adjust to the gloom.

"Sir?" she asked in a whisper.

A dark shape arose from where it sat on the floor. "I'm here."

She went to the stranger, careful not to trip. "I've brought ye some food. 'Twas all I could pilfer without arousing me father's suspicion." She unwrapped the bundle, revealing a hunk of bread, some cheese, and a small flask of water. The man's eyes widened with gratitude, and he reached for the offerings.

"Thank you," he said. "I could eat a horse."

Siobhan gave a small curtsy and suppressed a giggle at the thought of the man eating such an animal. She stepped back and settled herself on nearby hay, watching as Vincent ate with ravenous hunger. She fidgeted with the hem of her dress, her head full of questions.

After he'd eaten half the food, she asked, "Vincent, I must know. From where do ye hail? Yer garb, yer speech . . . they're like naught I've ever encountered."

Vincent swallowed hard, weighing his words carefully. "You wouldn't believe me if I told you," he said at last.

Siobhan's eyes flashed with a hint of defiance. "I might surprise ye. I've seen things that would curdle the blood of most folk. Your arrival 'twas not natural. I sense a great power about ye, though whether 'tis for good or ill, I cannot say."

Vincent chewed slowly, savouring the food Siobhan had brought. He couldn't believe how good it tasted. As he swallowed, he caught her expectant look and sighed. "Right. How do I explain?" The question was more for his benefit than hers.

Siobhan leaned forward, her green eyes bright with curiosity. "Start at the beginning."

Vincent took a deep breath. "I'm not from here. Not just this place, but this time."

Siobhan's brow furrowed. "This . . . time?"

"Aye. I'm from the future. Over two hundred years from now."

Siobhan's eyes widened, but she remained silent, waiting for him to continue.

"Where I'm from, we have machines. Devices that can do many things. Like that metal contraption back there, my steed – it's called a motorcycle. It's for travelling."

"Travelling?" Siobhan interrupted. "So it's a mechanical horse?"

Vincent rubbed his temples, searching for the right words. "Right. But it's powered by an engine."

Siobhan's face scrunched up. "En-gin? Diabhal é sin," she muttered, slipping into Irish.

Vincent sighed. This was going to be harder than he thought. He tried a different approach. "Look, I know this sounds mad. But I swear I'm telling the truth. I was riding my bike, and suddenly I was here. In your time." He left out the parts about suicide and the Devil.

Siobhan studied him, taking in his clothing and lingering on the pentagram tattoo visible on his forearm.

"I have seen strangeness," she said. "Things others would not believe. But this . . ."

Vincent nodded, understanding her scepticism. He wouldn't believe it himself if he hadn't lived it. "I know it's hard to accept. But I'm not here to cause trouble. I'm just . . . lost."

Siobhan's expression softened. "Lost in time. Like a spirit trapped between worlds."

Vincent blinked, surprised by her poetic interpretation. Maybe she understood more than he'd given her credit for.

Siobhan got up and pointed at a pile of hay in the barn's corner. "Sleep, while I think upon yer words."

"Sleep here?" Vincent guessed, pointing at the hay.

Siobhan nodded, her wild auburn hair bouncing with the movement. "I'll fetch a blanket tomorrow, if I can."

"Right, got it. Thanks."

She moved toward the barn door, looking back at him. "Rest well, stranger from the future."

Vincent settled into the hay. His mind whirled with the

day's events, trying to process everything that had happened.

"What the hell have I gotten myself into?" he muttered to himself, closing his eyes.

A soft giggle from the doorway made him look up. Siobhan stood there, her green eyes twinkling with amusement at his odd phrase. She pressed a finger to her lips, reminding him to be silent before disappearing into the night.

CHAPTER 18
A HARSH REALITY

Vincent's eyes fluttered open as the first rays of dawn crept through the cracks in the barn's weathered planks. For a moment, he lay still, confusion clouding his mind as he tried to make sense of where he was. The scent of hay and livestock filled his nostrils, a far cry from the stale air of his bedroom.

Then it all came back. The crash, the Devil, the portal, the girl in the woods with the wild auburn hair. He wasn't in his own time anymore.

Vincent sat up, his muscles protesting after a night spent on the makeshift bedding. He rubbed his eyes, trying to shake off the lingering disorientation. As he did so, movement caught his attention through a gap in the wooden slats.

Siobhan emerged from the small cottage, her hair a tangled mess and her dress rumpled from sleep. She moved with purpose, though Vincent could see the weariness in her steps. This obviously wasn't her first time rising with the sun.

He watched, fascinated, as she made her way to a

rickety chicken coop. She scattered feed on the ground, clucking to coax the birds out. The chickens emerged one by one, pecking at the offering.

Next, Siobhan turned her attention to a lean cow tethered nearby. She approached the animal with a wooden pail, speaking to it in a low, soothing tone before milking it, her hands moving in a steady rhythm.

The scene mesmerised Vincent. Like he viewed a living history book, so far removed from the world he knew. The timeless nature of the chores was comforting, a continuity that stretched across centuries.

The morning passed and Vincent noticed the slump in Siobhan's shoulders, the way she occasionally stretched her back. Despite her youth, this life of constant work had taken its toll.

The cottage door swung open with a creak. A man stumbled out, his gait unsteady and his eyes bloodshot. This must be Siobhan's father. The stench of stale alcohol wafted across the yard, reaching Vincent even in his hiding place.

The man's voice cut through the morning air, harsh and grating. "Siobhan! Where's me breakfast, girl? And don't forget to mend that fence in the north field today. Useless child."

The man's words grated at Vincent, and a nugget of anger grew. He'd seen his fair share of drunks in his time as a bouncer, but there was something particularly galling about watching a father treat his daughter with such disdain.

Siobhan's response was too quiet for Vincent to hear, but he saw her shoulders hunch further as she hurried into the cottage. Moments later, she emerged with a hunk of bread and a mug of something steaming. The man snatched them from her hands without a word of thanks and staggered off toward the fields.

As soon as he was out of sight, Siobhan's demeanour changed. She glanced around furtively, her eyes darting back and forth. Satisfied she was alone, she held out her hand, palm up. Vincent leaned forward, intrigued.

Siobhan's lips moved in a whisper, and the heavy bucket of milk she'd been struggling with earlier floated a metre off the ground. It drifted through the air, coming to rest on a nearby table without spilling a drop. A small smile played on Siobhan's lips, but it faded as she cast another nervous glance around the yard.

Vincent sat back. The contrast was startling – this girl, with power at her fingertips, reduced to a servant in her own home. He thought of his own daughter, Rose, and how he'd always encouraged her to stand up for herself. The idea of her cowering before him, afraid to use her talents, made his stomach churn.

As THE SUN dipped below the horizon, painting the sky in hues of orange and purple, Vincent's stomach growled. He'd spent the day hidden in the barn, alternating between dozing fitfully and pondering his bizarre situation. The hours had crawled by, marked only by the changing quality of light filtering through the cracks in the wooden walls.

Just as he was wondering if he'd been forgotten, Vincent heard the soft creak of the barn door. Siobhan slipped inside, her arms laden with a cloth-wrapped bundle. The scent of fresh bread and something savoury made Vincent's mouth water.

"I've brought ye sustenance." She knelt beside him,

unwrapping the bundle to reveal a hunk of bread, some cheese, and what looked like meat pie.

As Vincent accepted the food, Siobhan settled herself on a nearby hay bale. Her eyes darted toward the door before she spoke in hushed tones. "The day has been most trying. Father's mood was as foul as a rabid cur's. I feared he might discover ye."

As she spoke, Siobhan's hands moved restlessly, twisting a piece of straw between her fingers. "But 'twas not all darkness," Siobhan continued, a hint of excitement creeping into her voice. She leaned closer, her eyes shining. "In the deep woods, where the old ones whisper, I found a patch of rare herbs. Their power! 'Tis beyond imagining."

Vincent was glad that despite the hardships of her day, Siobhan had found some joy in her foraging. Her enthusiasm was infectious, and he smiled.

VINCENT WOKE to the sound of a rooster crowing. He stretched, his muscles aching from another night spent on his improvised bed. True to her word, Siobhan had brought him a threadbare blanket. His sleep had been the better for it.

Through a gap in the wooden slats, he watched as Siobhan emerged from the cottage, her hair still mussed from sleep. As the day progressed, Vincent found himself captivated by Siobhan's routine. She moved with purpose, her chores seeming to flow effortlessly. But her subtle flicks of the wrist and whispered words truly captured his attention.

The yard cleared on its own while Siobhan tended to

the chickens. Clothes on the line straightened as she passed. The heavy milk pails lightened in her grasp.

Vincent marvelled at the ingenuity. It was a practical magic. Almost innocent.

As the sun climbed higher, Siobhan slipped away to a secluded corner of the garden. Vincent shifted his position, curiosity piqued. Hidden behind a tangle of briars, Siobhan produced a small, leather-bound book. Her lips moved silently as she traced symbols with her hand. The surrounding air shimmered, leaves swirling in an unfelt breeze. For a moment, Vincent swore he saw sparks dancing at her fingertips.

The return of her father, Padraig, shattered the peace. He shouted across the yard, slurred but no less commanding, "Where's me dinner, girl? Don't tell me ye've been lazing about all day!"

Vincent flushed with anger as he watched Siobhan's shoulders hunch, her face falling as she hurried back to the cottage.

As dusk settled over the farm, Vincent's stomach growled. He'd spent the day alternating between dozing and keeping watch, always alert for Padraig's return. The barn door creaked open, and Siobhan slipped inside, a bundle clutched to her chest.

"I brought ye some supper," she whispered, her usual spark absent.

She stepped into a shaft of moonlight, and Vincent saw the dark bruise marring her pale arm. Memories of Deirdre popped into his head.

"What happened?" he asked, concern written on his face.

She glanced down, as if noticing the bruise for the first

time. "Oh, this? 'Tis nothing. Just caught meself on the door frame, clumsy as I am."

Her smile didn't reach her eyes, a brittle thing that made Vincent's heart ache. He'd seen that smile before, on Rose's face when she'd tried to hide her pain after Deirdre left.

"Are you sure?" Vincent pressed, keeping his voice gentle. "If he hurt you—"

"I said 'tis nothing," Siobhan cut him off, her tone sharper than he'd heard before. She thrust the bundle of food into his hands. "Eat up now, before it cools."

Vincent accepted the food, but his appetite had vanished. He watched as Siobhan busied herself, straightening his hay bed, her movements jerky and tense.

"I saw what you did," he said, changing the subject. "Earlier, in the garden. It's remarkable."

"Ye should not speak of it," she said, turning to face him. The moonlight caught the unshed tears in her eyes. "If father knew—"

Vincent nodded. He understood the burden of secrets. He wanted to comfort her, to promise protection, but the words stuck in his throat. What could he, a man out of time, offer?

VINCENT HUDDLED IN THE BARN, watching through a gap in the wooden slats as rain lashed the farmyard. The sky had opened up at dawn, turning the world into a grey blur. He shivered, pulling his leather jacket tighter around him.

Siobhan moved through the downpour like a ghost, her dress plastered to her. She struggled with a heavy bucket, her hair hanging in wet ropes around her face. He longed to help, to take the burden from her shoulders, but he couldn't risk being seen, for her sake more than his own.

Padraig stumbled out of the cottage, coat draped messily over his shoulders. He weaved his way down the muddy path. His unsteady gait betrayed his drunken state.

Hours crawled by. Vincent paced the barn, restless and worried. The rain showed no signs of letting up, and Siobhan had long since retreated inside. He wondered if she was warm, if she had dry clothes to change into.

As dusk approached, he heard the squelch of footsteps outside. Padraig trudged back up the path, his coat bulging. The clink of glass echoed in the farmyard as he stumbled, on the verge of losing his footing in the mud.

Vincent knew that sound – the telltale rattle of bottles, a chorus that had haunted his own life for far too long. Padraig disappeared into the cottage slamming the door behind him.

The rain continued to fall like an omen. Vincent stared at the cottage, his heart heavy with dread. He knew what those bottles meant, knew the storm that brewed inside those walls. He was powerless to stop it.

He was a ball of tension as night fell, bringing with it an eeriness broken only by the patter of rain on the roof. He paced restlessly, ears straining for any sound from the cottage. The silence unnerved him more than any noise.

Then it started. Muffled at first but growing louder – raised voices from within the cottage. Vincent pressed closer to the barn door to make out the words. He was sure most of it was Irish, and the language barrier frustrated him. He caught only the angry, fearful tone.

Padraig's voice boomed, slurred and vicious. Siobhan's replies came softer, pleading. Vincent's fingernails dug into his palms. He knew this dance – the rhythm of a drunk's rage, the futile attempts to placate.

The argument escalated, voices rising in pitch. Vincent's breath came faster, his body coiled like a spring. He wanted to rush in, to put himself between Siobhan and her father's wrath. But he held back, knowing his presence could make things worse.

A shattering crash split the air, followed by Siobhan's cry of pain. The sound lanced through Vincent like a knife.

He leapt to his feet. His body moved of its own accord, propelling him to the barn door. All caution, all thoughts of consequences evaporated in the face of that anguished cry.

Vincent sped across the muddy yard, rain pelting his face and obscuring his vision. His boots slipped and slid on the slick ground, but he pressed on, driven by his need to reach the cottage.

As he neared the window, the scene inside came into sharp focus. Siobhan lay crumpled on the floor, her auburn hair splayed out around her like a halo. Padraig towered over her, swaying as he glared down at his daughter. Vincent's stomach churned at the sight.

Time slowed as Vincent watched in horror. Padraig's arm drew back, his face contorted with drunken rage. The blow fell with a sickening force, connecting with Siobhan's shoulder as she shielded herself.

Vincent's vision went red. He'd seen this before, lived it before. The cocktail of fear and helplessness threatened to overwhelm him, but something else surged to the forefront – a burning, all-consuming anger.

Without conscious thought, Vincent's hand closed around a heavy stone lying in the mud. He hefted it, aware of its weight, as Padraig wound up for another strike. The drunk's wild swings became more erratic, more dangerous with each second.

Vincent's muscles tensed, ready to spring into action. Should he interfere? All he knew of time travel was from movies. Don't fuck with the past or you'll fuck up the future was a rule they all had in common. But as he watched Siobhan curl into herself, trying to protect her head from the onslaught, he realised he didn't care about consequences.

All that mattered was stopping this. Here. Now.

Vincent's hand tightened around the stone. The cottage door stood before him, a flimsy barrier between him and the violence unfolding inside. He was about to lunge for the handle when he caught movement. Through the rain-streaked window, Siobhan looked at him. Her green eyes, wide with pain and fear, met his with startling intensity. Despite the bruise blooming on her cheek and the blood trickling from her split lip, there was a fierce determination in her. Siobhan gave an almost imperceptible shake of her head. Her message was clear: Stay hidden. Don't intervene.

The silent plea hit him with the force of a punch. Every instinct screamed at him to burst through that door, to put himself between them. His fingers flexed around the stone, aching to use it.

But Siobhan held him back. It wasn't just fear – there was a spark of something else. Power? Defiance? Vincent couldn't name it, but it rooted him to the spot.

He stood there, frozen, as Padraig's muffled barks spilled from the cottage. The rain pounded against Vincent's back, soaking through his jacket, but all his focus was on Siobhan, on the silent battle of wills playing out between them.

Vincent sucked in a ragged breath. Inaction went

against every instinct within him. Memories of Rose, of his own failures as a father, threatened to consume him. He couldn't stand by and watch this happen. He couldn't fail another child.

And yet, Siobhan's eyes never wavered. She had such strength there, a resolve that Vincent couldn't help but admire. So he stood in the rain, suppressing his rage, every muscle screaming at him to move, while Siobhan's silent plea held him in place.

He watched as Padraig's fists continued to rise and fall. The sound of flesh striking flesh mingled with the patter of rain, creating a nightmarish symphony that tore at his soul. He flinched with each blow, his fingers tightening around the stone until their tips turned white. The stone was like an anchor, dragging him down into a sea of guilt and impotence.

His eyes never left Siobhan, willing her to look at him again, to give him permission to act. But she remained curled on the floor, enduring her father's assault with a stoicism that broke Vincent's heart.

After what seemed like hours, Padraig's rage burned itself out. The man staggered back, chest heaving, his face a mask of drunken confusion. Without a word, he turned and stumbled out of the cottage, lurching down the muddy path.

Vincent's grip on the stone tightened as Padraig retreated. The urge to follow and bring the rock down on the bastard's skull was strong. He took a step forward, then another, the stone raised halfway.

But he stopped and let his arm fall limp to his side. The rock slipped from his fingers, landing with a wet *SLAP* in the mud. Vincent turned back to the cottage and approached the door. He pushed it open and stepped inside.

The room reeked of alcohol and violence. Siobhan's crumpled form lay on the floor.

He rushed to her side, dropping to his knees. "Siobhan." His hands hovered over her, unsure where to touch without causing pain. "Let me help you."

Siobhan winced as she pushed herself up. Vincent supported her, his touch gentle against her bruised skin.

She looked up at him, her green eyes clouded with pain and fear. "Ye shouldn't be here," she mumbled, her words slurred from her swollen lip. "Too dangerous."

Vincent's anger flared, but he pushed it down, forcing his face into a mask of calm for her sake. He nodded, not trusting himself to speak without letting his emotions show. "It's all right," he managed after a moment, helping her up. "I'm making sure you're okay."

Siobhan's eyes darted to the door, her body tense. Vincent understood her fear. The constant dread of a drunk's return, the walking on eggshells, the desperate attempts to avoid setting off another explosion. He wanted to tell her it would be okay, that he'd protect her. But the words stuck in his throat. He knew better than to make promises he might not be able to keep.

Instead, Vincent focused on the immediate. He helped Siobhan to her feet, steadying her when she swayed. His eyes swept over her, cataloguing each visible injury with growing alarm.

Vincent wrapped his arm around Siobhan's waist, supporting her weight as they crossed the muddy yard. The rain had eased to a light drizzle, but each step was still treacherous. She shook against him, whether from cold or shock, he couldn't tell.

As they neared the barn, Vincent glanced down at Siobhan's face. Tears streamed down her cheeks, mixing with the blood from her split lip and creating pale tracks through the dirt and bruises. The sight stirred his protective instinct.

Vincent pushed open the barn door with his free hand, guiding Siobhan inside. The scent of hay, oil, and leather helping to mask the stench of violence that clung to the girl. He helped her sit on a pile of hay and knelt beside her. His hands hovered, unsure where to begin. Every visible inch of her seemed marred by her father's violence.

"Let me take a look," Vincent said. He cupped her chin with infinite care, tilting her face to the dim light filtering through the barn's cracks. His eyes roamed over her features, inspecting each injury with growing fury. A nasty bruise already bloomed along her cheekbone. Blood oozed from her split and swollen lip. He didn't think there were any fractures. Then he noticed how Siobhan cradled her left arm against her body.

"Your arm," he said. "May I?"

Siobhan nodded, her eyes downcast. Vincent's touch was feather-light as he examined her limb, looking for breaks or fractures. He breathed a sigh of relief when he found none, though the mottled bruising on the arm spoke of the force behind Padraig's blows.

Siobhan's body sagged against him, her composure finally crumbling. With each sob, her slight frame quivered against his chest as she sought comfort. For a moment, he froze, overwhelmed by the raw vulnerability of her sadness.

His arms automatically encircled her. One hand cradled the back of her head, fingers resting on her damp hair. The other pressed against her back, mindful of the bruises hidden beneath her dress. "That's it," he said. "Let it out. I've got you."

Siobhan clutched tight to his jacket. Her tears soaked through the fabric of his T-shirt, warm against his skin.

Vincent closed his eyes, fighting his own emotions. Allowing her to weep, each shuddering breath she took tore at him, fuelling his rage. He imagined Padraig stumbling back up the path and his arms tightened protectively around Siobhan, even as he conjured vivid images of retribution. He wanted to hunt the bastard down and make him pay for every bruise, every tear, every moment of fear he'd inflicted upon his daughter.

But Vincent pushed those thoughts aside, forcing himself to focus on the girl in his arms. She needed comfort, not vengeance. He gentled his hold, one hand moving in slow, soothing circles on her back.

As Siobhan's sobs quieted, Vincent's resolve hardened. The harsh reality of her life was now clear to him. He couldn't stand by and watch this continue. Somehow, someway, he had to protect her. He had to save the girl.

CHAPTER 19

SECRETS IN THE BARN

Vincent woke to the sound of the barn door creaking open. He blinked away the remnants of a fitful sleep. Siobhan slipped inside, a small bundle in her hand. The dim morning light caught her face, revealing the full extent of last night's brutality.

Helpless, he watched her approach. Every step caused her pain. The bruising to her face had darkened overnight, purplish on her pale skin.

"Morning," he whispered, not wanting to startle her.

Siobhan attempted a smile, but it came out as more of a grimace. "I've brought ye food," she said in a hoarse rasp.

Vincent sat up, his eyes never leaving her face. "Thank you." He accepted the bundle but had no desire to eat. Setting the package aside, he gestured for Siobhan to sit. She winced as she lowered herself onto the hay.

"How are you feeling?"

Siobhan's eyes darted away, her hands twisting in her lap. "I am well," she said. But her voice betrayed the truth beneath the surface.

Vincent took a deep breath, steeling himself for what he

needed to ask. "Siobhan, has this happened before? The way he treated you last night?"

Siobhan's shoulders tensed, and she looked away. The silence hung between them, heavy with unspoken pain. When she looked back, she saw the bundle of food. "Ye must eat," she said, reaching for the package. "It isn't much, but—"

He placed his hand on the bundle to stop her. "The food can wait. I'm more worried about you right now."

She withdrew her hand, averting her eyes again.

Vincent knew he was treading on dangerous ground, but he couldn't shake the memory of her father's drunken rage. "I know we've only met, and I'm a stranger to you, but I've seen— I've experienced . . ." he trailed off, memories of his past flooding back. He steeled himself before continuing. "My father wasn't a kind man either. He had a temper on him, especially when he drank. And my mother . . . she endured it."

Siobhan glanced at him, surprised.

"I was young, but I remember the shouting, the sound of things breaking." Vincent continued, emotion strangling the words, "I remember my mother's bruises, how she'd try to hide them with long sleeves even in the heat of summer."

Siobhan tugged her sleeves down.

"I'm not telling you this to make you feel sorry for me," Vincent said. "I'm telling you because I want you to know that you're not alone. What happened last night isn't your fault, Siobhan. And you don't deserve it."

Siobhan's lower lip quivered, her eyes shining with unshed tears. For a moment, Vincent thought she might open up, but then she shook her head, clearing the vulnerability away. "Ye don't understand," she said.

Her words trickled out, and he leaned in, careful not to

startle her, as though she were a frightened animal ready to bolt. "Mother died when she birthed me. Father couldn't forgive me for it."

Vincent ached for her voice. He wanted to reach out, to offer some comfort, but he held back, sensing she needed space to continue.

"He was not always as ye see him," Siobhan continued, her fingers tracing patterns in the hay. "There were days when he'd smile and ruffle me hair. But then the memory of Mother came, and his darkness would return." She paused, taking a shaky breath. "The cursed drink! It helps him forget, I think. Forget the pain, and Mother, and me." The last word caught on a sob. "When he remembers, all his anger comes back tenfold."

Vincent had seen this before – he'd lived it himself – and the familiar helplessness washed over him.

"I tried to be a good daughter," Siobhan whispered, her eyes finally meeting Vincent's. The delicate vulnerability caused his breath to catch. "I thought if I was quiet enough, helpful enough, Father might . . . he might love me."

Vincent swallowed hard, fighting back his own memories. He wanted to tell her again that she wasn't to blame, that she deserved better, but he knew from experience that such words often fell on deaf ears. Instead, he asked, "And your power? When did that start?"

Siobhan's eyes widened, a flicker of fear crossing her face. "I don't— I mean, I'm not—"

Vincent held up a hand. "It's okay," he said as gently as possible. "You showed me, remember? And I've seen you use it around the farm. I'm not here to judge or harm you. I only want to understand."

She nodded and her words stumbled, each one appearing to require effort. As she spoke, he noticed a subtle change in the surrounding air. A faint shimmer enveloped Siobhan. His eyes narrowed, focusing on her injuries. To his amazement, the angry red marks on her arms faded. The swelling around her eye decreased, the skin losing its angry purple hue. Siobhan didn't notice, her look distant as she spoke of her discovery of her abilities.

Transfixed, Vincent couldn't look away. He witnessed a healing unlike anything he had ever seen – no grand gestures or chants, just a gentle, almost instinctive restoration. The surrounding air pulsed with an otherworldly energy, almost like a heat haze.

He leaned forward, captivated by the display. Part of him wanted to point it out, to ask her about this remarkable ability. But he held his tongue, sensing that drawing attention to it might cause Siobhan to retreat into herself.

Instead, Vincent focused on her words, offering what comfort he could in listening. All the while, his eyes remained fixed on the subtle magic at work, marvelling at the power this young woman possessed – power she seemed unaware of wielding.

Siobhan finally sensed the healing, and her eyes widened as her hand flew to her face. She touched her cheek, confused. "What miracle is this?" She traced the outline of where a bruise had been moments before.

"The bruises. They're fading."

Siobhan's gaze snapped to meet his, wonder in her eyes. "But I willed it not . . ."

"Has this happened before?"

Siobhan thought about it for a moment before responding, "Sometimes, I awaken from rest and hurts from the day before have lessened. Not in such a way, whilst awake and speaking."

A smile tugged at the corner of her mouth, a hint of

pride shining through her usual guarded expression. Vincent was glad to see a moment of joy amid her struggles.

But as quickly as it appeared, the smile vanished. Siobhan's eyes darted away, her posture stiffening. Vincent recognised the shift – the instinct to hide vulnerability.

"Ye must eat," Siobhan said abruptly, gesturing to the forgotten bundle of food beside him. "Else it grows cold."

Vincent nodded, understanding her need to change the subject. He reached for the package, unwrapping it. The scent of fresh bread and cheese filled the air, making his stomach growl in anticipation.

Vincent kept his gaze on Siobhan while he devoured his meal. She seemed both relieved and unsettled by her unconscious display of power. He wanted to press further, to explore this newfound ability with her, but he held back. There would be time for that later, he hoped.

VINCENT WOKE to the sound of footsteps approaching the barn. He tensed for a moment, then relaxed as Siobhan's familiar silhouette appeared in the doorway.

"I wish ye a good morning," she said. "I've brought ye breakfast."

Vincent sat up, wincing at the stiffness in his muscles. He thought he'd never get used to sleeping on hay. "Good morning."

She settled beside him, unwrapping a bundle to reveal fresh bread, cheese, and what looked like wild berries. Vincent's stomach growled, and Siobhan laughed.

"Eat. Ye'll need yer strength."

As Vincent tore into the bread, Siobhan watched him

with curiosity. "I've been thinkin' about what ye told me," she said. "About where and when ye're from."

Swallowing a mouthful of food, he asked, "What do you want to know?"

Her eyes lit up. "Everything," she breathed. "But first, I thought ye might want to know more of where ye are now."

"I'd like that," he said.

Siobhan reached into her apron pocket and pulled out a small collection of objects. Her eyes sparkled as she laid them out on a clean patch between them. "I thought ye might like to see a bit of our world," she said, gesturing to the items.

The first thing that caught Vincent's eye was a crudely printed pamphlet. He picked it up, careful not to damage the delicate paper.

"What's this about?" he asked, squinting at the faded text.

Siobhan's brow creased as she peered at it. "That tells of troubles with the English landlords. Many can't read it, but it's passed around the village. Folk are angry about the taxes and such."

Vincent thought how different yet familiar the political concerns of this time were. He set the pamphlet down and picked up a small wooden whistle.

"This is lovely," he murmured, turning it over in his hands.

Siobhan's face lit up. "Aye, that's for our music. Ye should hear it played proper. 'Twould make yer heart soar."

Next, Vincent's attention was drawn to a tiny glass vial filled with clear liquid. "Holy water," Siobhan explained in a whisper. "From the church. Some say it wards off evil spirits."

Vincent raised an eyebrow, remembering his own

complicated history with religion. He set it down and picked up a small, worn coin.

"Is that . . . King George?" he asked, recognising the profile from history books.

Her expression darkened. "Aye, the English king. Not much loved around here, I'll tell ye that."

Finally, Vincent's fingers brushed against a delicate piece of lace. He marvelled at the intricate patterns woven into the fabric.

"This is beautiful."

Siobhan beamed with pride. "Made right here in the village, that is. Our lace holds great value far and wide."

Vincent examined each item, awed. These simple objects painted a vivid picture of a world both foreign and familiar, a world that in his time existed only in history books and museums.

He turned each object over in his hands, marvelling at the tangible pieces of history. He couldn't help but pepper Siobhan with questions, his curiosity getting the better of him.

"What about elections? Do people vote for their leaders?" he asked, forgetting himself for a moment.

"Vote? I don't understand. The landlords and the English decide."

Vincent winced, realising his mistake. He tried to backpedal. "I mean, how do people have a say in what happens?"

"We don't," Siobhan replied. "That's why there's so much anger."

As Vincent absorbed this information, a nagging question tugged at him. Why was he here? What purpose could he serve in this time?

The Devil's words came back to him then. *Go back and*

save the girl. She's one of us. Siobhan was the girl, he was sure of it, and her Father's treatment of her was vile, but was she in need of saving? As far as he could see, she handled her situation well. And what does 'She's one of us' mean?

"Siobhan, do you have any idea why I might have been sent here?"

She opened her mouth to respond, but before she could, a furious shout erupted from the cottage.

"Siobhan! Where are ye, ye lazy girl?"

The colour drained from her. "Oh no, Father is back," she whispered, hastily gathering up the objects. "I must go."

Vincent reached out, wanting to stop her, to protect her, but she was already on her feet.

"Stay hidden," she hissed, then darted out of the barn, leaving Vincent alone with his unanswered questions and a growing sense of dread.

OVER THE NEXT FEW DAYS, Vincent settled into an unusual routine. Siobhan would slip away from her chores whenever she could, bringing him food and spending precious moments in hushed conversation.

As they sat in the dim light of the barn, Siobhan painted a vivid picture of life in the 1800s. She spoke of the rigid social structure, where landlords held sway over the lives of tenant farmers. Vincent listened, careful not to betray his shock at the brazen inequality.

"There's a hierarchy, ye see," Siobhan explained. "The English and their loyal Protestant allies at the top, then the wealthy Catholics, and us common folk at the bottom."

Vincent nodded, comparing it to the class divisions of his own time.

Siobhan's eyes gleamed as she delved into the local superstitions. "Folk here believe in the fair folk, the banshee, and all manner of spirits," she whispered. "There's magic in the land itself."

Vincent thought of the supernatural forces that had sent him there. He wouldn't have taken the fair folk seriously, but recent experience made him wonder if there was more truth to these beliefs than he'd ever imagined.

One evening, Siobhan's voice dropped even lower as she spoke of recent history. "The rebellion of ninety-eight left its mark on us all. Father . . . he played his part, though he never speaks of it."

Vincent sensed the importance of this confession to her and paid heed.

"He has a pair of pistols hidden away." Siobhan went on, her words barely audible, "From those days. I've trusted no one with this before."

Vincent recognised the trust she placed in him with this shared secret. He wanted to reassure her, to tell her about the future where such rebellions were distant history, but he held his tongue.

As Siobhan continued to educate him about her world, Vincent catalogued the differences and surprising similarities to his own time. He was careful never to voice these observations, afraid of the danger of revealing too much about the future.

He leaned back against a weathered beam in the barn, his eyes distant as he searched for stories he could share without revealing too much. Siobhan sat cross-legged before him, her face eager in the flickering light of a scavenged candle.

"In my time," Vincent began, choosing his words carefully, "there are cities that stretch as far as the eye can see. Buildings taller than the tallest trees, reaching up to touch the sky."

Siobhan's eyes widened, her lips parting in wonder. "How do they stay upright?"

He smiled, remembering his own awe at seeing a skyscraper for the first time. "They're built with new methods," he said vaguely. "Strong as stone castles, but light as a bird's bones."

He described the bustle of city streets, the constant flow of people and vehicles, avoiding mention of cars or modern technology. Instead, he painted a picture of a world always in motion, alive with possibility.

"And the lights," Vincent continued, warming to his subject. "At night, the city glows brighter than day. It's as if the stars have come down to earth."

"It must be magical," she breathed.

Vincent chuckled softly. "Sometimes it feels that way," he admitted. "But it's just," – he struggled to find the word – "progress. People finding new ways to do things."

He described concerts and festivals where music could be heard anywhere, anytime, without mentioning recordings or electricity. Siobhan's face lit up as she tried to imagine it.

"And the people," Vincent said. "There are folk from all over the world living side by side. Different colours, different beliefs, all mingling together."

Siobhan's brow furrowed. "Do they not fight?" she asked, scepticism creeping in.

Vincent sighed, remembering the many conflicts of his own time. "Sometimes they do," he admitted. "But mostly, they learn from each other. Grow together." Describing it to her, Vincent saw his world through fresh eyes. The marvels he'd taken for granted were astounding when viewed through the lens of Siobhan's wonder.

He watched in awe as Siobhan closed her eyes and concentrated. The surrounding air thickened, crackling with unseen energy. Slowly, tendrils of shadow coalesced around her fingertips, writhing and twisting like living smoke.

"That is incredible," Vincent breathed, unable to tear his eyes away from the display.

Siobhan's eyes snapped open, glowing with an otherworldly light. "There is more," she whispered.

The shadows expanded, forming shapes in the air – birds, beasts, and stranger things that Vincent couldn't name. They danced around the barn, silent and ethereal, before dissipating like mist in sunlight.

As the last wisps faded, Siobhan sagged, the glow leaving her eyes. "I've shown none that afore."

The sight of such raw power stirred a surge of protectiveness within Vincent, though a subtle undercurrent of fear also gripped him. Pushing aside his unease, he reached into his jacket pocket.

"I want to show you something, too," he said, pulling out his smartphone. The screen was dark, but he powered the device on and it loaded onto the home screen. He opened his picture gallery. "This is for communication, but that won't work here. But it also captures images."

He turned the screen to face Siobhan, and her eyes widened as she looked at the images on the small screen, turning it over in her hands. "What manner of sorcery is this?" she asked, tracing the smooth glass surface.

"It's not magic, not really. It captures the likeness of whatever it's pointed at."

Their conversations drifted beyond the wonders of their respective worlds. Vincent shared his hopes for redemption, omitting the darker details of his past. Siobhan spoke of her dreams to escape her father's cruelty and explore the world beyond her village.

"Betimes I imagine leaving here," Siobhan confessed. "Taking to the road and never looking back."

Vincent nodded, understanding the pull of escape. "Where would you go?"

Siobhan's eyes lit up. "Everywhere," she breathed. "I would see it all."

As the days passed, Vincent grew increasingly protective of Siobhan. Padraig's drunken tirades set his teeth on edge and he itched to intervene.

As the days melted into one another, Vincent and Siobhan's clandestine meetings in the barn became a cherished ritual. The unlikely pair found solace in each other's company, their bond deepening with each shared secret and stolen moment.

Vincent saw echoes of Rose in Siobhan's fierceness and quick wit. The way her eyes lit up when she mastered a new spell reminded him of his daughter's excitement over her own achievements. Yet, he dared not voice these thoughts, even to himself. Losing Rose was still too recent, and the idea of substituting her felt like a betrayal.

Siobhan, for her part, found herself drawn to Vincent's strength and gentle guidance. He listened to her fears and dreams without judgment, offering words of encouragement that were the complete opposite of her father's constant belittlement. In her most private thoughts, she imagined what life might have been like with Vincent as her father. But a wave of guilt washed these musings away. How could she wish for a different parent when her own flesh and blood still breathed?

They found solace in their time together, but an undercurrent of melancholy shadowed it. Vincent assumed that his presence in that time was temporary; as soon as he fulfilled the Devil's request and saved the girl (who he assumed to be Siobhan), he figured he'd be returned to his own time. Each day that passed brought him closer to an inevitable departure, leaving Siobhan alone once more.

Siobhan, too, felt the looming spectre of separation. She fell deeper into a tangle of emotions she couldn't quite name. Vincent was unlike any man she'd ever known – kind, respectful, and fascinatingly alien. She both yearned for and feared the intensity of her growing attachment to this enigmatic stranger from the future.

As the sun dipped below the horizon, painting the sky in hues of gold and crimson, Vincent and Siobhan sat side by side in the barn. Strips of fading light filtered through the weathered slats, casting long shadows across the straw-strewn floor. They sat in comfortable silence, each lost in their own thoughts yet acutely aware of the other's presence.

CHAPTER 20

A DESPERATE BARGAIN

The morning air hung heavy with an unusual silence as Vincent waited for Siobhan's familiar footsteps.

As the sun climbed higher, Vincent's unease grew. He paced the barn, pausing occasionally to peer through the gaps in the walls. The farmyard remained still, save for a few chickens scratching in the dirt.

By midday, Vincent's stomach growled, a further reminder of Siobhan's absence. Where was she? Had something happened?

A memory surfaced: Siobhan mentioned a trip to the village for supplies. Vincent relaxed, but doubt lingered. She'd never been gone this long before.

He approached the barn door, hand hovering over the latch. The risks of venturing out weighed on him. If Padraig saw him, or worse, if someone from a neighbouring farm happened by and spotted a strange man lurking about . . . Vincent's fingers curled around the latch. Siobhan had risked everything to help him. He owed her the same courage.

Vincent froze as the distant clatter of hooves and wheels reached his ears. He crept back to the gap in the wall and peered out.

An ornate carriage rolled into view, its polished surface gleaming in the afternoon sun. Vincent's eyes widened at the armed soldiers flanking the vehicle, their red uniforms crisp and intimidating.

Fucking redcoats? thought Vincent.

The carriage came to a halt before the cottage. Vincent held his breath as the door swung open, revealing a woman whose presence commanded attention. She stepped down gracefully, her fine dress and regal bearing marking her as someone of importance.

The woman strode toward the cottage. Her auburn hair caught the light, and even from a distance, he could see the sharp intelligence in her emerald eyes. She carried herself with an air of authority.

The woman disappeared inside the cottage while the armed guards took up positions outside, their presence a clear warning against interference.

Who the fuck is she?

Vincent's fingers dug into the rough wood of the barn wall as he watched, helpless and filled with a growing sense of dread. Something told him this visit would change everything, and not for the better.

He crept from the barn, keeping low and using the sparse cover of scraggly bushes to approach the cottage. He pressed his back against the rough stone wall, inching toward a partially open window. The murmur of voices drifted out, and Vincent strained his ears to catch the conversation.

A woman's voice, cultured and refined, cut through the

air. "Now, Mr O'Connor, let's discuss the terms of our arrangement."

Vincent knit his brows together. The voice belonged to the auburn-haired woman. What arrangement was she referring to?

Padraig's familiar slur followed. "Aye, m'lady. Ye said ye'd clear me debts?"

"Indeed," the woman replied smoothly. "In exchange for what we discussed."

Vincent's stomach churned. Something about her tone set his teeth on edge.

"Siobhan?"

"Precisely," the woman said. "She will live with us, and we will put her talents to good use."

Vincent's blood ran cold. His eyes darted around the farmyard, searching for any sign of her, but she was nowhere to be seen.

"Lord Blackwood will be most pleased." The woman continued, "The organisation has been searching for someone with Siobhan's unique abilities for quite some time."

Lord Blackwood? The name tugged at his memory, dredging up fragments of information he'd once read about the area's history. Something about a club . . . a secret society . . .

"And ye swear no harm'll come to her?" Padraig's voice was thick with drink and a hint of reluctance.

"I assure you, Mr O'Connor, we will treat Siobhan with the utmost care. The club values her potential greatly."

What fucking club? wondered Vincent.

"I dunno, m'lady. She's me only child, y'see."

The clink of coins cut through the air, followed by a

sharp intake of breath from Padraig. Vincent knew how easily a desperate man could be swayed.

"Consider it an investment in your daughter's future, Mr O'Connor." Lady Scarlett's voice oozed false compassion. "And a solution to your financial troubles."

A heavy silence hung in the air, broken only by the sound of Padraig's calloused fingers running over the coins. Vincent's nails dug into his palms as he waited, praying the man would find some shred of paternal instinct.

But Padraig's resolve crumbled. "Aye, then. If ye swear she'll be cared for . . ."

Vincent's heart sank as Lady Scarlett's triumphant tone rang out. "Excellent decision, Mr O'Connor. I'm pleased to inform you that Siobhan is already in our care."

Vincent's breath caught. No, it couldn't be . . .

"We invited her to join us while she was in the village." Lady Scarlett continued smoothly, "She was quite eager for the opportunity, I assure you."

The village trip. Siobhan's unusual absence. It all made sense now.

Fuck!

"This arrangement truly is for the best." Lady Scarlett's voice dripped with false sincerity. "We will nurture Siobhan and help her realise her potential. She'll want for nothing under our guidance."

Vincent's fists clenched with such force he thought they might break. Rage and frustration coursed through him, threatening to explode. He'd been too late. He fought the urge to burst into the cottage, to confront Lady Scarlett and Padraig. But what good would it do? He was outnumbered, outgunned, and centuries out of his depth. Vincent's impotent fury threatened to choke him as he realised how powerless he was.

The reality of the situation crashed over him. Siobhan was gone, spirited away by this lady while he'd been hiding in the barn like a coward.

He watched from his hidden vantage point as Lady Scarlett emerged from the cottage. A satisfied smile played across her lips, a smile that spoke of victory and dark promises. Vincent's stomach churned at the sight of it.

Lady Scarlett paused at the carriage door, turning to survey the farmyard with a proprietary air. For a heart-stopping moment, Vincent thought she'd seen him, but her eyes swept past his hiding spot.

As Lady Scarlett climbed into the ornate carriage, a shroud of helplessness settled over Vincent. What could he do? He was a man out of time, with no resources, no allies, and no bloody idea where they might take Siobhan.

The carriage lurched into motion, flanked by the redcoats. It rolled away, taking with it any hope of an immediate resolution. Despite his best efforts, Vincent's attempts to conjure up a plan proved futile.

The hoofbeats, creaking wheels, and marching soldiers faded into the distance, leaving Vincent alone with his failure. He slumped against the cottage wall, his head in his hands. How had it all gone so wrong?

The door creaking open drew his attention back to the present. Padraig stumbled out, his gait unsteady and eyes unfocused. In his hand, a small leather pouch clinked with the sound of coins. The man who had just sold his own daughter fumbled with the bag, a look of drunken satisfaction on his face. Without a backward glance at the cottage, Padraig set off, no doubt headed for the pub to drown what little conscience he had left in cheap whiskey.

Vincent was furious. He wanted to confront Padraig, to make the miserable excuse for a father pay for what he'd done. He itched to grab the man's throat and crush the life from him. But the voice of reason cut through his haze of anger. He forced himself to take a deep breath, then another. As much as he wanted to unleash his fury on Padraig, it wouldn't help Siobhan. He needed information, a plan, something more than blind rage to guide his next move.

Vincent held himself back, watching Padraig's retreating form. The man was a bastard, no doubt, but he might be Vincent's only lead. But, confronting him when he was drunk would likely result in a brawl. Vincent needed to think, to gather information before acting. Lord Blackwood and Lady Scarlett were pieces of the puzzle he needed to understand. He needed a strategy.

Vincent waited until Padraig was out of sight and earshot before moving. He crept toward the cottage. The door creaked open, revealing a dim interior that reeked of stale alcohol and recent neglect. He looked around the sparse room for anything out of place. A rickety table caught his attention, its surface littered with empty bottles and scattered papers.

Vincent sifted through the detritus of Padraig's miserable existence. His fingers brushed against a crisp parchment, standing out among the crumpled notes and unpaid bills. He lifted it, noting an ornate seal pressed into black wax at the bottom of the page. The seal bore an intricate design – a stylised tree with twisted branches forming the letter *B*.

For Blackwood?

Vincent read the elegant script, absorbing every detail.

. . . pleased to inform you that Miss Siobhan

*O'Connor has accepted a position of employment at
Blackwood Manor . . .*

Vincent's anger built with each word. There was no way
Siobhan had agreed to this.

*. . . an advance of payment, as discussed, has
been provided for your consideration . . .*

The letter contained directions to Blackwood Manor,
several miles to the north. Vincent committed the words to
memory. The beginning of a rescue plan already forming.

He replaced the letter, ensuring it appeared undis-
turbed. He turned to leave, but a small, worn trunk tucked
beneath Siobhan's bed caught his attention. It probably
held her few personal possessions. Vincent hesitated before
kneeling beside the trunk. He couldn't take much, but
perhaps it contained something meaningful that he could
bring to Siobhan when he found her.

He'd hardly touched the lid when a cheerful whistle
pierced the air. He recognised Padraig's drunken tune.
Cursing under his breath, Vincent scrambled to his feet and
slipped out of the cottage, pressing his back against the
rough stone wall beneath the window again.

Padraig's heavy footsteps stumbled across the threshold, accompanied by a muttered grumbling. Vincent
strained to listen as Padraig rummaged around.

"Where'd I put the bloody thing?" Padraig slurred.

Vincent wondered what he'd lost. What could be so
important to him? The sound of drawers being yanked open
and papers shuffling filled the air.

From his hiding place beneath the window, Vincent thought of the impossibility of the situation. Siobhan was gone, whisked away for fuck knows what purposes. For the first time, he was utterly alone in this time that was not his own. He had no allies and no resources asides from his own capabilities.

He closed his eyes, forcing himself to breathe.

Think, for fuck's sake! He required information and had only one accessible source. The thought of confronting Padraig made his stomach churn, but what choice did he have? Every moment he hesitated was another moment Siobhan slipped further from his reach.

He prepared himself for what he had to do. The risks were immense – exposure, arrest, or worse. But the alternative, leaving Siobhan to whatever fate had in store for her, was unthinkable.

Vincent took one final deep breath, his resolve hardening. He'd face Padraig and force the truth from him if necessary. Whatever it took to save Siobhan.

The Devil's words echoed from memory. *Go back and save the girl. She's one of us.* Without a doubt, Siobhan needed saving now. Her fate was in his hands, and it was tightly bound to his. He had no choice but to step out of the shadows to save her.

CHAPTER 21
CONFRONTATION AND CONFESSION

Vincent paused at the door, steeling himself for the coming confrontation. Padraig's drunken mumbling filtered through the thin door. He remembered Siobhan's bruises and her stoicism in the face of her father's cruelty, and his resolve hardened.

He kicked the door, splintering wood. The *CRACK* of breaking timber echoed through the small cottage as the door flew open, slamming against the interior wall.

Vincent strode in, an imposing figure filling the doorway. His eyes locked onto Padraig, who scrambled back, almost toppling over a rickety chair.

"What in Christ's name?" Padraig slurred, his bloodshot eyes wide with fear and confusion.

"We need to talk about Siobhan." The words a low rumble. His broad frame cast a long shadow across worn floorboards. The acrid stench of stale alcohol and Padraig's unwashed body assaulted Vincent, but he kept his focus on the dishevelled man.

The cup in Padraig's hand clattered to the floor, spilling its contents across the dirty planks. Padraig's bleary eyes widened in surprise, then narrowed. "What do ye think yer doin'?" Padraig bellowed, his words slurred and thick with drink. He staggered to his feet, swaying as he glared at Vincent.

Every muscle in Vincent's body was taut. The urge to lash out, to make Padraig experience even a fraction of the pain he'd inflicted on Siobhan, was all-consuming. But he forced it down, reminding himself why he was there. "Where is she?" Vincent asked in a dangerous whisper. "Where's Siobhan?"

Padraig's face contorted with fury. "Ye've no right to come bargin' in here! This is me home, ye bloody—"

Taking a step forward, Vincent cut him off, "I said, where is Siobhan?"

The older man's anger faltered, replaced by something Vincent couldn't quite place. Fear? Guilt? But in a blink, Padraig's features hardened again.

"Get out!" he roared, spittle flying from his mouth. "Ye've no business here! The girl's gone and good riddance!"

Vincent's vision blurred red at the edges. He crossed the room in two long strides, grabbing Padraig by the front of his filthy shirt and slamming him against the wall. "Tell me where she is," Vincent snarled, his face inches from Padraig's. "Now!"

Vincent's grip tightened on Padraig's shirt, his knuckles turning white with the effort of restraining himself. The stench of cheap whiskey on the older man's breath made Vincent's stomach turn, but he held his ground, searching Padraig's bloodshot eyes for answers.

To Vincent's surprise, Padraig's anger evaporated, replaced by amusement. A bitter laugh bubbled up from the man's throat, catching Vincent off guard.

"Ah, I see now," Padraig wheezed, his lips curling into a smirk. "Yer the one she's been sneakin' off to see, aren't ye? Her secret lover, come to sweep her away?"

Vincent scowled, taken aback by the sudden shift in Padraig. He loosened his grip but kept the man pinned against the wall.

"Well, yer too late, boyo." Padraig continued, his words slurring together, "Someone else has claimed her, and for a fair price at that."

Vincent was sick to his stomach. "What do you mean, 'claimed her'? What have you done?" He wanted to hear the man say it.

Padraig's eyes gleamed with twisted spite. "She's gone to serve her betters, she has. Lady Scarlett saw her potential, offered a pretty penny for her services."

The memories returned of the beating Padraig had administered to Siobhan. The gentle girl's pain, her strength in the face of this monster's cruelty ignited a fire that threatened to consume Vincent. He roared as he threw Padraig. The man crashed to the ground in a tangle of limbs; the impact knocked the wind from his lungs.

Vincent followed and straddled Padraig, his fists a blur of motion. Each punch landed with a sickening *THUD*, fuelled by the memory of Siobhan's pain. The bruise on her cheek, her battered limbs, her acceptance of a life filled with fear – all of it poured into Vincent's fists.

"You bastard!" He pummelled Padraig's face again and again. "She trusted you! She needed you!" Vincent's fists rained down. Padraig's attempts to fight back were pitiful, his swings easily deflected by Vincent's superior strength and fury.

Padraig soon faltered, his arms falling limply to his sides. Blood streamed from his nose and mouth, but

Vincent couldn't stop. The red haze of fury clouded his vision, driving him forward.

Flashes of his past intruded upon Vincent. Deirdre's angry voice, Rose's lifeless body, the guilt that had haunted him for years – all of it merged with the present moment, intensifying his anger. "Where is she?" he roared, punctuating each word with another devastating blow. "Tell me where they've taken her!"

Padraig's face was a mess of blood and bruises, his eyes swollen near shut. Yet still, he spat out a mouthful of blood, a defiant gleam in his one open eye. "Go to hell," Padraig slurred, his words barely intelligible through his battered lips. His laugh was a wet gurgle. "Ye'll never find her," he wheezed. "She's where she belongs."

Vincent's rage crystallised into cold, calculated fury. His assault became more focused, each strike targeted with brutal precision. Years of street fights and bouncer work had honed his instincts, and now he put that knowledge to use.

He drove his knee into Padraig's solar plexus, expelling what little air remained in the man's lungs. As Padraig gasped, Vincent's elbow connected with the side of his head, sending a shock of pain through the drunk's skull. Vincent's fists found the soft spots: kidneys, liver, the delicate bones of the nose. Each impact elicited a pained grunt or whimper from Padraig, whose bravado crumbled under the relentless onslaught.

The defiance in Padraig's eyes flickered and died, replaced by naked fear. His arms raised to shield against the fury raining down upon him.

Vincent saw the change, the moment when Padraig's spirit broke. It should have satisfied him, should have quelled the rage burning inside. But it only fuelled the fire, driving him to extract every ounce of information from this wretched excuse for a father.

He seized Padraig by the throat, pinning him to the floor. He leaned in close, his face inches from the terrified man's battered visage. The stench of blood, sweat, and fear filled his nostrils. He thought the man might have soiled himself.

"Last chance," Vincent said. "Where. Is. Siobhan?"

Vincent's grip tightened around Padraig's throat, his hands shaking with the effort of restraining himself from crushing the man's windpipe.

There was a look of abject terror in Padraig's eyes. "Please. I'll tell ye. I'll tell ye everythin'."

Vincent loosened his hold. "Talk."

Tears mixed with the blood on Padraig's cheeks as he sobbed, "I-I sold her." He choked out his words, slurred with pain and alcohol. "To the Hellfire Club. I knew— I knew what they were."

Vincent's stomach lurched at the confession, but he needed more. "The Hellfire Club?"

Padraig nodded. "Blackwell and all those lords an' ladies." The man hawked and spat a bloody glob of phlegm. "They do The Divil's work on Mountpelier."

The pieces fell into place for Vincent. The Hellfire Club lodge on Mountpelier wasn't far from his village. He'd read a write-up about it in the local newspaper years ago. A secretive group of aristocrats rumoured to dabble in the occult. He had no recollection of when they operated, but if the Hellfire Club existed in this time, and they wanted Siobhan . . . The Hellfire Club's reputation was dark, filled with whispers of debauchery and black magic – human sacrifice even.

Bile rose in his throat. "You knew?" The way he spoke

sent a clear message of danger. "You knew what they'd do to her?"

Padraig's sobs intensified, his body shaking beneath Vincent's weight. "Aye," he admitted in a broken voice. "I heard the whispers . . . the things they do. But I didn't care. I just— I needed the money."

Vincent's grip on Padraig's throat tightened. The man gasped, his eyes widening in panic.

"The debts." Padraig struggled to speak. "They would take everythin'. No choice but to take the coin they offered."

Vincent's stomach churned with disgust, but he eased his grip on Padraig's throat. The broken man gasped for air, his words tumbling out in a desperate, drunken babble, "She— She came in a fancy carriage," Padraig said, his eyes unfocused. "That Lady Scarlett, with a purse full of coin. She said Siobhan'd be well looked after . . . but I knew."

Vincent wanted to tighten his grip again, to silence the pathetic creature. But he needed more information. "Where?" Vincent asked. "Where is she?"

"The Blackwood estate," he mumbled. "Two miles north, past The Devil's Glen. A huge stone mansion, all dark and forbidden like." Padraig's confession wound down, dissolving into incoherent mumblings and choked sobs.

The man repulsed Vincent, but he also held a grudging pity for this wreck of a man. Padraig was a monster, no doubt about it. The things he'd done to Siobhan, the years of abuse and neglect, and this betrayal – they were unforgivable. And yet, looking at the blubbering creature beneath him, Vincent couldn't help but see a glimpse of his own past. The desperation, the poor choices, the descent into darkness – all too familiar.

Vincent rose to his feet, his chest heaving after the violence. He scanned the cottage, taking in the sparse furnishings and general squalor. Siobhan had mentioned something about weapons hidden away, and Vincent was determined to find them. He began his search, checking under loose floorboards and behind rickety furniture.

As he moved a decrepit chest of drawers, Vincent's keen ears caught the sound of something shifting behind the wall. He ran his fingers along the rough wooden planks until he found a loose board. He pried it free, revealing a small, hidden compartment.

Nestled in a bed of old rags lay a pair of flintlock pistols. Vincent retrieved them. They were heavier than he expected, the metal cold against his skin. He turned the weapons over, examining them. The craftsmanship was impressive, even to his untrained eye. Intricate engravings adorned the barrels, and the wooden grips felt smooth from years of handling. Vincent studied the pistols and realised he didn't know how to load or fire them. The mechanisms were foreign.

Vincent frowned, frustration creeping in. These pistols could be invaluable in his quest to rescue Siobhan, but only if he could figure out how to use them. He turned to Padraig, pistols in hand. "Where's the powder and shot?"

Padraig, still dazed from the beating, blinked up at Vincent. He lifted a shaking hand, pointing to a small wooden box perched on a shelf.

Vincent retrieved the bin. It was heavier than he expected, and as he opened it, he found it contained the tools of destruction neatly packed away: gunpowder, lead balls, and wadding. He returned to where Padraig lay crumpled on the floor and placed the pistols and box at his feet.

"Load them."

Padraig looked up, his battered face fearful. "What?"

Vincent towered over Padraig. "Load the pistols. Now!"

Padraig's hands shook as he reached for the weapons and supplies.

Vincent knelt on his haunches and watched. He needed the pistols loaded correctly if he was going to have any chance against the Hellfire Club. And who better to do it than the man who owned them? The air was thick with tension as Padraig got to work.

"Start with the powder," he said. He opened the box, spilling a few grains onto the floor before pouring a measure into the barrel of the first pistol.

Vincent committed each movement to memory. He'd never loaded a flintlock before, but his life – and Siobhan's – might depend on mastering the skill.

"Now the wadding," Padraig continued. He pressed a small piece of cloth into the barrel. "It will keep the black powder in place." The man's fingers shook as he picked up a lead ball, rolling it between his palms before dropping it into the barrel. "The ball goes in next. Ye want it snug against the wadding."

Vincent felt a grudging appreciation for the knowledge Padraig imparted.

"Then prime the pan." Padraig showed how to add a pinch of powder to the pan. "When ye pull the trigger, it will spark and ignite the main charge."

Vincent took in each detail. As Padraig finished loading the second weapon, Vincent knew he'd witnessed a skill that could mean the difference between life and death.

He took the pistols from Padraig and turned them over, examining the firing mechanism critically. They were unfamiliar, yet he saw their deadly potential.

He glanced down at Padraig, still lying on the floor, a pathetic heap of bruises and regret. For a moment, Vincent felt a flicker of pity, extinguished by the memory of what this man had been a party to.

Without a word, Vincent tucked the pistols into his belt and walked to the door. His hand reached for the handle, fingers brushing the cool metal, when he heard a familiar voice.

"He can't live, Vincent. You know this."

Vincent froze, his hand resting on the door handle. It was the voice that had haunted him since Deirdre's betrayal, the one that had urged him to kill Declan.

He turned his head, looking back at Padraig from the corner of his eye. The man lay there, broken and defeated, no longer a threat. And yet . . .

The voice was right. Padraig knew too much. He'd seen Vincent, could identify him. More importantly, he knew the Hellfire Club had Siobhan. If left alive, he could warn them, could jeopardise any chance Vincent had of rescuing the girl.

Vincent's hand dropped from the door handle, his fingers twitching as they brushed against the butt of one pistol.

CHAPTER 22

DARK JUSTICE

Vincent turned back to Padraig. The pistols were a reminder of the choice he had.

Padraig, sprawled on the floor, caught the change in Vincent. His eyes flickered, understanding dawning in their bloodshot depths. The danger wasn't over. He tried to push himself upright, his face contorting in pain as his battered body protested. He whimpered.

The sound should have stirred pity in Vincent. But he felt nothing. The voice urged him on.

"You know it's the only way, Vincent."

Vincent's fingers curled around the cold handles of the pistols. They felt familiar, almost comforting in his hands. He raised them, pointing them at Padraig.

Fear etched deep lines into Padraig's weathered face. He opened his mouth, lips trembling as he tried to find words. A strangled sound escaped his throat, but no coherent plea followed.

Vincent's face was an expressionless mask, yet beneath the surface, a storm raged. The memory of Siobhan's bruises, followed by an image of Rose's smiling face. His finger twitched on the trigger.

Then a flicker of doubt. Was this who he'd become? A man who could coldly execute another, no matter how despicable?

The voice slithered into his thoughts, smooth and persuasive.

"He's a loose end, Vincent. And a waste of good air."

The voice had a point. Padraig was dangerous, a liability. He'd sold his own daughter without a second thought. What was to stop him from revealing Vincent's presence to others?

Vincent's expression hardened, his grip tightening on the pistols as he reached his decision. The darker part of him stirred, awakening like a beast from slumber, and a cold resolve settled over him. His eyes, once filled with conflict, now burned with terrible purpose. He'd made harder choices before, hadn't he? This was just one more soul to add to the tally. The metal gleamed in the dim light, a harbinger of death.

The fog of alcohol cleared from Padraig as terror took hold. He saw his fate reflected in the cold metal of the pistol and the matching eyes of the man holding it. A whimper as he realised Vincent's intention.

Vincent's finger curled around the trigger, the pressure building. He could almost hear the mechanism inside the flintlock, ready to spark and ignite. The world narrowed to this moment, this choice.

Padraig's mouth opened and closed like a fish gasping for air. Words failed him as he stared down the barrel of the gun. His hands scrabbled weakly at the floor, seeking an escape that didn't exist.

Vincent pulled the trigger. The flintlock's report thundered through the small cottage, leaving his ears ringing. The acrid smell of gunpowder filled the air, mixing with the stench of fear and alcohol.

Padraig howled in pain, his body jerking backwards as the shot struck him in the chest. Blood blossomed on his filthy shirt, spreading like spilled wine. His eyes, wide with shock and agony, locked onto Vincent's face.

Without a word, Vincent stepped closer. The presence of the second pistol in his hand felt right, its purpose clear. He raised it, pointing at Padraig's head.

Padraig writhed on the floor, his hands clutching at the wound in his chest. Gurgling escaped his throat, an attempt at words that never formed. His eyes, once clouded by drink, now shone with a terrible clarity as they fixed on the barrel of the second pistol.

Vincent's finger tightened. There was no hesitation, no flicker of doubt. The second shot rang out, louder than the first. Padraig's head snapped back at the point-blank gunshot, then lay still.

The noise faded, and silence descended. Vincent stood motionless, the smoking pistol still aimed at what remained of Padraig's head. The only sound was the faint dripping of blood onto the worn floorboards.

Vincent's expression was a blend of grim satisfaction and detachment. He gazed down at the body, disconnected from the scene. The acrid smell of gunpowder mingled with the metallic tang of blood.

Vincent sat at the small table, setting down the empty pistols with a soft thud. His hands, steady and sure, moved of their own accord as he reloaded. The physical task brought comfort, his fingers deftly measuring out the powder. He tamped it down with wadding, his movements methodical. The lead ball followed, nestling snugly into place. As he worked, a part of Vincent's mind acknowledged the practicality of this impromptu practice. The unfamiliar weapons demanded respect and understanding if he hoped to use them.

The click of the frizzen snapping into place echoed in the silent room. Vincent's eyes flicked briefly to Padraig's dead body, then back to the pistol in his hands. He repeated the process with the second weapon, his movements no less precise for the grisly tableau.

Vincent stood, the loaded pistols a comfort at his sides. His eyes swept across the grim scene, taking in every detail with cold detachment. A pool of blood spread around Padraig. Pieces of brain spattered the walls. The man had definitely shit himself. There was no possible disguise for this, it was clearly a cold-blooded execution.

He assessed the situation with ruthless efficiency. The cottage, once merely shabby, now bore the unmistakable marks of violence. Every surface screamed of his murderous deed. Vincent realised the impossibility of concealing what had transpired here.

He looked around, searching for anything that might aid him in dealing with the aftermath. His gaze flicked from the meagre furnishings to the grimy windows, considering and discarding options in rapid succession.

The glint of metal caught his eye. In the room's corner, leaning against the wall, stood a shovel. Its wooden handle was worn smooth with use, the metal blade dulled and rusted at the edges. Vincent's eyes locked onto it, a plan forming.

He picked up the shovel, testing its weight in his hands. The handle was rough against his palms, much different than the smooth metal of the pistols he'd just used. He turned the tool over, examining the rusted blade. It wasn't ideal, but it would serve its purpose.

His gaze shifted from the shovel to Padraig. The pool of blood seeped into the worn floorboards. Vincent calculated the effort it would take to move the corpse and clean up the mess. His eyes darted to the door, gauging the distance and considering the best route to avoid detection.

Taking a deep breath, Vincent prepared himself. The air, thick with the scent of gunpowder and death, filled his lungs. He exhaled slowly, pushing aside any lingering doubts or regrets. This was necessary, he reminded himself. A loose end tied up, a monster removed from the world.

Vincent tucked the pistols into his belt. He gripped the shovel, studying it. The tool, once used for honest labour, would now serve a darker purpose.

CHAPTER 23
THE AFTERMATH

Vincent stepped out of the cottage, blinking as the low sun assaulted him. The farmland stretched away, a patchwork of fields and hedgerows that went on forever. He scanned the horizon, searching for any sign of life. The land appeared deserted, but Vincent knew better than to trust appearances.

The gentle breeze carried the scent of fresh-cut hay and distant livestock, a far cry from the acrid smell of gunpowder that clung to his clothes. Vincent considered his options for disposing of Padraig's body. The soft earth of a nearby field? The dense woods that bordered the property? Each possibility came with risks.

The sun hung low in the sky. It wouldn't be long before dusk settled over the land. A plan formed in his mind. He'd wait until the light faded, not out of fear of passersby on this isolated stretch, but to ensure farmers had retired for the day.

Vincent re-entered the cottage, his eyes falling on Padraig. The sight didn't stir any emotion in him; death was an old acquaintance by now. He surveyed the scene with a clinical detachment, assessing the task at hand.

Vincent's hands were steady as he reached for an old blanket draped over a nearby chair. He shook it out, dust motes dancing in the light.

Vincent wrapped Padraig's body in the blanket, tucking in the edges and ensuring complete coverage. The heaviness surprised him; Padraig had been a large man in life, and death had done nothing to diminish that.

As he worked, Vincent thought of Siobhan. *Would she mourn this man despite his cruelty? Or would she feel a twisted sense of relief, knowing she was free from his abuse? Did she even need to know?*

With the body wrapped, Vincent took a deep breath, preparing to lift it. Before he did, he saw the shovel and cursed under his breath. He grabbed it and tied it to the wrapped body with a length of rope. Then he dragged the body from the cottage to the barn until he was ready for it later.

He returned to the cottage to deal with the rest of the mess. The blood which had pooled around Padraig's body had seeped through gaps in the floorboards. He found a stack of old rags near the hearth and grabbed them, along with a bucket of water that sat by the door.

On hands and knees, Vincent wiped away the evidence. He dipped a rag into the cool water, wringing it out before attacking the crimson stains. The cloth quickly turned pink, then red as he worked.

Vincent's movements were efficient, born of experience he'd rather forget. He'd done this before, in another time, another place. The memories threatened to surface, but he pushed them down, focusing on what he was doing.

With the last visible traces of blood wiped away,

Vincent looked for any spots he might have missed. Satisfied with his work, he stood, muscles protesting after the prolonged crouch.

He retrieved a small sack of sand from near the fireplace, likely kept there to absorb spills. He scattered it liberally over the damp areas, watching as it soaked up the remaining moisture. The sand would disguise any faint stains that escaped his notice.

Vincent saw the secluded spot where he'd buried Declan – the damp earth, the eerie silence, the shovel in his hands. He shook his head, forcing the image away. It wasn't the time for such thoughts. He had to keep it together while he removed all traces of what had transpired in the cottage.

The aftermath of Deirdre's departure came to him. He recalled the meticulous way he'd cleaned the house, removing every trace of her presence. He'd scrubbed until his hands were raw, as if he could erase the pain along with the physical reminders.

He recognised the similarities between then and now, the anger and betrayal he'd felt when Deirdre . . . left. The betrayal was second-hand this time around.

He moved through the cottage, eyes sharp for any missed detail. It was a skill he'd never wanted to gain, yet here he was, applying it with the precision of a professional.

Vincent paused at Siobhan's small trunk. A pang of guilt struck him – he was taking so long to come to her aid. His fingers traced the rough wood, imagining the meagre possessions she'd left behind. What little comfort had this place offered her? And what danger awaited her at Blackwood Manor?

He shook his head, pushing the thoughts aside. The

sooner he disposed of Padraig's body, the sooner he could go to Siobhan.

The setting sun elongated the shadows across the farmyard, signalling it was time to move the body. Vincent peered out the grimy window, watching as the golden light faded to a deep orange. The distant fields were empty with no sign of life, save for a few crows pecking at the freshly turned earth. Night would come quickly now, and he didn't relish getting lost in the dark. It was time.

Vincent returned to the barn and pulled out Padraig's blanket-wrapped body. He grunted as he dragged it out of the farmyard, his muscles straining against the dead weight. The isolation of the farm, once oppressive, was now a blessing. No prying eyes to witness his nefarious task, no chance encounters to explain away.

The rough ground caught at the blanket-wrapped corpse, threatening to unravel his handiwork. Vincent paused, readjusting his grip. The chill of the evening air raised goose bumps on his skin, as sweat beaded on his brow.

As he neared the edge of the woods, he looked about for any sign of movement. Only the rustling of leaves and the occasional hoot of an owl broke the silence. He plunged into the dense undergrowth, pushing deep in search of a spot secluded enough for his dark purpose. The similarities to that night with Declan were impossible to ignore. The crunch of leaves underfoot, the loamy smell of damp earth, the guilt but also a sense of justice served – all unnervingly familiar.

I wish I had Murph's Ford.

After a few minutes, Vincent found a clearing, hidden from view by a thick copse of trees. He dropped Padraig's body to the ground, his breath coming in ragged bursts.

He untied the shovel and drove it into the soft earth, the metallic scrape echoing in the stillness. His muscles burned as he dug deeper, the repetitive motion allowing his mind to wander, formulating plans for Siobhan's rescue. According to Padraig and the supposed offer letter, Blackwood Manor wasn't far, so he'd get there on foot. Then he'd see the lay of the land.

The shovel struck a rock, jarring Vincent's arms. He cursed under his breath, leveraging the stone out of the hole. As he tossed it aside, his thoughts turned back to Blackwood Manor. Its layout and defences were unknown, and going in blind was a risk, but waiting might prove fatal to Siobhan.

Vincent paused, leaned on the shovel and wiped sweat from his face.

Fuck it! It's deep enough.

He climbed out and grasped the edge of the blanket, unravelling the bundle toward the grave. The corpse tumbled in. *THUMP.* Another life ended by his hand. Another burden he'd carry forever.

Shaking off the moment of introspection, Vincent set to filling in the grave. Time was of the essence; full night would make the task near impossible. He worked fast, shovelling the earth back into the hole with grim efficiency. The piled dirt grew, obscuring Padraig's makeshift shroud, and Vincent's thoughts returned to Siobhan. He hoped she was safe, or as safe as she could be in the clutches of the Hellfire Club. The sooner he could reach her, the better.

Vincent trudged back to the cottage, his muscles aching from the gruesome task. The last trace of twilight clung to the sky, casting long shadows across the farmyard. He paused at the threshold, steeling himself for one last sweep of the place.

With methodical precision, he scanned the room, eyes darting from corner to corner, searching for any telltale signs of his presence. He moved through the small space, his footsteps loud in the stillness. The floorboards creaked, too, and he winced at each sound. Vincent's gaze fell on the spot where Padraig had fallen. No trace remained of the violence that had occurred there, yet the memory of it hung in the air like thick fog.

Satisfied that he'd left no obvious trace, Vincent returned to the door. He paused, his hand on the rough wooden frame, and took one last look at the cottage interior. He could do no more. Pulling the door behind him, he left it ajar, as he had found it.

The cool evening air carried with it the scent of damp earth, livestock, and the promise of rain. He stood for a moment, listening to the distant call of a night bird. These ordinary sounds felt surreal to Vincent, as if the world should have stopped turning after what he'd done.

Why would it? It never has before.

Slipping back inside the barn, Vincent let the darkness envelop him like a shroud. His legs gave way beneath him, and he collapsed onto his makeshift bed. The prickly stems jabbed at him through his clothes, but he was used to it by now. Every muscle in his body ached, but the emotional exhaustion took a greater toll. His body wanted rest, but his mind refused to quiet. He lay on the straw, eyes fixed on the barn's shadowy rafters, as plans and contingencies whirled through his thoughts.

There's no time for rest! Siobhan needs you, for fuck's sake!

He pushed himself back up. His body complained, but

he forced himself to move. He went to where the Yam stood, a hulking anachronism in the dim light. He ran his hands over the bike, checking for any damage from their tumultuous arrival. Satisfied all was in order, he turned his attention to his meagre supplies.

The pistols lay where he'd left them, wrapped in a scrap of cloth. Vincent unwrapped them, the metal cool against his skin. He checked the powder and shot, grateful for Padraig's lesson. His fingers brushed against his phone, and he pulled it out, staring at the black screen. Useless here, but he couldn't discard it.

He sorted through the rest of his belongings, making an inventory of useful items. No matter how he looked at it, he was ill-equipped for a rescue mission. He needed an edge. He thought back over his time there for anything useful. Between the farmyard and the cottage, there had to be something. He refused to consider the shovel a worthy weapon.

All Padraig was good for was drink and empty bottles.

Empty bottles! An idea came to him and he ran across the farmyard and into the cottage. One by one, he checked all the bottles. Most bottles were drained, and a few had a few mouthfuls of sour wine within them. That wouldn't do.

He searched behind the furniture. Nothing. The cupboard contained only cups and plates. But tucked down the side of the bed, he found what he sought.

An addict always has a stash. He lifted out a large bottle of clear liquid, corked tight. Easing the cork out, he took a whiff, and it near blew his head off. *Good man, Padraig. Poitín.* It would burn like kerosene.

He placed the bottle of poitín to one side and studied the empty bottles again. Three would do, solid but breakable. He selected them and set them beside the poitín.

One more ingredient. Laundry soap. He'd last seen Siobhan use it while washing clothes in the yard. It was wrapped in paper and stored in a cupboard with other cleaning supplies. Using a paring knife, he made three piles of soap shavings. His arm was sore by the end.

Back to the poitín, he distributed the liquid between the three bottles. He used a crude paper cone to funnel a pile of soap into each one. Thumb-sealing the bottles, he shook each in turn to mix the concoction. Torn rags plugged the bottles, and he sat back to admire them. His lips quirked, amused.

"Homemade napalm, motherfuckers. I'll show you cunts hellfire."

CHAPTER 24

RECONNAISSANCE AND PREPARATION

Vincent stirred as the first light of dawn crept through the cracks in the barn. His body was stiff from the previous day and night.

He had no time to spare; Siobhan needed him. He gathered his belongings, securing the pistols inside his jacket. He checked the saddlebag where he stored his science experiment from the night before. The three bottles stood upright, wrapped in old towels from the cottage.

Snug as fucking bugs, he thought. *I'll be the snug one if I crash.*

He buckled the saddlebag tight, took a last look around the barn, and stepped out into the misty morning.

The world outside was awash in soft greys and muted greens. Dew clung to every blade of grass, wetting the bottom of his jeans as he trudged across the field.

Vincent paused at the edge of the property, recalling Padraig's slurred directions. "Follow the old road north," he muttered to himself, scanning the horizon. There, faintly visible through the morning haze, he spotted the worn path cutting through the countryside.

He set off, his footsteps crunching on the road's surface, the unfamiliar landscape unfolding around him. Fields gave way to dense woodlands, the trees pressing close on either side of the road, many more than in his own time.

Vincent's eyes darted from landmark to landmark, matching them against Padraig's descriptions. "Past the crooked oak," he murmured, spotting the gnarled tree ahead. Its twisted branches reached for him, a reminder of the ancient oak at The Devil's Corner.

The sun climbed higher, burning away the morning mist. Vincent wiped sweat from his forehead, unused to the hike. He crested a small hill to catch his breath and get his bearings. In the distance, he saw the next marker: a weathered stone cross jutting from the earth. He was on the right path.

VINCENT CROUCHED low in the undergrowth, his eyes fixed on the imposing structure of Blackwood Manor. The grand house stood before him, its stone walls a fortress against the outside world. He'd found a vantage point on a nearby rise hidden within a copse of trees, giving him a clear view of the main entrance and surrounding grounds. He settled in, prepared for a long wait.

The sun climbed higher, and he observed a steady stream of activity. Servants scurried to their duties, entering and exiting through a side door. A gardener tended the manicured lawns. Twice, the attendants welcomed elegantly dressed visitors and escorted them inside with grand ceremony. His eyes narrowed as he saw Lady Scarlett, her crimson dress unmistakable, stride in with her head held high.

The hours crawled by. Vincent saw patterns in the manor's routine. The changing of the guards, the rotation of servants, the timing of deliveries – all fell into a predictable rhythm.

When the sun dipped low on the horizon, painting the ground with shadows, Vincent made his move. He crept from his hiding place, using the darkness as cover. With as much stealth as possible, he slunk down the slope, keeping to the tree line.

Close to the manor wall, he paused behind a large oak, scanning for signs of alarm. The grounds remained quiet, the staff likely preparing for the evening meal. After taking a deep breath, he darted across an open stretch of lawn, pressing himself against the cool stone of the manor wall. He inched along it, alert for any disturbance. A barred window caught his attention. He peered inside, straining to see into the dark interior.

Vincent froze as two well-dressed gentlemen strolled along the garden path on the other side. Their voices carried to him on the evening breeze. "... the ritual must be performed at the stroke of midnight tomorrow," one said, his aristocratic tone clipped and precise.

"Do you believe the girl possesses the power we need?" the other asked, a note of doubt there.

"Lady Scarlett assures me she does. The Mountpelier clubhouse is prepared, per Lord Blackwood's instructions.

Vincent's breath caught in his throat. Mountpelier clubhouse. He filed away the location, already planning.

Their voices faded, but Vincent remained frozen in place, processing what he'd overheard. A ritual. Midnight. And Siobhan at the centre of it all. Determination coursed through him. This was his chance to save her, but he'd have to be careful. He didn't have backup or the luxury of a second chance.

As darkness fell, Vincent kept watch, cloaked in shadows. Flickering lights illuminated the windows and the muffled sounds of a dinner party drifting from within. All the while, he pieced together what he knew of the Hellfire Club's plans.

When the last servant retired, and the grounds lay silent under a blanket of stars, Vincent stirred. He crept away from the manor, his senses on alert for signs that he had been detected. But all was still. The only sound was the soft rustle of leaves in the gentle breeze.

VINCENT ENTERED THE BARN, breathing hard from the hurried return trip from Blackwood Manor. The familiar scent of hay and leather greeted him like a warm blanket. He leaned against the weathered wood of the barn door, allowing himself a moment to rest before his mind kicked into overdrive.

A rescue plan. He needed a rescue plan.

Vincent's eyes swept the barn, landing on his possessions. The smartphone, useless for calls but still a potential source of light. A Swiss Army knife, small but versatile. He wore his leather jacket, sturdy and intimidating, and had the pistols too. His three improvised incendiary devices were tucked away in a saddlebag. Each one held potential, waiting to be used for his desperate mission.

He picked up the smartphone, turning it over in his hands. The battery was low, but it might last long enough to serve as a distraction if needed. Vincent tucked it into his pocket, along with the knife. He had his lighter in his hip pocket too. Every advantage, no matter how small, could make the difference between success and failure.

He looked at the Yam, its chrome gleaming dimly. He approached it, running his hand along the smooth curves of the fuel tank. This machine, so out of place in this time, might be his greatest asset. Crouching beside the bike, his practiced hands moved over every inch of the machine. He checked the tires and made sure they were properly inflated. The chain received a thorough inspection, each link tested for weakness. He checked the oil and fuel levels and concluded they were good.

As he worked, Vincent mulled over scenarios. The Yam would provide a quick getaway, but its roar would attract unwanted attention. He'd need to time its use carefully, balancing speed against stealth.

Vincent hefted one of the flintlock pistols. He turned it over, examining the intricate mechanism. The smell of gunpowder still clung to the weapon.

Deciding he needed practice, Vincent left the barn and entered the woods beyond. The foliage closed in around him, muffling the sounds of the outside world. He found a clearing where a thick tree trunk would serve as a target.

Vincent raised the pistol, squinting down its length. He pulled the trigger, and the weapon kicked in his hand with a deafening roar. Bark splintered off the tree, a good foot to the left of where he'd been aiming.

Loading the pistol again, Vincent took more care with his aim. The second shot was closer, and by the third, he hit close to the centre of his imaginary target. Each blast echoed through the woods, but Vincent hoped the dense foliage would contain the noise.

Returning to the barn, Vincent felt more confident. He could handle the pistols now, but the limited shots and slow reload time made him acutely aware of their limitations. He had his other surprise to fall back on.

He turned his attention to the Yam, packing the saddlebag with essentials. Water, what little food he had, the pistols and ammunition – each item carefully considered and placed.

As he rummaged through the farm tools, Vincent's hand closed around a small hand axe. He lifted it, testing its weight and balance. It wasn't much, but it could be a useful backup if things went sideways. He tucked it into one saddlebag, hoping he wouldn't need to use it, but grateful for its solid presence.

Vincent paused before Siobhan's small trunk, his hand hovering over its worn surface. After a moment's hesitation, he lifted the lid. Among the meagre belongings, a splash of colour caught his eye – a vibrant hair ribbon. He plucked it from the trunk, running the soft fabric between his fingers. Without overthinking it, Vincent tucked the ribbon into his jacket pocket, a reminder of his mission. Just as he was about to close the trunk, he noticed Siobhan's notebook. He took it too.

Back at the Yam, he reorganised the saddlebags. He placed the flintlock pistols within easy reach, followed by the hand axe and extra gunpowder, shot, and wadding. His modern tools – the Swiss Army knife and the nearly dead smartphone – found their places alongside the period weaponry. He tucked Siobhan's notebook in there too.

As he packed, he mentally rehearsed the motions of loading and firing the pistols to make the process more familiar. He silently recited the steps: pour the powder, add the wadding, insert the ball, ram it down. This way, he cemented the sequence in his memory. The thought of fumbling them in a moment of crisis unnerved him.

With everything packed, Vincent took a step back, surveying his preparations. One saddlebag bulged, but nothing would fall out during the ride. He patted his pocket, feeling the reassuring presence of Siobhan's ribbon . . . and something else. From his pocket, he took the small, smooth stone given to him by Siobhan when they first met. He traced the occult symbols with his finger, still thinking them familiar but not knowing why. The stone itself was cool in his palm and grounded him. He slipped it into his jacket's inside pocket, where it would be close to his heart.

"For luck," he said. "Can't fuckin' hurt."

VINCENT WAITED IN THE FARMYARD, his body tense with anticipation, as the first hint of pre-dawn light crept across the sky. The world around him slumbered, unaware of the intruder in its midst. He straddled his motorcycle, feeling its familiar weight beneath him.

He turned the key. The engine roared to life, shattering the silence like a thunderclap. He winced, aware of how out of place the sound was in this era. But there was no turning back.

Vincent eased the bike onto the narrow country lane, the headlight cutting through the gloom. The rough terrain posed a challenge; the motorcycle bucked and shuddered beneath him as he navigated around potholes and over uneven ground. He gritted his teeth, hands gripping the handlebars tightly as he fought to maintain control.

The noise of the engine echoed from tree and hillside, amplifying its alien presence. Vincent looked left and right, checking if he'd attracted unwanted attention. But for now, the lanes remained empty.

The sky lightened, and he passed the first stirrings of life. Farmers, toiling in their fields, stopped and stared as the strange machine roared past. Their faces, illuminated by the growing light, were masks of shock and disbelief. Some dropped their tools, mouths agape. Others made the sign of the cross, no doubt believing they witnessed a demonic apparition.

Vincent hunched lower over the handlebars, avoiding eye contact with the startled onlookers. He left a trail of bewildered witnesses in his wake, but he couldn't afford to slow down or stop. Every moment counted if he was to reach the clubhouse on Mountpelier in time.

THE YAM'S roar cut through the early morning stillness as Vincent neared Mountpelier. He couldn't risk drawing attention to himself, not when he was so close. He flicked his wrist and killed the engine.

Sweat beaded on his brow as he dismounted, muscles straining as he pushed the heavy machine along the rough path. He scanned the area, his eyes darting around, searching for movement.

After an age of waiting, Vincent saw a small clearing within a cluster of trees off the main path. *Perfect.* He wheeled the bike into the undergrowth. Every crunch beneath the tyres set his teeth on edge.

He gathered fallen branches and handfuls of leaves to drape over the Yam, disguising its alien shape. He stepped back to survey his handiwork and allowed himself a nod of satisfaction. Unless someone stumbled upon it, the bike would remain hidden.

With his transportation secured, Vincent turned his

attention to Mountpelier itself. He made out the shape of the lodge building through the trees, its imposing silhouette a dark smudge against the lightening sky.

He steadied himself, then checked his pistols, feeling their reassuring weight against his side. With careful steps, he began his approach.

Vincent moved like a shadow, each footfall placed to avoid snapping twigs or rustling leaves. He scanned constantly, taking in every detail. The slightest movement, the faintest sound, could spell disaster.

Drawing closer to Mountpelier, his senses heightened. Every nerve in his body thrummed with tension. He was painfully aware of how exposed he was, how visible he was if someone glanced out of a window.

He sighed when he reached a gnarled tree and crouched low behind it. He surveyed the clubhouse. It was a hunting lodge with dark stone walls that taunted him with untold secrets. A large, ornate door dominated the front.

Too obvious, Vincent thought. His attention shifted to a smaller side entrance, partially obscured by overgrown shrubbery. *Better.*

He noted a series of tall windows along the upper floor. Possible escape routes, if things went pear-shaped. He grimaced at the thought. He couldn't afford to fail Siobhan.

As dawn's first light crept across the grounds, Vincent's keen eyes picked out several potential hiding places. A dense thicket of bushes near the east wall could provide decent cover. An old groundskeeper's shed, its paint peeling and door hanging askew, stood a stone's throw from the main building. Vincent filed these locations away knowing they might prove crucial later.

A sleepy-eyed servant emerged from the side door, stretching and yawning before shuffling to a well. The man drew water, his movements slow and predictable. Vincent noted the timing. If this was a daily routine, it could provide a window of opportunity.

As the morning progressed, Vincent observed a gradual increase in activity. More servants appeared, going about their usual tasks. He noted their patterns, the paths they took, the frequency of their movements. Each detail was another piece of the puzzle, another potential advantage.

Vincent's muscles ached from holding his position, but he dared not move. He needed more information, more time to understand the rhythm of this place. Only then could he plan to infiltrate the clubhouse. Observing the comings and goings around Mountpelier, he drew parallels between the security measures he saw and those he was familiar with in his own time.

No CCTV cameras here, he thought. *But the principle's the same – eyes watching, always watching.* He noted how the servants moved about, constantly sweeping the grounds. Not just going about their duties, but serving as a human surveillance system.

Vincent's lips twitched in a grim smile. In some ways, this was more challenging than a modern setup. Cameras were predictable, their blind spots easily mapped. People were unpredictable. A servant might turn to take a different route across the grounds.

He considered the locks he might encounter. No electronic keypads or biometric scanners here. But that didn't mean they'd be easy to bypass. Vincent had heard tales of the intricate lock mechanisms of this era, marvels of engineering in their own right. He'd need to be prepared for that.

As he watched, Vincent pieced together the social hierarchy at play. The way certain servants carried themselves, the deference shown by some to others, all painted a picture of the complex social dance of nineteenth-century Ireland. The groundskeeper barked orders at a young lad lugging gardening tools, the boy's head bowed in submission. Yet when a well-dressed man – likely one of the club members – strode past, the groundskeeper's attitude changed. His back straightened, his tone became deferential.

Vincent considered the implications. In his time, he might have been able to bluff his way past security with a confident attitude and the right clothes.

He thought of Siobhan, of the life she must have led. The constant awareness of one's place, the rigid expectations. No wonder she had turned to magic, he mused. It was probably the only aspect of her life where she had control.

Once he'd gathered enough information, he crouched behind the tree, eyes darting between the clubhouse and the surrounding grounds. With quick strokes, he sketched a rough map of Mountpelier and its surroundings in the dirt. He marked the main entrance, the side door he'd spotted earlier, and the windows on the upper floor. The groundskeeper's shed and the dense thicket of bushes were noted as potential hiding spots.

As he drew, Vincent's thoughts churned with rescue scenarios. The most straightforward approach would be to wait for nightfall and sneak in through the side entrance. But that assumed the door was unguarded and unlocked – a risky assumption at best.

If Siobhan is even in there yet.

Another option presented itself as Vincent watched a delivery cart trundle up to the main entrance. He could disguise himself as a servant or tradesman, bluffing his way inside. But the social intricacies of this era made that plan fraught with danger. One wrong word or gesture could give him away.

He looked to the upper windows. Scaling the building was a possibility, but it would leave him exposed during the climb. And still no guarantee he'd find Siobhan once inside.

He considered the possibility of creating a distraction. A small fire set on the grounds might draw enough attention to allow him to slip inside unnoticed. But the risk of the fire spreading gave him pause.

As Vincent sketched and planned, he tried to anticipate potential obstacles. Guards were an obvious concern; he marked their positions on his map as he saw them.

Then there was the matter of Siobhan herself. Vincent had no way of knowing where she was being held within. He threw the stick he'd used to sketch with to the dirt in disgust. There were too many factors, and he knew too little. Every plan he'd concocted seemed to have a fatal flaw, a weak point that could spell disaster for both of them.

He leaned back against the oak tree, his eyes fixed on Mountpelier. The building seemed to mock him with its secrets, its hidden dangers. Vincent's jaw tightened as he considered his options once more.

Then, like a bolt of lightning, clarity struck. The one thing he did know was that Siobhan would be where the biggest gathering was at midnight. That's when he'd strike. And fuck stealth.

A grim smile played across Vincent's lips as the plan crystallised in his mind. He'd come kicking down the door, guns blazing. It was reckless, dangerous, and probably stupid. But it was also unexpected. These pompous bastards wouldn't know what hit them.

Vincent's hand moved to the pistols at his side, feeling their reassuring weight. He'd have to time it perfectly, waiting until the ritual was underway, when they would be distracted and vulnerable. The element of surprise would be his greatest weapon.

He thought of the chaos he'd unleash and smiled. It wasn't a perfect plan, far from it. But it was a plan he could execute with the skills and tools at his disposal. And most importantly, it gave Siobhan the best chance of escape in the ensuing mayhem.

CHAPTER 25

THE WITCH'S PROCESSION

Siobhan's eyes fluttered open, her vision hazy as she tried to make sense of her surroundings. Gradually, the room came into view, unveiling its grandeur. Ornate wallpaper adorned the walls, and lavish velvet curtains concealed tall windows. She blinked, confused as she realised she wasn't in her cottage.

She touched the silken sheets beneath her, a luxury she'd never known. A mahogany wardrobe stood in the corner, its polished surface reflecting the faint light that seeped between the curtains. The air was thick with the scent of beeswax and lavender, so different from the earthy smells of home.

Her head pounded as she sat up. Her limbs were leaden. She struggled to piece together how she'd got to the unfamiliar room. As she rubbed her temples, a vivid memory burst forth, sharp and clear amidst the fog of her mind.

～

Siobhan remembered the village market. The air had been thick with the scent of fresh bread and ripe fruit, the chatter of haggling villagers filling her ears. She'd clutched her woven basket close, handpicking vegetables and herbs for the coming week.

As she'd moved from stall to stall, a prickle of unease had crept up her neck. She'd glanced over her shoulder and picked out two men standing apart from the crowd. Their fine clothing and haughty expressions marked them as outsiders, and they watched her with an intensity that made her skin crawl.

Siobhan paid for her purchases, coins clinking as she dropped them into the merchant's palm before quickening her pace and weaving through the throng of market-goers. The men's stares followed.

She ducked down a quiet lane that led toward home. The sounds of the market faded, replaced by the swish of her skirts against the cobblestones. She allowed herself a small sigh of relief, thinking she evaded the unwanted audience.

Then, without warning, a hand clamped over her mouth from behind. Siobhan's basket tumbled to the ground, apples rolling across the lane.

Siobhan struggled against her captor's iron grip. She clawed at the hand clamped over her mouth, nails digging into flesh, but the man's hold didn't waver. Panic surged through, instinct screaming at her to fight.

A sickly sweet scent filled her nostrils as a cloth pressed against her mouth and nose. Her eyes widened in recognition. Ether. She'd seen the local doctor use it once to ease the pain of a man with a broken leg. The knowledge that it was being used on her sent a fresh wave of terror through her.

She thrashed wildly, her legs kicking out, desperate to connect with her assailant. But he held her fast, his arm viselike around her waist. Siobhan tried to summon her magic, to call forth the shadows that usually danced at her fingertips. But fear clouded her mind, scattering her focus.

The world tilted and swayed. She blinked rapidly, trying to clear her vision, but the alleyway blurred into a haze of muted colours. Her limbs grew heavy as if weighed down by invisible stones. She tried to lift her arms, to push away the cloth, but they refused to obey.

A distant part of her registered voices, low and urgent, but she couldn't make out the words. They seemed to come from far away, echoing strangely in her ears. Siobhan's eyelids drooped, each blink lasting longer than the last.

She fought against the encroaching darkness with every ounce of her remaining strength. But the battle was lost. The world spun, fading at the edges. Her last thoughts were of her father, of the cottage, of Vincent hidden in the barn. Then, like a candle being snuffed out, all went black.

SIOBHAN SHUDDERED, the phantom scent of ether lingering in her nostrils. She blinked, trying to banish the memory and focus on her current situation. Pushing herself up to a sitting position, she noticed the unfamiliar fabric draped across her. She glanced down and her breath caught. Gone were her worn, homespun clothes. In their place was an elaborate gown of deep crimson silk embroidered with intricate golden symbols that writhed in the dim light. It had an air of magic about it.

A ritual gown? But for what purpose?

Siobhan reached for her magic, seeking the comforting

embrace of shadows that had always been her ally. But where she expected a wellspring of power, she found only emptiness. Panic clawed at her as she tried again and again, each attempt more desperate than the last.

Her magic was gone.

Siobhan panicked, her heart pounded, and her breaths came in quick gasps. She'd never felt so vulnerable, so defenceless. Even in her darkest moments, her power had always been there, a silent promise of protection.

As she pushed her hair back from her face with a trembling hand, something caught her attention. A bracelet encircled her left wrist, its metal gleaming softly. It was a simple thing, a band of what looked like iron, but Siobhan knew at once that its purpose was far from benign.

She tugged at it, her nails scrabbling against the smooth surface, but it remained firmly in place. With each failed attempt to remove it, her fear grew. This was no mere ornament but a cage, trapping her magic within her own body, rendering her powerless.

The door creaked open, and Siobhan's heart leapt to her throat. Two figures glided in, their faces hidden behind ornate masks, bodies shrouded in heavy robes. They moved with an eerie grace, not uttering a single word as they approached her.

Siobhan scrambled back and pressed against the head-board, her fingers clawed at the sheets. She opened her mouth to speak, to demand answers, but her voice failed her. The figures reached out, their hands pale and long-fingered, grasping her arms with surprising gentleness. "Leave me be!"

They ignored her pleas and pulled her to her feet, then led her from the room. Her bare feet touched the cold stone floor, sending a shiver through her. The chill seeped into her very bones.

They moved through the manor's winding corridors and Siobhan took in more of the opulent surroundings. Tapestries depicting grotesque scenes adorned the walls, their images writhing in the flickering candlelight. Mirrors in intricate frames reflected distorted versions of her, a stranger in a crimson gown.

They passed by a partially open door, and snippets of conversation drifted out.

" . . . the great ritual must begin at midnight . . ."

". . . power beyond our wildest dreams . . ."

". . . the Devil-touched girl is the key . . ."

The voices spoke of Siobhan; she was certain. A 'great ritual'? Her fear, already a living thing inside her chest, grew teeth and claws. What did they plan to do with her? And who were these people who spoke of rituals and power with such ease?

As they descended a grand staircase, Siobhan thought of Vincent, wondering if he'd noticed her absence. Would he seek her out? Or was she alone in this nightmare?

She stumbled as they led her out of Blackwood Manor, the cool night air a shock against her skin. Her eyes widened at the sight of an ornate carriage waiting in the courtyard, its black lacquered surface gleaming in the moonlight.

The masked figures guided her to the carriage, their grip on her arms unyielding. They ushered her into the plush interior. Within, she sat among several robed figures, their faces hidden behind grotesque masks. As the carriage door slammed shut, a wave of claustrophobia washed over her. The scent of incense and something darker, something that made her skin crawl, hung heavy in the air. She tried to steady her breathing, aware of the silent figures all around her.

The carriage lurched into motion, the rhythmic clop of horses' hooves echoing in the night. Siobhan's fingers dug into the velvet seat as the carriage picked up speed, each turn and bump making her more aware of the growing distance between her and Blackwood Manor.

Where are they taking me?

Minutes stretched into hours. Siobhan attempted to piece together a map of their journey, but heavy curtains covered the windows, leaving her blind.

The silence inside the carriage was oppressive. None of the robed figures spoke or moved, their stillness unnatural. Siobhan looked from one mask to another, searching for a hint of humanity behind the grotesque facades. She found nothing, only empty sockets stared back at her.

Siobhan's thoughts turned to her father, a storm of emotions churning within her. Anger flared hot and bright, memories of his drunken rages and cruel words searing through her mind. The bruises he'd left on her skin had faded, but the ones on her heart remained.

Yet, beneath the anger lay a current of sorrow. For all his faults, Padraig was still her father. The man who'd taught her to fish in the nearby stream, who'd once sung her to sleep with old Irish ballads. Where was he now? Did he even notice she was gone? A bitter laugh threatened to escape. Of course, he'd noticed. Who else would cook his meals and clean up after his messes? But would he care enough to look for her?

Pushing thoughts of her father aside, Siobhan closed her eyes, focusing inward. She reached for her magic once more, seeking that familiar warmth. But where there should have been a roaring fire, she found only cold ashes.

The iron bracelet seemed to tighten around her wrist, mocking her powerlessness.

Sweat beaded on her brow as she strained, pushing against the invisible barrier that kept her magic locked away. It was like trying to break through a stone wall with her bare hands. Exhaustion swept over her, leaving her feeling hollow and more afraid than ever.

As Siobhan slumped back against the seat, she caught snippets of whispered conversation between two nearby figures.

"The vessel is strong," one murmured, voice muffled behind the mask.

"Indeed," replied the other. "Lord Blackwood chose well. Her power will serve our purpose admirably."

Siobhan's blood ran cold. 'The vessel'. She was nothing more than a tool to these people, a means to an end. But what end? What terrible purpose did they have in mind for her?

The carriage climbed, its wheels creaking as they navigated a steep incline. Siobhan's stomach lurched with each turn, a mix of motion sickness and dread. She pressed her hands against the seat to steady herself as the vehicle swayed.

Through a gap in the curtains, Siobhan caught her first glimpse of their destination. The Hellfire clubhouse on Mountpelier crouched against the night sky, a dark silhouette that swallowed the surrounding stars. Its imposing structure sent a chill down her spine, and she held her breath.

The carriage jolted to a stop at the base of the hill, and the door swung open. Cool night air rushing in as rough hands grasped her, pulling her into the darkness. Her bare feet touched damp grass, and she stumbled, only to be hauled upright by her captors.

Siobhan's eyes adjusted to the gloom, and she saw they weren't alone. Dark-clad figures emerged from the surrounding trees, their faces hidden behind masks similar to those worn by her escorts. They moved with an eerie synchronicity, forming a loose circle around her.

Siobhan searched one masked face after another for any sign of humanity, any hint of mercy. But she found only blank, emotionless stares. She had no choice but to move at the centre of the macabre procession, masked figures flanking her, their robes rustling in the night breeze. She shivered, aware of her vulnerability in the thin silk gown.

The path leading to the clubhouse stretched up the hill, a winding trail of loose stones and gnarled roots. Siobhan's bare feet ached with each step, sharp pebbles digging into her soles. She stumbled more than once, only to be hauled upright by the silent guards.

She searched left and right for an opportunity to break free, but the terrain offered no refuge. To her left, the hillside fell away in a steep drop, promising only injury if she dared to flee in that direction. To her right, the slope rose sharply, too treacherous to climb. Besides, the guards pressed close, their grip on her arms unyielding. Siobhan's heart beat a frantic rhythm, echoing the steady tread of feet. She tried to swallow her fear, but it lodged in her throat.

As they climbed higher, the air grew thinner. Siobhan's lungs burned with the effort of the ascent. She longed to stop, to catch her breath, but the procession moved relentlessly onward. The clubhouse above grew larger with each torturous step.

The surrounding figures moved with a singular purpose

and never faltered. An impenetrable wall of bodies that trapped her, hemming her in on all sides.

She looked to the vast expanse of countryside stretching out below. Rolling hills and dark forests for as far as the eye could see, bathed in silvery moonlight. The sight made her long for home. Her little cottage, nestled in the valley, seemed so far away.

Her eyes stung with unshed tears, but she blinked them back. She wouldn't give her captors the satisfaction of seeing her cry. Instead, she stared ahead at the clubhouse. Its windows glowed with an otherworldly light, pulsing in a rhythm that matched her heartbeat. The eerie radiance cast long shadows across the hillside, turning familiar shapes into monstrous silhouettes.

Dread grew inside Siobhan. The bracelet on her wrist grew heavier, a reminder of her powerlessness. Yet, as they drew near the clubhouse, something else came into existence – a fierce, defiant spark that refused to be extinguished.

Siobhan squared her shoulders, lifting her chin despite the fear twisting her gut. Whatever awaited her beyond those glowing windows, she would face it with all the strength she could muster. Despite her powerlessness, she wasn't broken.

As they reached the base of the clubhouse steps, Siobhan's eyes locked onto a figure standing at the top. Unlike the others, this one wore elaborate robes embroidered with symbols that writhed and twisted in the flickering light, much like the gown she wore. A mask of polished gold concealed their features, revealing only two empty eye sockets staring into Siobhan's soul.

Her heart sank as she recognised the figure. Lord Blackwood's cruel eyes sent chills down her spine, gleaming with malicious intent from behind his golden mask. She had seen him only once before, at a village gathering, but his presence had left an indelible mark on her memory.

As the guards led her up the steps, each one felt like a step closer to doom. The stone beneath her bare feet was cold and unyielding. Siobhan's legs trembled with exhaustion and fear, but she forced herself to keep moving, refusing to give Lord Blackwood the satisfaction of seeing her falter.

At the top of the stairs, Siobhan stopped, her eyes drawn to the night sky. The stars twinkled, unbelievably remote and indifferent to her plight. She took in the surrounding landscape again, the rolling hills and dark forests stretching below. The familiar contours of her homeland, now so far out of reach, made her heart ache. Siobhan took a deep breath, memorising every detail of the scene. The cool night air on her skin, the faint scent of heather carried on the breeze, the soft whisper of wind through the trees – all of it seemed precious, knowing what awaited her inside.

Before she could linger any longer, rough hands grasped her arms, propelling her toward the entrance. Lord Blackwood's eyes never left her as she passed, so she lifted her chin, meeting his look with defiance.

As she crossed the threshold, the warmth and flickering light from within washed over her. The heavy doors swung shut with a resounding *THUD*, the sound echoing through the cavernous interior. Siobhan flinched at the finality of it, feeling as though those doors had sealed her fate.

CHAPTER 26

THE DEVIL RIDES OUT

Vincent crouched in the shadows, his eyes locked on the clubhouse entrance. He watched Siobhan being led up the steps, her tiny figure dwarfed by the masked men flanking her. Every fibre of his being screamed at him to rush forward, to snatch her away from their grasp, but he forced himself to remain still. The time wasn't right. Not yet.

The heavy doors of the clubhouse swung shut behind Siobhan with an ominous *THUD*, the sound echoing in the night air like a death knell.

Vincent's nails dug into his palms. "Fuck!" He leapt to his feet, throwing caution to the wind. He abandoned his hiding spot, the urgency of the situation overriding any semblance of a plan.

Sprinting from his observation point, he headed for the Yam's hiding place. Leaves crunched beneath his boots, branches whipping at his face as he tore through the underbrush. His lungs burned with each ragged breath, but he pushed on, driven by the image of Siobhan's frightened face.

As he ran, fragmented ideas tumbled through his thoughts. Would the bike's roar be enough of a distraction? He was betting on it.

Vincent burst into the small clearing where he'd hidden the Yam, his chest heaving with exertion. The bike lay on its side, covered in a hasty camouflage of branches and leaves. Without pause, he flung himself at it, his hands grasping at the foliage. Twigs snapped and leaves rustled as he tore away the makeshift cover. His fingers worked frantically, driven by urgency. Each second gave fresh images of what might happen to Siobhan inside that hellish clubhouse.

The last branch fell away and Vincent gripped the Yam's handlebars. Grunting with the effort, he heaved the bike upright and engaged the stand.

He fumbled with the flintlock pistols, cursing under his breath, willing himself to focus.

"Come on, come on," he muttered, his eyes darting between the weapons and the clubhouse in the distance.

He checked the first pistol, his movements hurried. The pan was primed, the flint cocked back. It seemed ready, but doubt gnawed at him. Had he loaded it properly? Was the powder distributed correctly? He couldn't remember, his mind a whirlwind of panic and determination.

No time. No bloody time.

Vincent moved to the second pistol, his inspection even more cursory than the first. Siobhan's fate urged him to act now. To rush in, guns blazing.

He shoved both pistols into his jacket, the cold metal pressing against his skin through his shirt. Vincent's eyes fell on the hand axe in the saddlebag. He snatched it up and tucked it into his belt, the blade reassuring against his hip.

Vincent swung his leg over the bike and he disengaged the stand. The bike wobbled beneath him, nearly toppling as he settled onto the seat. He cursed under his breath, steadying the Yam with his feet planted on the ground.

His hands shook as he reached for the key, fingers fumbling with the small piece of metal. Sweat beaded on his forehead as it slipped from his grasp once, twice, before he finally slotted it into the ignition.

"Come on, you bastard," he said, twisting the key with more force than necessary.

The motorcycle's engine roared to life as he thumbed the starter, the sound shattering the eerie silence. The noise reverberated through the trees, startling a flock of birds from their roost nearby.

Vincent revved the engine again, the aggressive growl echoing through the night. Stealth was no longer an option, but he didn't care.

He gripped the handlebars tight. The familiar vibration of the motorcycle beneath him grounded him, a touchstone of his own time in the madness of this era.

He took a deep breath, the cool night air filling his lungs. Vincent closed his eyes for a moment, trying to centre himself. Images flashed through his mind: Siobhan's frightened face, the masked figures leading her away, the ominous clubhouse in the distance. Each one stoked the fire of his resolve.

Vincent opened his eyes, his jaw set. He was about to unleash chaos upon the Hellfire Club, and he welcomed it. The flintlock pistols at his sides, a reminder of the violence to come. The hand axe at his hip was a promise of retribution. And he'd brought his own hellfire.

He flexed his fingers on the throttle, the engine's low hum rising to a roar. Vincent thought of his fragmented plans and half-formed strategies. None of it mattered now.

All that mattered was getting to Siobhan, tearing through anyone who stood in his way.

Vincent sat poised on his motorcycle, a man out of time ready to storm the gates of Hell. There was no turning back from this moment. Whatever happened next would change everything.

With one final, steadying breath, Vincent kicked the Yam into gear and twisted the throttle, aiming the bike at the Hellfire clubhouse doors.

CHAPTER 27
CHAOS UNLEASHED

Rough hands shoved Siobhan farther into the high-ceilinged chamber. The air hung thick with incense, stinging her nostrils. Robed figures stood in the shadows, their faces hidden behind ornate masks. She squinted, willing her eyes to adjust to the gloom.

Jet-black drapes covered the walls, absorbing the light from the many candles that served as illumination. An imposing altar dominated the far end of the room, its surface gleaming with strange symbols etched in gold. Black candles burned at each corner.

Behind the altar hung an inverted crucifix. At first, she thought someone painted Christ's hanging body red, but the liquid was wet and flowed from his wounds to drip from his crown of thorns.

Before the altar stood an X-shaped frame made from rough-hewn wood. At the extremity of each point hung a thick rope.

"No," she whispered. She dug her heels in, but her captors dragged her forward. Siobhan thrashed wildly, her movements desperate, as the frame came closer. She reached for her magic – a reflexive action – only to feel the cold bite of the bracelet on her wrist.

"Let me go!" she snarled, twisting in their grip. One of the robed figures chuckled, the sound devoid of mirth.

They forced her against the frame, rough hemp biting into her wrists and ankles as they bound her tight. Siobhan strained against the ropes, but they held fast. She stood, spread-eagled, vulnerable, her chest heaving with panicked breaths. She looked from face to face, searching for a hint of mercy, finding only blank masks staring back.

She watched helplessly as the anonymous congregation formed a semi-circle around her and the altar. Their hidden eyes watched as she struggled against her bindings. Blinking away sweat, she refused to show fear despite it eating her up inside.

The crowd parted, and a figure emerged that made Siobhan's blood run cold. Lord Blackwood approached the altar, his elaborate robes swirling about him like living shadows. The golden mask that concealed his features caught the flickering candlelight, transforming his visage into something terrible.

Flanking Lord Blackwood were two figures Siobhan recognised. Lady Scarlett glided forward, her figure-hugging crimson gown unlike anything in the sea of dark robes. In her hands, she cradled an ornate chalice that pulsed with otherworldly light. It drew Siobhan's gaze as a sick fascination battled with her terror.

On Blackwood's other side strode Sir Reginald Hawthorne, his tall frame stooped as if weighed down by the ancient volume he carried. The symbols on the book's cover made Siobhan's eyes water when she tried to look at them.

As the trio reached the altar, Siobhan strained against her bonds once more. The ropes gnawed at her flesh, but she ignored the pain. She searched for a way out, a glimmer of hope in this nightmare.

Blackwood raised his arms, his golden mask gleaming in the torchlight. The congregation fell silent, their attention fixed on their leader. Blackwood's voice filled the chamber, resonant with dark authority.

"Brothers and sisters, tonight we stand on the precipice of greatness. With this ritual, we shall harness powers beyond mortal comprehension."

Siobhan's eyes darted around the room, searching for an opportunity to escape. She focused inward, reaching for her magic. The bracelet on her wrist grew icy cold, sending painful jolts up her arm. She bit back a cry, unwilling to give them the satisfaction of hearing her pain.

Blackwood's words took on a sinister cadence as he began the ritual. *"In nomine Satanas, nos invocamus potentiam tenebrarum,"* he said in a guttural growl.

The air in the chamber grew heavy, pressing down on Siobhan like a physical weight. She gasped for breath, her skin crawling with revulsion as the satanic invocation continued. The symbols on the altar glowed with an eerie, pulsing light.

Lady Scarlett stepped forward, raising the chalice high. Sir Reginald opened the ancient tome, his fingers tracing lines of text. A dark, malevolent energy built in the room.

Blackwood's chanting grew louder, the words twisting and distorting until they barely resembled human speech. Siobhan's head throbbed, each syllable feeling like a hammer blow against her skull. She squeezed her eyes shut, offering a silent plea for it to stop, for someone to intervene.

Siobhan sensed movement close by and opened her

eyes to see Lady Scarlett circling her, the woman's emerald eyes glinting with malicious intent. In her hand, a ceremonial dagger caught the flickering light, its blade wickedly sharp. Scarlett traced intricate symbols in the air around Siobhan, each movement precise.

The air shimmered where the dagger passed, leaving faint, glowing trails that hung suspended for a moment before fading. A chill crept over her skin, gooseflesh rising in the wake of each symbol. She tried to follow the patterns with her eyes, but they twisted away, defying comprehension.

To her left, Sir Reginald busied himself at the altar, arranging objects with painstaking care. Siobhan caught glimpses of strange artefacts: a curved bone that looked unsettlingly human, a black candle that seemed to absorb light rather than cast it, a small vial filled with a swirling, opalescent liquid.

As the ritual progressed, Siobhan noticed an odd sensation. It started as a faint tug, infinitesimal amidst her fear and confusion. But with each symbol Lady Scarlett traced, with each item Sir Reginald placed, the feeling intensified.

It was as if gossamer threads were attached to every part of her, gently but insistently pulling outward. She gasped as the sensation deepened, her essence stretching beyond the confines of her physical form. She struggled against her bonds again, desperate to escape the invasion.

The pull grew stronger, and Siobhan felt a part of herself – not her body, but something deeper, more fundamental – unravel. Panic clawed at her as she realised what was happening. They were draining her, drawing out her life force, her magic, her soul.

The congregation chanted in unison, a low, guttural sound that penetrated Siobhan's bones. The intonation reverberated through her body, each syllable pulsing in time with her heartbeat. She gritted her teeth, trying to block out the invasive noise, but it wormed its way into her skull, clouding her thoughts.

Lord Blackwood's voice cut through the chanting, rising in both volume and intensity. His words, a twisted blend of Latin and something far older, corrupted the surrounding air. The power built, pressing against her like a physical force.

As the ritual reached a peak, Siobhan's vision blurred. The room swam and the masked figures melted into indistinct shapes. She blinked to clear her sight, but the haziness persisted. A bone-deep weariness crept through her limbs, each breath becoming a monumental effort.

Her strength ebbed away. Her essence was being siphoned off, drawn out by the relentless pull of the ritual. She struggled against her bonds, determined to fight until the last, but she grew weaker. Her arms leaden, her legs trembling with the effort to remain upright.

Despite her fading strength, Siobhan refused to give in. She twisted her wrists, ignoring the bite of the ropes, searching for any hint of slack. But her efforts were feeble, her once fierce struggles reduced to faint twitches. Despair threatened to overwhelm her as she realised how powerless she had become.

The chanting grew louder, as if it pressed against her ears like a physical force. The dark energy built in the air, thickening it until each breath was like drawing in syrup. Around her, the power swirled, a malevolent maelstrom of intent draining the last remnants of her feeble strength.

Siobhan's head lolled forward, her chin dropping to her chest. She fought to keep her eyes open, but her eyelids felt impossibly heavy. She tried to focus, to cling to conscious-ness, but it slipped away.

In her fading vision, the room tilted and swayed. The chanting came from everywhere and nowhere at once, echoing inside her head. Siobhan blinked slowly, struggling to make sense of the scene before her.

From the haze, a shape materialised, towering over her – Lord Blackwood in his golden mask, catching the flick-ering light. Siobhan watched, her mind sluggish and uncomprehending, as he raised his arms high above his head.

In Blackwood's hand, something glinted. Siobhan's eyes struggled to focus on the object. As her vision cleared for a moment, she saw the athame, its blade sharp and etched with strange symbols. The sight sent a jolt of fear through her, piercing the fog that clouded her mind.

Siobhan's eyelids fluttered. Her consciousness flowed away like sand through an hourglass. The chanting had become a dull roar, her body numb and unresponsive. She faded as she fell into an abyss of darkness.

Then, through the haze, a sound penetrated. At first, it barely registered amidst the ritual's chaos. But it grew louder, a deep, mechanical roar unlike anything Siobhan had ever heard.

The strange noise cut through the chanting, causing it to falter. The ritual's power lessened. There was movement in the arranged bodies as the congregation's focus wavered.

Murmurs of confusion rippled through the chamber. Siobhan heard the uncertainty in voices, the rising tide of fear. The roar grew louder still, shaking the very founda-tions of the building.

Lord Blackwood's voice rose above the din, sharp with

anger. "Continue the ritual!" But there was a tremor in his tone that betrayed his own unease.

Without warning, the massive doors at the far end of the chamber crashed open. The thunderous sound reverberated through the room, shaking Siobhan to her core. A gust of cool night air rushed in, dispelling the cloying incense.

A spark of hope ignited within her. With monumental effort, she summoned the last of her strength. Her muscles screamed in protest as she raised her head.

Through bleary eyes, she struggled to focus on the doorway. Her vision swam, the scene before her a blur of motion and confusion. But there, in the chaos, was the impossible. Framed by the shattered doorway was a man astride a monstrous metal beast which growled and snarled, belching smoke and fire. Its two wheels spun, spraying debris as it advanced into the room. The congregation scattered before it, their chants replaced by cries of terror.

Siobhan was certain her mind played tricks on her, but as the beast came into clearer focus, recognition dawned. The broad shoulders, the determined set of the jaw, the fierce look in his eyes – it was Vincent. He looked like an avenging demon, his face contorted with rage as he surveyed the scene.

A wave of relief washed over Siobhan, cutting through the fog that clouded her mind. Her parched lips parted, and she tried to call out to him, but all that came out was a whisper. Her strength was all but spent.

"Vincent," she murmured, the name inaudible even to her own ears.

As if hearing her feeble call, Vincent's gaze swept across

the room, finally landing on her. Their eyes met, and Siobhan saw the recognition in his fierce expression. In that moment, a spark of hope ignited.

CHAPTER 28
HELLFIRE

Vincent fought to control the Yam on the slick stone floor of the clubhouse. The noise of splintered wood, screaming cultists, and the bike's roaring engine assaulted him. He gripped the handlebars in a death grip, willing the machine to obey as it fishtailed wildly.

He scanned the room, taking in the chaos he'd unleashed. Robed figures scattered like startled birds, their masks hiding expressions of terror and disbelief. Some stood frozen, jaws agape at the impossible sight before them. Despite the mayhem, his eyes found Siobhan. She hung limply from an X-frame at the far end of the room; her face was luminous, surrounded by dark robes.

Their eyes met across the chaos. Vincent saw a flicker of recognition. The spark of hope that ignited there, despite her weakened state, sent a jolt through him, as if an electric current had passed between them. Her slumped posture and the unnatural pallor of her skin made Vincent's blood boil. Whatever dark ritual these bastards were performing, he'd arrived just in time.

Vincent locked onto a clear patch of floor near the altar. He leaned into the turn, guiding the Yam toward it. The bike's tires shrieked in protest as they slid across the polished stone, leaving dark rubber streaks in their wake.

The world around him blurred into a chaotic whirl of motion and sound, but Vincent remained laser-focused. The bike wanted to slip out from beneath him, its weight threatening to topple at any moment.

As he bore down on the altar, he tensed his muscles, preparing for the next crucial moments. In one fluid motion born of years of riding experience, he kicked out the bike's stand while pushing off the saddle with his legs. The transition from seated to standing happened in the blink of an eye, leaving the Yam to slide a few inches but remain upright.

Vincent's boots hit the ground hard, sending a jolt through his legs. He stumbled but kept his footing. Behind him, the bike's engine continued to rumble, filling the chamber with its anachronistic roar.

A fleeting prayer to some dark god flashed through Vincent's mind as he glanced back at the bike. He willed the machine to keep running, knowing that its continued noise would add to the confusion and give him a precious advantage. The last thing he needed was for it to sputter out.

Vincent reached into his jacket and withdrew the pistols. He strode toward the altar, his eyes locked on Lord Blackwood. The aristocrat's mask had fallen off in the commotion, and his face was all shock and indignation. The lord's elaborate robes were in disarray as well.

Vincent's gaze never wavered as each step brought him closer to Siobhan and the man responsible for her captivity. His voice boomed through the chaos, "Let her go, you cunt!"

Every cultist in the room trained their eyes on Vincent, but he focused only on Blackwood and Siobhan.

Lord Blackwood, recovering from the shock, sneered contemptuously. His initial surprise gave way to arrogant disdain as he regarded Vincent. "And who might you be, sir, to make such bold demands?"

Without hesitation, Vincent raised one pistol and fired. The shot rang out, deafening in the enclosed space. The acrid smell of gunpowder filled his nostrils as smoke curled from the barrel.

Blackwood staggered back, his face contorting in pain. He clutched his arm where blood seeped between his fingers, staining his robe.

Wasting no time, Vincent stepped up to the altar area. His other pistol swung in a smooth arc to stop at Lady Scarlett and Sir Reginald. They paled when confronted by the cold barrel.

"Now, you fucking pricks," Vincent said in a dangerous voice. "Let her go right fucking now, or I swear to Christ, I'll end you."

The modern expletives would be strange to them, but Vincent couldn't have cared less. His eyes darted between the three cult leaders, daring them to disagree.

"I said NOW!" he roared.

Vincent kept the pistol steady, aware of Siobhan's limp form behind him. Every second counted, and he prayed the shock of his entrance and the threat of his weapons would be enough to make these bastards comply.

Lady Scarlett composed herself, her initial shock giving way to a practiced allure. She stepped forward, her voice dripping with honey. "As you wish, my Lord," she said, her eyes locked on Vincent's.

The unexpected address threw him. He blinked, his grip

on the pistol tightening as he processed her words. He snorted in disbelief before he could stop it. "Keep your panties on, love."

Confusion rippled across Lady Scarlett's face, her seductive mask slipping to be replaced by a look of utter bewilderment. Even Lord Blackwood, still clutching his wounded arm, raised an eyebrow at the unfamiliar phrase.

Vincent suppressed a grimace, realising how out of place his modern vernacular must sound to their nineteenth-century ears. But he pushed the thought aside, focusing on his goal.

He looked between the three Hellfire Club leaders, muscles tense and ready for any sudden moves. He had the pistol trained on Lady Scarlett but kept Lord Blackwood and Sir Reginald in his peripheral vision. In addition, he maintained a watchful eye on the nearby cultists, searching for any courageous or reckless individuals.

Vincent thought of how he must look to them. The combination of his long hair, unkempt beard, and modern clothing gave him the appearance of a demon. His attire of black leather jacket and jeans was outlandishly out of place against theirs. He felt like an intruder from another world, which, he supposed, he was. He almost laughed, but the gravity of the situation kept his face grim.

An eeriness fell over the room. Vincent heard his own heartbeat thundering in his ears as he took in the frozen figures around him. Most of the cultists stood stock-still, their eyes wide with terror behind their masks. They radiated fear, and he realised they might genuinely believe him to be the Devil incarnate.

His eyes met Siobhan's again, her look a complex mix of emotions: relief at seeing a familiar face, fear of their precarious situation, and something else he couldn't place. Hope, perhaps?

A surge of protectiveness washed over him. Siobhan looked so vulnerable, so out of place among these sinister figures. Vincent tightened his grip on the pistol, his resolve strengthening. He'd get her out of there, no matter what it took.

Vincent's muscles tensed as Lord Blackwood gave a desperate command. The aristocrat's voice cracked with pain and fury as he shouted, "Seize this infernal intruder! Subdue him at once!"

Vincent assessed the threat level of the room. Most of the cultists remained rooted to the spot, their masks unable to hide the terror in their eyes. But a handful, driven by twisted loyalty or sheer madness, moved toward him with menacing intent.

Time slowed as Vincent's combat instincts kicked in. His grip tightened on the pistol, aware that he had only one shot left. He cursed himself for not bringing one of the poitín bottles.

Too late now.

The first attacker, a burly man in a dark robe, lunged forward with surprising speed. Vincent's world narrowed to a pinpoint focus on the threat. Without hesitation, he raised the loaded pistol and squeezed the trigger.

The gunshot rang out, and the weapon kicked as it discharged. At such close range, there was no chance of missing. The cultist's mask shattered, revealing a face frozen in shock for a split second before the round tore it apart. The man dropped to the ground.

Smoke curled from the barrel of his now empty pistol. He had no time to process what he'd done before the other attackers advanced. It would take too long to reload, so he tossed the gun at the nearest attacker and drew the hand axe. His muscles tensed, ready for the onslaught.

He rushed to meet the first attacker, who swung a wild punch. Vincent ducked under it with ease, years of barroom brawl experience kicking in. He drove his fist into the man's solar plexus, feeling a crack under the impact. The cultist wheezed and crumpled.

Two more rushed him from different angles. Vincent spun, the axe whistling through the air. It bit deep into one attacker's shoulder, eliciting a scream of agony. Without pausing, Vincent wrenched the weapon free and brought the back of it crashing into the other man's face. Teeth and blood sprayed across the polished floor.

The brutality of his actions shocked even Vincent. The people he faced weren't hardened criminals but soft aristocrats playing at dark rituals. They had no idea how to handle an actual threat.

A woman lunged at him, a ceremonial dagger raised. Vincent caught her wrist, twisting until a bone snapped and the weapon clattered to the ground. He head-butted her hard, feeling her nose shatter beneath his forehead. She stumbled back, clutching her ruined face.

Vincent fought like a man possessed, each movement chosen for maximum effect. He saw the fear and awe in the eyes of those who dared approach him. To them, he was an avenging demon, all violence and unstoppable fury.

The hand axe rose and fell, cutting through expensive robes and soft flesh alike. Blood slicked the floor, making the footing treacherous. But Vincent moved with deadly grace, each step purposeful as he carved a path through them.

Cultists fell, broken and bleeding. Some tried to flee, only to slip in the gore of their fallen comrades. Vincent struck them down with no remorse. These people had kidnapped Siobhan, had tried to use her in some dark ritual. They deserved no mercy.

As he turned back to the altar, Vincent locked eyes with Siobhan. She was pale and weak, but there was a fire in her gaze that gave him strength. He moved to her side, assessing the bindings holding her to the X-frame. Thick rope secured her wrists and ankles.

He raised the hand axe and brought it down on the rope holding her right wrist. The sharp blade sliced through it with a satisfying *THUNK*. Vincent worked methodically, hacking through each restraint while keeping one eye on the chaos behind him.

A cultist, braver or more foolish than the rest, charged toward them. Vincent spun, axe at the ready. The man's eyes widened in terror as he realised his mistake, but it was too late. The axe connected with a sickening *CRUNCH*, cleaving the top of his skull off.

Like a boiled fucking egg, thought Vincent. The man dropped to the floor.

Vincent turned back to Siobhan, freeing her remaining binding. She slumped forward, her legs giving way beneath her. He caught her in his arms, feeling how light and fragile she was.

"I've got you," he said, supporting her weight as she struggled to find her footing.

Siobhan's eyes met his, clouded with exhaustion but still alert. She managed a weak nod, her fingers gripping his jacket as she tried to steady herself.

Vincent glanced at the Yam still running at the far end of the room. Fallen cultists and debris littered the path to it, creating a treacherous obstacle course.

"We have to move," he said, adjusting his grip on her. "Can you walk?"

She attempted a step, her legs shaking with the effort. It was clear she wouldn't make it on her own. Vincent dropped the axe and scooped her up, one arm under her knees and the other supporting her back. Siobhan's head lolled against his shoulder as he moved.

He carried her toward the motorcycle, his muscles straining with the effort. He picked his way through the carnage, aware of how vulnerable they were. The remaining cultists were too shocked or terrified to approach, but that could change in an instant.

The Yam continued its steady rumble, growing louder as they approached. The ride with Siobhan in her weakened state would be a problem, but they had to reach the bike first.

Lady Scarlett stood frozen, her usual poise shattered. Sir Reginald cowered behind the altar, his spectacles askew. Neither made any move to stop Vincent.

As they neared the bike, Lord Blackwood's voice rang out, shrill with fury, "You'll pay for this, demon! The Hell-fire Club will hunt you to the ends of the earth!"

Vincent ignored the threats, focusing on getting Siobhan safely onto the motorcycle. He lowered her onto the seat, steadying her with one hand as he swung his leg over in front of her.

"Hold on tight," he murmured, guiding her arms around his waist.

He leaned back and pulled one of the poitín bottles from the saddlebag, then lit the hanging rag with his lighter. The alcohol took the flame. *WHOOSH*. He looked to where Blackwood stood at the altar and shouted, "Fuck you!"

Vincent hurled the bottle overarm in the direction of the altar. It fell short but when it hit, the liquid exploded in a wall of flame. The laundry soap had the desired effect and stuck to everything in a ten-foot radius. Cultists caught in it screamed as their robes and exposed skin burned.

He kicked the bike into gear. The engine roared, the sound amplified in the enclosed space, but the screams of the burning cultists almost drowned it out.

Vincent angled the bike toward the exit. He revved the engine, and Siobhan pressed against his back as they prepared to make their escape. He gunned it, feeling the Yam surge forward. The roar of the machine now ate the cultists' screams as they sped for the shattered doorway. Bodies scrambled out of their path, robes fluttering in the wake of their passage.

The cool night air hit Vincent as they burst out of the clubhouse. Siobhan's grip tightened around his waist, her body pressed against his back. The girl's strength was fading fast. They needed a safe place, and soon.

As they careened down the hill away from Mountpelier he wondered, where could they go? The cottage wasn't an option. It was the most obvious place for the cultists to search first. They needed somewhere to hide, somewhere to regroup and figure out their next move.

The darkness enveloped them as they sped along the winding country trail. Vincent's senses were hyper-aware of every bump and turn. Despite the absence of pursuit, Vincent knew the Hellfire Club would regroup soon enough.

Siobhan's head rested against his shoulder, her breathing shallow but steady. He'd got her out, but now what? In this unfamiliar time, with limited resources and a weakened companion, their options were few. The motorcycle ate up the miles as they fled into the night, leaving behind a scene of chaos and terror. All he could do was ride.

CHAPTER 29
ESCAPE

Vincent guided the motorcycle through the darkness, the engine's roar echoing off the trees. He risked a glance over his shoulder, his stomach clenching at the sight of flickering torches in the distance. The Hellfire Club wasn't giving up. Vincent twisted the throttle, urging more speed from the bike as they sped down the narrow country lane.

The cool night air carried with it the scent of damp earth and wood smoke. They needed shelter – a hiding place where Siobhan could recover – but Vincent didn't know where to find one.

A new sound reached him, the rhythmic thunder of hooves. The Hellfire Club had mounted a pursuit and was gaining ground.

The country road twisted and turned, a treacherous ribbon of darkness illuminated by the bike's headlight. Every bump and dip sent shockwaves through the frame, threatening to throw them off balance.

Siobhan stirred, adjusting her hold on Vincent. A wave of relief washed over him at her renewed strength.

"Vincent!" she said, shouting above the engine noise. "Where do we travel?"

He shouted back over his shoulder, "The spot where I first arrived. It's not far . . . I think."

The forest where he'd come into this time was worth checking out. It was the only idea he had. If they could make it there, perhaps they could lose their pursuers in the dense undergrowth.

The hoofbeats grew louder, spurring Vincent to risk pushing the bike harder. He leaned into each turn, the tires skidding dangerously close to the edge of the road. The engine roared, but he ignored it, focused on putting distance between them and their pursuers.

As they crested a hill, Vincent caught sight of a familiar tree line silhouetted against the night sky. They were close. Just a little farther, and they might have a chance.

His eyes combed the landscape. A subtle shift in the world around them made him uneasy, like a distant storm brewing on the horizon. The countryside took on an unsettling quality, as if reality was bending. He blinked hard, certain his eyes played tricks on him. A modern streetlamp flickered into existence by the roadside, only to vanish a moment later.

Vincent focused on the path ahead. Trees wavered, their outlines blurring and reshaping. He glimpsed buildings that had no right to be there – a petrol station, its neon sign glowing briefly before melting back into the darkness of nineteenth-century Ireland.

Siobhan tensed, and she dug her fingers into his sides. A sharp inhalation, then, "Vincent! The land . . . it changes!"

No fucking shit, he thought, but didn't respond. The way ahead warped as tarmac bled through the dirt track.

Vincent struggled to keep the bike steady as the ground shifted.

The thunder of hooves drew nearer. A glance back confirmed his fears – the riders had gained ground.

He gritted his teeth, looking for an escape route. Ahead, the woods, their dark silhouette promising cover. Vincent wrenched the handlebars, veering off the main path and into the tree line.

The Yam slid and skidded on the uneven ground as they plunged into the woods. Vincent hunched low, willing the bike to stay upright as they weaved between the trunks. The engine's roar shattered the peace of the woods.

The strangeness continued as the forest writhed around them like a living entity. Trees that had been there moments before vanished, only to reappear in different locations. Shadows danced and twisted, playing tricks on Vincent's eyes as he struggled to navigate the ever-changing terrain.

"Vincent, watch out!" Siobhan's voice cut through his concentration.

Vincent looked up as a thick bough materialised. He ducked, feeling the rough bark graze his back as they passed beneath.

"They are all about," Siobhan shouted. "The branches appear and disappear!"

Vincent's eyes flickered from one side to the other. He swerved to avoid another low-hanging limb, only to have it vanish as they passed. The forest had become a maze of shifting obstacles, each turn bringing new dangers.

Vincent burst through the tree line into a moonlit clearing. Fear and exhilaration coursed through him in equal measure. Was this where he'd first arrived in this time?

Behind them, the hoofbeats grew louder. Another

risked glance caught flickering torches through the trees. The Hellfire Club closed the gap.

"Hold on!" Siobhan's arms tightened around him.

The motorcycle began to sputter and jerk. Vincent's stomach dropped as he realised the cause. The fuel gauge confirmed his fears; they were running on empty.

With practiced movements, Vincent reached down and flipped the fuel valve to the reserve tank position. The engine coughed once, twice, before roaring back to life.

"What is it?" Siobhan called out, panicked.

"Low on fuel! There's a bit left! It'll be enough!"

"Vincent! Look ahead!" She pointed.

He inhaled sharply when he saw what she did. A strange distortion in the air ahead. It shimmered and wavered, like heat rising from the sun-baked tarmac but far more intense.

"I see it!" The distortion looked like the portal that had brought him there. Could it be? Was another gateway forming right before their eyes?

The thundering of hooves grew deafening. The Hellfire Club riders were mere yards behind them. Their faces were twisted masks of fury, torches held high as they closed the gap.

One rider, a burly man sporting a thick beard, grasped for Siobhan. His fingers grazed her sleeve, and she flinched at Vincent's back.

"Hold on!" Vincent roared, twisting the throttle to coax every ounce of speed from the struggling motorcycle.

Vincent aimed for the centre of the shimmering portal. The Yam roared beneath him, vibrating with the strain of pushing its limits. Siobhan pressed against his back. Her fear mirrored his own, but there was no turning back.

They rode headlong at the vortex. Vincent gritted his

teeth, bracing for the impact. As if they'd slammed into a wall of water, the entire bike lurched when the front wheel hit first. White-knuckled, he refused to allow the sudden resistance to tear the handlebars from his grip. Then they were through.

Time slowed as they entered. The world dissolved into a swirling chaos of light and shadow. Echoes of the past and whispers of the future blended into an incomprehensible roar. Colours bled and merged, forming impossible patterns that hurt their eyes.

Vincent struggled to keep the bike upright as they hurtled through the time stream. The laws of physics warped as its forces pulled them in multiple directions at once. His arms ached from the effort of controlling the motorcycle. Each second was an eternity as they journeyed through. Siobhan's grip on him weakened, and fear gripped him. If they became separated in the maelstrom, he might lose her for good.

Gritting his teeth, Vincent fought against the chaotic forces threatening to tear them apart. The bike bucked and weaved, but he refused to let go. Through force of will, he kept them on course, plunging deeper into the unknown.

Vincent risked a glance over his shoulder. The shimmering portal shrunk, the pursuing riders little more than silhouettes against the chaotic swirl of light. He felt a surge of relief as the distance between them and their enemies increased.

As the portal closed, he heard a familiar voice.

"Well done, Vinny."

Vincent's blood ran cold. He knew that voice well, but he didn't dwell on it. The portal snapped shut with a sound like a thunderclap, leaving their pursuers stranded in the past.

He focused his attention back on controlling the Yam. It bucked and weaved as they hurtled through the vortex, surrounded by a dizzying array of lights and sounds. Echoes of different times came to him: snippets of conversation, the clash of swords, the rumble of engines, the roar of crowds.

He was glad Siobhan was with him. Despite the chaos surrounding them, her presence was an anchor, reminding him of why they'd taken this desperate gamble.

As they continued through the swirling maelstrom, Vincent wondered where they'd end up, and when. The uncertainty of their destination worried him. He'd navigated nineteenth-century Ireland well enough, but what if they landed somewhere even more unfamiliar?

The vortex stretched on, time losing all meaning as they sped through its twisting corridors. Vincent's arms ached from the strain of keeping the motorcycle steady, but he dared not let go. He and Siobhan were still in transit, their fate hanging in the balance as they hurtled into an unknown future.

CHAPTER 30

RETURN TO THE PRESENT

Vincent's stomach lurched as they burst from the swirling vortex, the Yam's tyres slamming onto solid ground. The sudden transition from chaotic timelessness to tangible reality left him disoriented, his senses reeling as they tried to adjust.

Damp grass whipped beneath them as Vincent fought to control the bike's trajectory. The smell of wet earth filled his nostrils, distinctly different from the otherworldly scents of the time stream.

Siobhan still held onto him for dear life.

Vincent's arms burned with the effort of keeping the Yam upright as it fishtailed across the field. The bike's wheels struggled for purchase on the slick grass, threatening to send them both flying. He gritted his teeth as he wrestled with it.

Slowing, his eyes locked onto a familiar sight – the ancient oak tree stood ahead. Its gnarled branches reached out like skeletal fingers against the grey sky. A landmark he'd seen countless times before, usually with dread. Tonight it was a bitter yet welcome sight.

They stopped yards from the oak's massive trunk, and Vincent cut the engine. The sudden silence deafened after the roar of their journey. He gulped deep breaths of cool, damp air.

Siobhan's arms trembled, and even though they'd stopped, she didn't break her hold on his waist.

Blinking away the disorientation, Vincent looked around. The familiar landscape came into focus. There, just a stone's throw away, was the ragged gap in the hedgerow where he'd plunged through earlier. Broken branches and trampled grass marked his reckless path.

The same fucking night? Relief engulfed him as understanding dawned. They'd returned. Not just to the same place, but to the moment he'd left. The grey sky above held the same brooding clouds; the air carried the same hint of impending rain. It was as if no time had passed at all.

Vincent let go of the handlebars. He let out a shaky laugh, equal parts disbelief and gratitude. They'd made it. They'd fucking made it.

Vincent kicked out the stand and swung his leg over the bike, his boots sinking into the damp grass after he dismounted. His legs quivered jelly-like. He took another deep breath, steadying himself against the bike's frame for a moment.

Turning to Siobhan, he saw her wide-eyed expression. She remained perched on the motorcycle pillion, her hands gripping the leather seat in front of her in his absence. She looked around at the familiar yet alien landscape.

"It's all right, love. We're back," Vincent said.

He reached out, offering his hand to help her dismount. Siobhan blinked, focusing on Vincent's face as if seeing him for the first time. She nodded, her movements jerky and uncertain as she took his hand.

As Siobhan slid off the bike, her legs buckled. Vincent wrapped an arm around her waist, steadying her against his side. Her entire body shook, the adrenaline crash hitting her hard.

"Easy now," he said, concerned. He guided her a few steps away from the motorcycle, making sure she was steady on her feet before loosening his grip. "You all right?"

Siobhan nodded again, more firmly. "I-I believe so," she whispered with a slight shake. "That was . . . quite the journey."

Vincent squeezed her shoulder before turning his attention back to the Yam. He circled it, looking for damage. The frame was intact, no obvious dents or scratches from their wild ride. He crouched down, checking the tyres and suspension, relieved to find everything operational.

He turned back to Siobhan, seeing her wide, fearful eyes. She stood rooted to the spot, looking between him and their surroundings, overwhelmed by the sudden shift in location.

"Siobhan," he said, waiting for her to look at him. "I know this is a lot to take in, but we're safe. We're in my time."

He watched her for signs of comprehension. Her brow furrowed, lips parting as she processed his words. He saw the gears turn as she reconciled the impossible journey they'd experienced.

"Your . . . time?" she whispered. There was disbelief and a hint of awe there too.

Vincent nodded, offering what he hoped was a reassuring smile. "Aye, the future. Well, my present. It's a lot different from what you're used to."

He weighed their options. They couldn't linger in the open, exposed. The chill night air nipped at his skin, reminding him of the need for shelter and warmth. Siobhan shivered, too, clad as she was in only a silk dress.

His home. It wasn't much, but it was secure and familiar. At least there, they could regroup and figure out their next move without fear of discovery.

"Listen," Vincent said, touching Siobhan's arm to recapture her attention. "We can't stay here. My place is nearby. We'll be safe there. It's . . . different from what you know, but I'll explain everything once we get there. All right?"

Siobhan hesitated for a moment before nodding, her trust in him clear despite her apprehension.

As Vincent guided her back to the Yam, a fresh worry occurred to him. How would Siobhan react to the modern world? The sights, sounds, and technology of his time would be alien to her. He'd have to gradually introduce things, careful to avoid overwhelming her further.

Vincent scanned the field one last time, his eyes piercing the darkness for any sign of movement. The night remained still, save for the gentle rustling of leaves in the breeze. No shimmering portals, no pursuing cultists. They were alone.

Satisfied, he turned back to Siobhan. Her face was pale in the moonlight, a mix of fear and wonder there. Vincent prepared himself, knowing the next hour wouldn't be easy.

"My home's not far, but . . ." – he paused, choosing his words – "we have to ride through the village to get there."

Her eyes widened at this, a flicker of panic crossing her face. Vincent pressed on. "It's going to differ from anything you've ever seen. Lights, buildings, things you can't even imagine. But I promise you'll be safe with me."

Siobhan swallowed hard, but after a moment, she gave a small nod. Her jaw set determinedly despite the fear in her eyes.

Vincent moved to the Yam, gesturing for Siobhan to follow. She hesitated, eyeing the machine, wary of its potential to spring to life and attack at any moment.

"It's all right," Vincent said, placing a reassuring hand on her shoulder. "Just like before, yeah? Hold on tight to me, and I'll get us there."

He swung his leg over the seat, settling onto the Yam, then turned, extending his hand to Siobhan. She stared at it for a long moment, then reached out and grasped his hand.

Vincent helped her onto the back of the bike, and she settled behind him. Her arms wrapped around his waist, clinging to him in a way that spoke volumes of her fear.

"Ready?" he asked, his hand hovering over the ignition.

Her forehead pressed against his back as she nodded, her grip tightening further.

Vincent turned the key, and the motorcycle roared to life. The familiar rumble vibrated through his body, breaking the eerie silence of the field.

Siobhan squeezed him and he felt a sudden wave of protectiveness that reminded him of the responsibility he now bore for this young woman from another time.

He cast one last glance at the ancient oak tree. The memory of losing Rose resurfaced, but it mingled with the fresh pain of his attempted suicide earlier that night. A maelstrom of emotions churned within him: sorrow for Rose, guilt over his recent actions, fear for Siobhan's safety, and an odd sense of purpose he hadn't experienced in years. He forced his attention back to the immediate goal. They had to get to safety.

Vincent revved the engine, feeling Siobhan flinch at the noise. He patted her hand before grasping the handlebars. He rode the Yam toward the gap in the hedgerow.

They passed through the broken branches, leaving the

field behind. The village lay ahead, a gauntlet of modern sights and sounds that might overwhelm the girl. He'd have to navigate carefully, shielding her as best he could from the shock of this new world while ensuring their safe passage to his home.

CHAPTER 31
A NEW WORLD

Siobhan clung to Vincent as the metal beast beneath them roared to life. Fear and exhilaration coursed through her as the world blurred into a dizzying array of unfamiliar sensations.

The road stretched ahead, smooth and dark as polished obsidian. She marvelled at how effortlessly they glided along its surface, so unlike the rutted paths she was familiar with. The steady thrum of the motorcycle vibrated through her body, a reminder of the strange magic that propelled them.

Overwhelmed by the sensory assault, Siobhan buried her head in Vincent's back, inhaling the scent of his leather jacket and body odour. The fabric was strange against her skin, unlike the rough-spun wool she knew.

Curiosity soon got the better of her, and she peeked out from behind Vincent. She stared as they passed structures of glass and metal, their surfaces reflecting the moonlight like ethereal beacons.

The air was different too – thick with strange scents and an underlying buzz of energy that set her teeth on edge. Her fingers twitched for her magic, but the bracelet still enchained it.

As they sped through the alien landscape, questions occurred to her. Everything she thought she knew about the world was askew. She alternated between pressing her face into Vincent's back for comfort and peering out in fascination at the wonders they passed.

Rounding a bend, Siobhan's eyes widened in astonishment. Tall poles lined the street, each crowned with a glowing orb that cast an otherworldly light upon the ground. She gasped, her grip on Vincent's waist tightening.

"Sweet Mother Mary," she whispered, but the wind carried her words away.

The lights made a uniform procession of artificial stars. Their brightness rivalled that of the moon, banishing the darkness with an eerie, constant glow. Siobhan had never seen anything like it. Even the grandest manor house of her time couldn't boast such consistent, powerful illumination.

Beneath the lights, Siobhan marvelled at how they transformed the night. Shadows danced and retreated, revealing details of the strange world with startling clarity. She found herself both frightened and fascinated by this unnatural daylight.

A monstrous roar abruptly filled the air. Siobhan's heart leapt into her throat as a metal behemoth hurtled past them on the opposite side of the road. Its speed was terrifying, far surpassing that of the swiftest horse. Bright eyes blazed from its front, cutting through the night like twin beams of sunlight.

"Lord have mercy," she breathed, her eyes wide with fear and wonder.

Red taillights disappeared into the distance, and Siobhan struggled to comprehend what she witnessed. It resembled nothing she had ever known – a horseless carriage zooming at unimaginable speeds. The ingenuity of future folk awed her, and their creations' unbridled power terrified her.

More horseless carriages appeared as Vincent steered them toward a busier part of town. Siobhan dug her fingers into Vincent's sides. The growl of engines, the blur of lights, and the sheer number of people and vehicles threatened to overwhelm her.

Her senses reeled as they entered a bustling part of town. Even at that late hour, the sounds assaulted her. Strange, mechanical roars filled the air, punctuated by distant wails that made her skin crawl. Music, unlike any she'd heard before, poured from the buildings they passed, a chaotic blend of rhythms and instruments she couldn't name.

Her eyes were like saucers at a busy intersection. Lights danced before her, red and green and amber, hanging in the air like magical sigils. Bright signs adorned the buildings, glowing with an inner fire that pulsed and flickered. The colours reflected in her eyes, painting her face with a multi-hued glow.

Unfamiliar smells assailed her, making her wrinkle her nose in confusion. A sharp, acrid scent stung her throat – the breath of the metal beasts, she realised. Another smell wafted past, rich and greasy, setting her stomach growling despite its strangeness. Underlying it all was a cocktail of scents she couldn't identify, each one more bewildering than the last.

As they slowed for a moment, Siobhan watched the people on the street. Their clothing shocked her – women in trousers, men in short sleeves, fabrics and styles she'd never imagined. Several people clutched small, glowing rectangles to their ears, engaging in conversation and laughter as if it were the most ordinary thing in the world. Others hurried past with purpose, their eyes fixed on some unseen destination.

The behaviour of these future folk baffled her. They moved with a brisk, impatient energy, weaving around each other without a word or nod of acknowledgment. In her village, such rudeness would have been unthinkable. Yet here it seemed the norm.

A group of young women caught her attention, their laughter ringing out above the din. Their skirts were scandalously short, their hair dyed in vibrant hues that put the brightest flowers to shame. Siobhan envied their carefree spirits, so different from the constant wariness she'd lived with.

Her eyes darted from building to building, her mind struggling with their glass structures, surfaces reflecting light like shimmering mirrors. How could people use such fragile material in construction? She marvelled at the smooth, unbroken facades, so unlike the rough stone walls of her time.

Some buildings defied gravity, their upper floors jutting out at precarious angles or curving in ways that should have sent them toppling to the ground. Yet they stood firm, perhaps by way of arcane knowledge beyond her wildest imaginings.

As Vincent navigated the streets, the world around them moved at a dizzying pace. Siobhan's head spun at the charged urgency in the air. The constant motion, coupled with the assault on her senses, took its toll. Her stomach churned, a wave of nausea washing over her. The world tilted and swayed as the scene blended into a kaleidoscope of confusion.

Unable to bear it, Siobhan squeezed her eyes shut. She pressed her forehead against Vincent's back, seeking some semblance of stability in this chaotic new world. The darkness behind her eyelids provided a momentary respite, but it couldn't block the noise entirely or the lingering scents that assailed her.

The mechanical beast's roar softened to a gentle purr. Siobhan relaxed her rigid muscles. The din of the town centre faded, replaced by a quieter area where the assault on her senses subsided. She breathed more freely, but the relief was fleeting as a new apprehension took root. Where were they going? What new wonders – or terrors – awaited her?

The beast slowed further, and Siobhan saw a strange structure standing tall and proud, its walls smooth and uniform, painted in a pale colour that glowed in the moonlight. Large, gleaming windows reflected the streetlights, giving the impression of eyes watching their approach.

As Vincent guided the metal beast to this alien building, realisation dawned on Siobhan. This must be Vincent's home. The thought both fascinated and unsettled her. How different it was from the humble thatched cottage she had left behind! There was no garden to speak of, just a small patch of grass bordered by a low wall. A paved path led to the front door, flanked by neatly trimmed shrubs.

Vincent brought the beast to a stop, and Siobhan's eyes immediately focused on the neighbouring structures. They mirrored Vincent's home almost exactly, creating a bizarre sense of repetition. How could so many homes look so alike? Where was the individuality, the personal touch that made each dwelling unique?

Siobhan's legs wobbled as Vincent helped her off the metal beast. She focused on the home in front of them. The walls rose smooth and unblemished, lacking the rough texture of stone or the grain of wood. The size and clarity of the windows defied belief. How could glass panes so large exist without shattering under their own weight? In her time, even the grandest manors boasted only small, imperfect panes. These gleamed like still water, reflecting the world around them with mirror-like precision.

She looked up at the crisp lines and angles of the roof. No thatching or wooden shingles adorned this dwelling. Instead, uniform tiles lay in perfect rows, their edges sharp enough to cut the eye.

As Vincent guided her toward the entrance, Siobhan's heart raced. What lay within? She watched, transfixed, as Vincent reached into his pocket and withdrew a small metal object. It gleamed in the moonlight, its surface etched with intricate patterns.

Vincent inserted the object into a hole in the door, a concept so foreign that Siobhan struggled to process it. In her world, heavy iron locks or simple wooden latches were used to secure doors. This seemed more akin to magic than a mechanical device.

A sharp *click* pierced the night air, causing her to jump. The sound was crisp and decisive, unlike the dull thud of a dropping latch or the scrape of a key in an iron lock. Vincent turned the handle, and the door swung open with silent ease.

Siobhan hesitated at the threshold before crossing it. Inside, the alien interior stunned her. She looked from object to object, baffled by what she saw.

The floor beneath her feet was smooth as glass. Strange furniture dotted the room, their shapes and materials foreign to her. A large, black rectangle hung on the wall, its purpose a mystery.

Vincent moved past her, his hand reaching for something on the wall. Suddenly, the room filled with a soft, warm glow. Siobhan gasped. The light emanated from nowhere and everywhere at once, so different from the flickering flames of candles or oil lamps. She searched the ceiling for its source. No flames, no wicks, no smoke, just pure, unwavering light, as if Vincent had captured the sun and tamed it.

A low humming sound caught her attention, its origin a mystery. Siobhan's brow furrowed as she tried to place the noise, unaware it came from household appliances she couldn't fathom.

"I don't know about you, but I could eat a horse's arse." Vincent's crude phrase, so at odds with the magical surroundings, startled a small laugh from Siobhan.

He walked to the back of the house, calling back, "Make yourself at home."

Siobhan stood rooted to the spot, unsure of the invitation. Make herself at home? In this place of wonders and impossibilities? She glanced around, her eyes settling on a plush-looking chair. Tentatively, she approached it, her hand hovering over its surface, marvelling at its softness. She'd never touched fabric quite like it before. Just as she was about to sit, Vincent returned, carrying a tray laden with unfamiliar items.

"I made us some tea and a few sandwiches," he said, offering her a steaming cup.

Siobhan accepted it gingerly, the warmth seeping into her palms. She peered into the liquid, its rich amber colour reminding her of the herbal brews she often made back home.

Vincent added, "Hot, sweet tea is good for shock. Just in case..."

Siobhan nodded, taking an experimental sip. The taste was strong yet oddly comforting. The heat spread through, chasing away some of the lingering chill from their ride.

They sat in silence, the importance of their journey settling over them. Siobhan had many questions. They'd escaped the immediate danger, yes, but what now? This strange new world was as alien to her as the depths of the ocean.

"Vincent," she said, "what are we to do now? We've escaped, but . . ." she trailed off, unsure how to express the magnitude of their situation.

Vincent looked at her, his eyes tired but kind. "There'll be plenty of time to figure shit out in the morning." A hint of reassurance softened his gruff tone.

Siobhan nodded, taking another sip of tea. The warmth in her hands anchored her to the present, a slight comfort in this sea of uncertainty.

CHAPTER 32

THE DEVIL'S DUE

Vincent sat in the dark living room, a glass of whiskey in hand. While swirling the tumbler, lost in thought, the amber liquid danced. The past days played through his mind like a fever dream – time travel, magic, a chaotic rescue, the fucking Devil? All too fantastical to be real, but Siobhan, asleep in the spare room, said otherwise.

Anxiety twisted his guts. A young witch from the past was in his home, in a world she'd find hard to understand. Was he up to the task of guiding her? He sipped the whiskey, its burn a welcome distraction.

What was he to do with her? Even if he knew how, he couldn't very well send her back to the life she'd left behind.

Not since you murdered her auld fella.

He ignored the thought. Could Siobhan fit into this world? What sort of life would she have? Vincent rubbed his eyes, feeling every bit of his age and then some.

The house creaked, and Vincent's head snapped up, alert for danger, but it was the settling of old wood, nothing more. He was on edge. By bringing Siobhan here, had he opened the door for others?

He stood, wincing as his battered body protested. He crossed to the window. The street outside appeared deserted and nothing looked out of place. But he knew better than most how quickly normalcy could shatter.

The room turned icy cold, causing Vincent to shiver. The hair on the back of his neck stood on end, and his breath misted. He knew what this meant. A visitor.

His hand stilled on the whiskey glass, he fixed on the scene outside the window. He refused to turn around and search for the source of the presence. His encounters with supernatural phenomena were enough to last a lifetime.

"*Vincent Burke*," said the Devil, smooth as silk and cold as ice. "*Did you think your little jaunt through time would be the end of it?*"

Vincent took another swig of whiskey, relishing the burn as it travelled down his throat. It grounded him in reality as the impossible once again intruded upon his life.

"*Your journey isn't over. It's only just begun.*"

Vincent sighed. After what he'd been through – Rose's death, Declan's murder, the journey into the past, Siobhan's rescue – how much more could he endure?

"Haven't I paid enough?" Vincent asked. He turned to the empty room. "What more do you want from me?"

The Devil chuckled, the sound emanating from everywhere and nowhere, filling the room with its eerie presence.

"*Oh, Vincent. The past holds secrets you've yet to uncover, and the future . . . Well, that remains unwritten. We're on track.*"

Vincent's thoughts tumbled over one another as he grasped at the meaning of the Devil's words. What secrets?

The ones he knew of and held tight to or secrets he knew nothing of? He grimaced at the beginnings of a headache.

"What the fuck are you saying?" he asked. "That all of this . . . everything that's happened . . . it's all part of some plan?"

The air grew colder as the Devil's rich laughter sounded out. "*A plan? Perhaps. Or perhaps it's merely the confluence of choices and consequences, rippling through time like stones cast into a pond.*"

Vincent's brow furrowed as he tried to make sense of the cryptic words. He thought of Siobhan's magic, of the Hellfire Club's dark rituals, of his journey through time. How much was planned, and how much was coincidental?

"And what of Siobhan?" A protective edge crept in. "What role does she play?"

The Devil's response was vague, "*The witch-child's path intertwines with yours in ways yet to be revealed. She is both catalyst and consequence, a spark in the darkness.*"

Vincent's mind whirled with possibilities and implications. He thought of Rose, of the eerie similarities between her and Siobhan. Was there a connection there, something he'd missed?

His frustration boiled over; cryptic messages and supernatural intrusions wore his patience thin. He slammed his empty glass down on the nearby table, the sharp sound reverberating through the quiet house.

"Enough with the riddles," he growled. "What the fuck do you want from me? Haven't I suffered enough? Haven't I lost enough?"

"*Want? Oh, Vincent, this isn't about what I want. It's about balance. We must set the scales right.*"

"What scales? What are you on about?"

"*Souls, Vincent. Souls lost in time. Threads of fate unrav-*"

elled and tangled. Your journey through the years has left . . . ripples. Consequences."

Vincent thought of Declan, of Padraig, of the lives he'd taken. Was this a cosmic punishment? "What about my past? What's that got to do with anything?"

"Your past, Vincent Burke, is not as deeply buried as you'd like to believe. There are truths yet to be unearthed, secrets that refuse to stay hidden. But I have a solution."

Old memories and half-forgotten fears bubbled to the surface. He was afraid to ask the Devil what he meant. Were all his secrets laid bare to this being?

What fucking solution?

The chill in the air dissipated as suddenly as it had appeared, leaving Vincent alone with his thoughts. He exhaled, realising he'd been holding his breath during the entity's last words. The living room settled back into its familiar warmth, but the comfort it usually brought was absent.

Vincent thought again of Siobhan. The young witch slept, unaware of the supernatural conversation that had taken place. He wondered how much more she'd have to endure.

Turning back to the shadows of his living room, Vincent thought about the Devil's words.

Souls lost in time, threads of fate unravelled. What the fuck is he on about?

He thought of the murder of Declan in a moment of rage. Of Padraig, left buried in a shallow grave centuries in the past. Were these the souls the entity spoke of? The consequences of his actions rippling through time? Or was it another dark deed?

Vincent's hand shook as he reached for the whiskey

bottle, pouring another measure into his glass. He took a sip, letting the burn ground him.

The first rays of dawn light crept into the room, painting the walls in a soft, golden hue. The new day brought fresh challenges. He rubbed his tired eyes, the events of the night replaying behind them. The Devil's cryptic words echoed in his thoughts, a reminder that his dance wasn't over.

Vincent sat there, bathed in growing sunlight, considering how the flames of Hell might have forged him anew. The trials he'd faced, the impossible journey through time, the lives he'd taken – all of it had changed him, moulded him into something different. But what shape would he ultimately take?

He moved back to the window and watched the growing light chase away the remnants of night. His reflection in the glass caught his eye, and he studied it intently. The man looking back at him seemed both familiar and strange. The lines on his face spoke of the hardships he'd endured and his apprehension for what was to come, but they were tempered by a steely resolve. Whatever challenges lay ahead, whatever the future held, he would grab it by the balls and squeeze.

EPILOGUE: MATERNAL INSTINCT

Margaret Kenny's manicured fingers traced the columns of numbers on the financial report before her, her sharp eyes scrutinising every detail. The antique desk she sat at was a family heirloom passed down through generations.

The study exuded an air of refined power, its walls lined with leather-bound books and priceless artwork. Margaret's domain was a testament to the Kenny family's influence, both in the criminal underworld and in the legitimate business sphere.

She reached for her fountain pen to make a note, and her eyes fell upon the framed photograph on her desk. Declan's cocky grin stared back at her, a moment frozen in time. Her lips pursed, the only outward sign of the turmoil beneath her composed exterior.

"Where are you, my boy?"

Margaret's eyes hardened as she forced her attention back to the ledgers. The family's empire wouldn't run itself, and she'd be damned if she let sentiment cloud her judgment. Yet, as she pored over the figures, her mind kept circling back to Declan's disappearance.

A sharp rap on the door jolted her from her reverie. She closed the ledger, her face settling into its usual mask of calm.

"Come in."

Sean burst through the door, his face flushed and hair dishevelled. Margaret noted the wild look in his eyes, the shake of his hands as he gripped the doorframe. Her husband was a bundle of nerves, so unlike the intimidating figure he presented to the outside world.

"Still nothing." He paced the room like a caged animal. "Not a bloody word."

Margaret kept her emotions carefully tucked away. She'd expected as much, but Sean's outburst confirmed it. No news was rarely good news in their business.

"The police are useless," Sean continued, his voice rising. "And our own people are feck all good either. It's like Declan's vanished into thin air!" He punched the wall, the sharp *CRACK* making Margaret wince. She'd have to get that fixed later.

"Sean." Her tone was soft but firm. "That's quite enough."

He whirled to face her, mouth opening to protest, but Margaret cut him with a look she'd perfected over the years, a silent command that even Sean, in all his bluster, couldn't ignore.

"We'll find him. But this . . . display . . . helps no one. Least of all, Declan."

Sean deflated, the fight drained out of him. He looked like a lost child. For a moment, Margaret sympathised but she quashed it. Weakness was unacceptable, especially not now.

"Go to bed, Sean." She turned her attention back to the ledger. "Get some rest. I'll handle things from here."

He hesitated, perhaps considering arguing with her, but Margaret had already dismissed him. His heavy footsteps retreated, the door closing behind him with a soft click.

Once alone, Margaret allowed her carefully constructed facade to slip. Her fingers trembled as she reached out to touch Declan's photograph, tracing the outline of his face. The mask of the formidable crime matriarch cracked, revealing the anguished mother beneath. She closed her eyes and took a deep breath to steady herself. When she opened them again, her gaze fell on the bottom drawer of her desk. Margaret hesitated, then pulled it open with a soft creak.

Inside lay Declan's unfinished school project – a half-completed family genealogy. She carefully lifted it out as if handling a precious artefact. Declan's messy scrawl filled the pages, with notes on great-grandparents and distant cousins scribbled in the margins.

Her throat tightened as she flipped through the pages. She remembered Declan's excitement when he'd started the project, his eagerness to uncover the Kenny family's roots. He'd pestered her for days, asking about long-dead relatives and family legends.

As she studied the incomplete family tree, an idea formed in Margaret's mind. Perhaps . . . perhaps she could continue Declan's research. It would serve as a distraction from the gnawing worry that threatened to consume her, and in a way, it might help her feel closer to her missing son.

Margaret rose from her desk, her movements graceful. She approached a large oil painting on the far wall, an austere portrait of her great-grandfather. She swung the frame aside, revealing a state-of-the-art safe hidden behind it.

Her fingers danced across the keypad, inputting a complex code known only to her. The safe clicked open, and Margaret extracted a dusty cardboard box filled with yellowed papers and faded photographs. At the desk, she sorted through its contents, her keen eyes scrutinising each document. Birth certificates, marriage licences, and old letters passed through her hands as she created neat piles. She connected names and dates, piecing together the puzzle of her family's history, pausing occasionally to jot down notes in crisp handwriting.

Her hand froze as it brushed against something at the bottom of the box. Frowning, Margaret reached in and pulled out an old, leather-bound diary. Cracks and wear marked the cover, and the pages had turned yellow with age. She ran her fingers over the embossed initials on the front: E.B.

Margaret opened the diary with delicate precision, parting the fragile pages. The musty scent of aged paper filled her nostrils as she peered at the faded ink on the first page. Her eyes widened as she deciphered the elegant script: *Property of Lord Edmund Blackwood, 1800.*

A frisson of excitement ran through her. This was far older than she'd anticipated, predating even her great-grandfather's time. Margaret leaned closer, devouring the words as she read.

The diary's contents drew her in. Lord Blackwood's account of the Hellfire Club contained tantalising details of secret meetings, occult rituals, and whispered conspiracies. The vivid descriptions of masked figures gathered in candlelit chambers, voices raised in arcane chants, captivated Margaret. She linked the centuries-old events to her own family's history. Could there be a relationship between the Blackwoods of old and the Kennys of today? She made mental notes, already planning how to incorporate this newfound information into Declan's genealogy project.

The events of 1800 unfolded through Blackwood's flowery prose. He wrote of a powerful ritual, one that promised to grant the participants unimaginable power. Margaret read about a young witch forcibly brought to the Hellfire Club to serve as a sacrifice.

Her fingers tightened on the diary's edges. This went beyond family history; it was a glimpse into a hidden world – one that might still exist beneath the surface of modern Dublin. The possibilities were both thrilling and terrifying.

She turned the page to find a detailed sketch that sprawled across both pages. The image depicted a figure labelled *"The Devil"* astride what Lord Blackwood described as his *"infernal steed"*. She studied the drawing, taking in every line and shadow.

The figure's features were obscured by shadow, yet there was something strangely familiar about the posture, the way he confidently sat astride the beast. Margaret leaned closer, her nose almost touching the yellowed paper. The *"infernal steed"* bore an uncanny resemblance to a motorcycle, its form sleek and mechanical despite the archaic style of the sketch.

She shook her head, trying to dispel the notion. It was impossible, of course. It would take another century for motorcycles to be invented. Yet the similarity was striking, and Margaret couldn't shake the feeling that she was looking at a biker from her own time.

She turned to the next page, eager to read more. Lord Blackwood's elegant script described a ritual gone awry, his words tinged with fury and disbelief. Margaret's eyes widened as she read about a demon bursting into the chamber atop a roaring metal beast, disrupting the ceremony and snatching away the young witch they had captured. Many died in the fire he left in his wake.

Margaret made connections between the sketch and this account. Could it be the same figure? But how was that possible? She read on, as Lord Blackwood described the chaos that ensued, the screams and confusion as the intruder and the witch vanished into the night while the congregation burned.

The final entry spoke of the young witch's disappearance, how she had vanished without a trace along with the mysterious intruder. Lord Blackwood's words dripped with frustration and a hint of fear, lamenting the loss of such a powerful magical asset.

Margaret sat back, her thoughts whirling with the implications of what she'd just read. She needed a second opinion, someone who might recognise the figure in the sketch. And didn't Sean mention that the bouncer Declan had had a run-in with was a biker? She called out, steady but with an undercurrent of urgency.

"Sean! Come here, please."

Sean's heavy footsteps approached, followed by a tentative knock on the door.

"What is it, Margaret?" Sean asked as he entered, his earlier frustration replaced by curiosity.

Margaret gestured for him to approach her desk. "I need you to look at something."

As Sean drew near, Margaret turned the diary so he could see the sketch. She watched his face, searching for any flicker of recognition.

"Does this look familiar to you?" She tapped the image with a manicured nail. "The man on this . . . steed. Does he remind you of anyone? Perhaps the fellow Declan had trouble with at the nightclub?"

Sean leaned in, his brow furrowing. He squinted at the yellowed page. Margaret held her breath, hoping against hope that her hunch was correct. If this mysterious figure from the past had any connection to Declan's disappearance, it could be the breakthrough they needed.

After an eternity, Sean shrugged, his expression a mixture of confusion and mild interest. "There's a rough similarity, I suppose," he said, gesturing vaguely at the image. "The beard, the long hair . . ."

Margaret leaned forward, her fingers gripping the edge of the desk. "Go on."

Sean scratched his chin, tilting his head to the side. "It looks a bit like Vincent Burke, I suppose," he added, almost as an afterthought.

A spark of excitement flared in Margaret's chest, but she kept her face impassive. She was about to press further when Sean continued, his tone dismissive, "But I can't see what a sketch in an old book has to do with Declan going missing." He straightened up and shook his head.

Margaret's eyes narrowed at Sean's dismissal. She had hoped for more, for some flash of insight that might connect the same dots she was seeing. But Sean, as usual, couldn't see beyond the surface.

She pushed down her frustration. Now wasn't the time to argue or explain her theories. Sean wasn't in the right frame of mind to grasp the potential significance of what she'd discovered.

"Thank you, Sean," Margaret said, her dismissal crisp and final. "That will be all."

She turned back to the diary. The discussion was over, at least for now. As she heard Sean's footsteps retreating, Margaret leaned back in her chair. The connection between the mysterious figure in Lord Blackwood's diary and

Vincent Burke was perhaps a stretch, but she had no other avenue to explore, and she was desperate.

Margaret's lips thinned as she thought of her son. Declan's safety was paramount, but she couldn't deny the potential advantage the information in the diary might bring to their family. If there truly existed a supernatural element, it had the potential to create fresh opportunities for power and influence for the Kennys. But first, she needed to confirm her suspicions. Margaret's eyes hardened with resolve. She would have to meet this Vincent Burke face to face, to look into his eyes and see for herself what lies were in them.

She reached for her phone, her fingers hovering over the keypad. They could arrange a meeting away from prying eyes. Margaret would use all her skills of observation and interrogation to uncover whatever secrets Burke might be hiding.

As she contemplated her next move, she closed the diary. Whatever it took, she would sort this out and find her son. And if Vincent Burke stood in her way, he would soon learn the folly of crossing Margaret Kenny.

THANKS FOR READING

Thanks for reading Hellfire. I hope you enjoyed it and will consider leaving an honest review on Amazon, Goodreads, or wherever else you choose.

As an indie author, reviews are one of the best ways to raise visibility and find more readers like you.

Best,

B.C.

Acknowledgments

I would like to thank my family, once again for their patience and understanding.

Thanks to my editor, Dani, who did a wonderful job again, making what you hold in your hands so much better.

Thanks to my beta readers, Andy, Kirsten, and Dylan, who provided excellent feedback on the early draft and made the story tighter and better.

Last but not least, the reader, for taking the time to read this story. Without you, I'd just be writing into the void.

B.C. Hollywood
October, 2024

BIBLIOGRAPHY

ABOUT THE AUTHOR

B.C. Hollywood is an Irish author of dark fiction, fantasy, and horror. He spends much of his spare time battering raw stories into shapelier form.

He writes novels, short stories, flash fiction, screenplays, poetry, and tabletop games. He is the author of *The Darkle Chronicles* series.

To connect with B.C. and for news of his upcoming titles, you can check out his website at www.bchollywood.com, join his newsletter, and follow his Facebook author page.